Beyond Solstice Gates

WHERE THE SUN GIVES
NO LIGHT
AND THE MOON THROWS
GREAT DROPS OF BLOOD
...
SINGING OF BOTH
A GREAT AND TERRIBLE
DAY

Ahelia Publishing

Helena, Montana

VEILED SUN

BLOOD MOON

Kimm Reid

BEYOND SOLSTICE GATES

Veiled Sun Blood Moon

Second Edition 2018

ISBN—978-1-988001-00-5

1. Supernatural 2. Science Fiction 3. Fiction 4. Religion

Published in the United States of America
Printed in the United States of America

www.aheliapublishing.com
kimm.reid@outlook.com

Table of Contents

1

SURPRISE VISITOR

"Time goes by too quickly, don't you think, Judah?" Jennifer had to look up when she asked the question because, in the past number of months, Judah had grown immensely tall in size as well as in knowledge and understanding of the beings of the air; those unseen by the eye but who, nonetheless, hovered close by. Judah's voice had grown deeper, and sometimes the strength of it caught people by surprise.

"You sound like Daddy," Jennifer would often say. At first, this was hard to get used to. But now, after many months of hearing it, Jennifer and Bella had both grown to be rather fond of the sound.

"I like being reminded of Theo," Bella would say. Once in a while, though not often, Bella's tongue would slip and accidentally call Judah by his father's name. At first, it was completely by accident, but lately, it began to be more and more on purpose. It was this deep voice that responded to Jennifer's question this morning, and the girl's ears were delighted at the sound.

"I suppose it does," he sighed. "I hadn't thought much about it, I guess."

The twins were walking … taking their usual route to school … and they had nearly arrived; only a couple more blocks to go. They would have arrived, too, if not for a semi-familiar voice coming from a few steps behind them.

"Judahhhh," the voice rang out. "Jenniferrr," it called sweetly. Jennifer looked up at her brother, and he looked right back down at his sister. They both stopped dead in their tracks and watched as pleasant grins crossed the other's face.

"Kaija Mae!" They squealed simultaneously and spun around. Sure enough, the chubby face of the only slightly familiar girl was a few steps behind them, and with the twins now standing still, she quickly caught up.

"I thought I'd never catch up with you," she laughed. "I stopped at your house and Bella said I'd find you here and … well, here you are."

"Here we are," Jennifer smirked. The twins hadn't gotten to know Kaija Mae in Trilleah because Jennifer had spent the last part of their journey unconscious and unaware of everything—and everybody. In fact, she didn't recall much of their last journey at all, but somewhere deep in her subconscious, she'd heard Kaija Mae's voice, singing tenderly over her. That was how she was able to recognize the voice now.

She had asked Judah about that day many times since it seemed odd to her that she couldn't remember smashing her head into the floor, or her brave brother wielding a sword and disintegrating the hideous beast called Choshek. She had no recollection whatsoever of being carried through Malleana Forest or of being watched by the Trows.

"Like vultures waiting to feast," Judah had told her recently.

The one thing—in fact, the only thing—she remembered about the entire incident, was a voice; this voice.

Unrecognized at the time, Jennifer recalled it now as Kaija Mae had called to them. Undoubtedly, it was the same voice, and it carried her mind back to the song it had sung and the peace that poured over Jennifer as the words surrounded her back in Asphelia's Hollow. The words, or perhaps the melody, had licked at Jennifer's wounds like a soothing ointment and brought considerable relief. No; there was no way she'd forget that voice.

As far as Jennifer was concerned, it was the voice of a real live angel. Jennifer remembered briefly now, as she listened to Kaija Mae chitter-chatter with Judah, that as the girl sang over her, back in the Hollow, something had reached out and touched her; something very real but altogether unseen and forgotten about until this moment.

Jennifer had been excited to know the one to whom that mysterious voice belonged, and now … here she was.

Judah, on the other hand, had spent only a small amount of time with Kaija Mae, since he'd been fighting in Choshek's Hollow. He didn't know her well and had not met many of the others who had been with her. He, too, remembered her voice, however, because of the song she sang. Even though the words were unrecognizable in an unknown language, the voice is what stood out. There was something about it that was altogether … quite completely … simply … well, simply unforgettable. Judah and Jennifer had discussed it countless times.

"It was as if her words carried a peculiar power of some sort," Jennifer would recall.

"Like her song pulled in peace from somewhere far away," Judah would add.

Jennifer would reply, "I don't know the words she sang, but it felt like they went straight into my soul and washed it clean."

Then both would say, "Odd," at the same time and that would be the end of their discussion until the next time. The next time the conversation would be nearly the same as the last time, and so on and so forth.

Bella, on the other hand, had been able to spend a fair amount of time with Kaija Mae and the others while they waited for the twins to return from Choshek's Hollow. The twins' auntie often spoke of Kaija Mae and the others, as though they were the best of friends …

like they'd known each other forever. Now, it didn't sit well with either Judah or Jennifer that Bella hadn't mentioned anything of a possible visit from Kaija Mae.

"I don't wish to sound rude, but why are you here?" Judah asked in his deep voice. Kaija Mae giggled at the change.

"Didn't your auntie tell you I was coming?" the visitor asked. The poor girl did seem to be genuinely confused. "She and I made plans when we were in Trilleah that I'd come visit you all."

Now it was the twins who looked puzzled.

"Auntie Bella never mentioned it," Jennifer said. "At least not to me," and she glanced at Judah.

"She never said anything to me either," he shrugged and returned Jennifer's confused look.

"Hmm." Kaija Mae put her hands on her hips and made her lips twist up as though she was deeply pondering something of great importance. First her lips twisted up to the left, then they twisted up to the right. She said, "hmm" and "humm" umpteen times, and finally stepped between the twins. She looped her left arm through the right arm of Judah and her right arm through the left arm of Jennifer. "Makes no difference, I suppose. I'm here now, and you're both here, and that's what matters, after all."

Again, the twins looked at each other and without speaking any words, both knew what the other was thinking.

WHY is she here?

Kaija Mae also seemed to know the thought that passed between the twins and she answered it immediately.

"Oh, I'm sorry," she blurted out and walked a little quicker. "I assumed that Bella would have explained it to you." Kaija Mae looked puzzled, but the look disappeared and was replaced by an explanation of some sort, although, it was a very uninformative explanation, to be sure.

"I know a few things about Trilleah. I've been there a long, long time; longer than anyone else, I suppose. Longer than most of the cursed souls have been stuck in the forest, I'd say. Positively longer than any of the Travelers have been riding their Shailmas through the Gates of Solstice. Quite nearly as long as King Shrailzhar himself." As she spoke, Kaija Mae seemed to ponder her words carefully before letting them leave her lips.

Now it was the twins whose faces smeared with puzzlement … and confusion … and bewilderment … and trepidation. If this girl had been in Trilleah since the king, did she know him? Was she one of his army? How is it that she could cross from Shrailzhar's land to theirs? If she could cross over, could the rest of the army? Could the king?

A million questions tumbled in their minds. If one question did not pop up in Judah's mind, it most certainly showed up in Jennifer's. Any thoughts that couldn't find a space to be heard in Jennifer's cramped mind quickly squished themselves into Judah's.

Kaija Mae watched the two of them carefully, as though she could see through their eyes and into the swirling thoughts that were crowding their minds. Anxiety was growing quickly in the twins' hearts but was not given time to develop fully into fear. Before it had the chance, Kaija Mae spoke again, addressing the words that neither of them had spoken.

"No need to panic or wonder," she said. "I've nothing to hide and will answer every one of the questions that you have for me … so long as we have the time." Kaija Mae had a sweetness to her that would not allow their anxiousness to remain; as if her voice came out like a broom and swept away any remnants of fear or anxiousness. The curiousness stayed, however, and the twins determined to ask as many questions as they could come up with, but all ideas of fear, uncertainty, and doubt fluttered away.

"Do we have to go to school today?" was Judah's first question.

Kaija Mae laughed. "Of course, you're not going to school today. That's why I came looking for you, silly Judah."

"Phew," he sighed dramatically.

They came upon a T in the road just then which, if they took the right turn would lead them straight to their big brick school building. However, if they took the left turn they could go back home or to the malt shop on the corner. "Martha's Maltz," not only had the best malts to ever tingle a taste bud, it also had some of the twins' favorite snacks.

"Martha's Maltz it is," Jennifer squealed.

"Yes, please," Kaija Mae giggled. They turned to the left and ran toward the malt shop.

Even though both of the twins were thinking that skipping school and sipping on malts and munching on Martha's chicken fries and pickle chips was a fantastic alternative, neither had forgotten what Kaija Mae had said. Neither twin could even imagine what else she might have to say, and neither Judah nor Jennifer wasted any time playing out possible scenarios in their curious minds.

It only took a few minutes to arrive at the malt shop and find a seat—it wasn't exactly crowded this early on a school day. Judah and Jennifer knew exactly what they wanted, but had to wait a few minutes for Kaija Mae to look at the list of flavors so she could decide. Once their orders had been taken and Martha had disappeared through the swinging doors to prepare their snacks, Judah looked straight at the girl—who really was a stranger to them both—and asked the most basic question. However, this one basic question was only peeling back the lid on a box that contained a thousand other not-so-basic questions.

"Why have you come here? To Westlock, I mean?" Judah asked.

"Just to find us?" Jennifer added. "I wonder why Bella didn't tell us," she huffed. Jennifer was always suspicious of things she didn't understand. Ever since the unexplainable train accident that had taken her parents, Jennifer had become overly suspicious of even the most explainable things.

"Well," Kaija Mae said, taking a long sip of her malt, "I don't know why Bella didn't mention it, but I suppose she had her reasons. I do know why I am here, though," she said. "Shekinah brought me this morning … long before the sun was up."

"Shekinah is your Shailma, I guess?" Jennifer asked the question, even though she already knew the answer. Kaija Mae nodded and kept sipping her malt. The three of them chitter-chattered on for a while about many things that made no difference whatsoever, until finally the malts were nearly gone.

"Tell us why you're here, Kaija Mae," Judah spoke sternly. He was getting impatient; possibly because since the last time they'd been to Trilleah, he had taken it upon himself to find out as much as he could about the land, Malleana Forest, and the creatures that lived in the air—which were mostly unseen by the natural eye. Judah had learned a lot from books, although most of the things he read in the library said all these things were fictional.

He knew, for certain, they were not.

2

TELLING SECRETS

More than just studying on his own or reading what someone else had written about things they may have had no understanding of, Judah had begun spending long amounts of time with his Shailma. Shemaiah was very informative and helped Judah understand many things. He secretly hoped this was the reason Kaija Mae had come to Westlock—to provide Judah with even more understanding of such things; things that were otherwise beyond any reasonable understanding.

Since their last trip to the dark and detestable land when he had to use his own sister's blood to defeat the deplorable Choshek, Judah had become very interested … and very confused … and very determined.

"What if I hadn't heard Shemaiah? What if I chose to let my fear in the circumstances be stronger than my trust in the Shailma? What if Miriam had gone into the Hollow with Jennifer instead of me?" Judah would often become so overwhelmed by all his "what if's," that he finally decided to find answers the best he could. He worked hard to gain as much wisdom and information from Shemaiah outside of Trilleah as he could, so that when the Solstice Gates opened again and they were called to return, Judah would be armed with the necessary equipment, which was not equipment at all.

No; not equipment such as swords or guns or weapons that one would carry on their backs, although if those things were necessary, he'd most certainly take them as well. The equipment Judah most needed to be armed with was wisdom and knowledge of not only the land, but of the beasts that skulked about behind the veil and their underhanded, scheming ways. Most of all, he needed to know about King Shrailzhar and his marching armies. It seemed there'd come a day when he and the other Travelers would meet the king face to face. Judah was unwilling to go into such a meeting unprepared … or unarmed.

"OK, Kaija Mae," Judah said sternly and repeated his question from earlier. "Tell us why you're here." He let his spoon fall into the empty glass. The clanking it made from the metal hitting the glass was louder than he'd expected. The noise startled Jennifer and she jumped in her seat.

"Judah," she snarled, throwing him a fowl glare.

"Sorry," he said before turning back to their visitor. "Kaija Mae, please … what do you have to tell us?" He sounded impatient, so Kaija Mae tucked her spoon inside the glass and pushed it aside.

"Yes," she apologized. "I got distracted. As I was saying," she started, "I've been in Trilleah as long as Trilleah has existed. You see, I was among the first of the souls stolen by the Trows—or the first that they tried to steal, I suppose. There was a time long ago when an evil and despicable man dwelled on the earth." She could see by the looks on the twins' faces they were already confused.

"Long before you, or your aunt Bella, or even your parents were born," she said. Both Judah and Jennifer nodded in understanding—even though they had no understanding whatsoever —so Kaija Mae continued.

"A long time ago, a man—the most evil of all men—lived in my country. He was so vile that he gathered hundreds of thousands of people who he'd decided had no right to exist and proceeded to eliminate them from the earth; wiping them out entirely was his goal, I suppose." Again confusion crossed their faces. "I realize this may be hard for you to understand and even harder for you to believe," said this chubby-faced girl whom they barely knew.

"Anyway, please do try," she said and continued.

"King Shrailzhar was just beginning to set up his kingdom, and so for the first time, the Trows were deployed to steal souls and oh, they stole many. Those Trows gathered souls like a child gathers candy at Halloween, locking them all away in Malleana Forest with great excitement. The more souls they stole, the more they wanted to steal. They got an appetite for it, I suppose you could say. Before this time in history, Trilleah already existed, although there were no souls in its forest. Just a king without a throne, I guess you might say."

Here is where Jennifer finally interrupted. "How was there a Forest of Waiting Ones without any ... well … without any Waiting Ones?" The question made sense in her mind, but as she tried to put words together to ask it, she was aware that it didn't make much sense outside of her mind.

"Pardon?" Kaija Mae asked.

Jennifer huffed, feeling exasperated. "The Malleana Forest is made up of stolen and cursed souls, so if none of their souls had been stolen and hidden in the forest, how could there be any forest at all? Were there trees but no souls or were there not even trees? Did the souls enter the trees or did they become the trees? Were the trees in the forest before the souls were cursed? I don't understand any of this."

"Oh, I think I know what you're asking. Good question, I suppose," Kaija Mae replied, pondering for a moment before giving an answer. "I guess there was no forest until the souls of the ones I was with here were stolen and taken there." She saw Jennifer's mind was reeling with more questions along the same rabbit trail and stopped her before she could continue in a direction that had no purpose for this particular discussion.

"Jennifer, that makes no difference right now. There were no Waiting Ones before this time I'm speaking of. But then, in one quick moment, the Trows stole thousands of souls—my friends, family, strangers—and carried us off to Trilleah. We were all imprisoned by the curse and stuck in the Dark Land. In an instant, there was a Malleana Forest and the dreadful curse was spoken over it to keep the souls locked in its grip.

Again, Jennifer's face contorted as she tried to make sense of this, for indeed, it seemed senseless. "Jelly Bean," Judah finally spoke. "I don't think *how* the forest became a forest matters." He took his spoon out of the empty glass and licked it for the umpteenth time. "Be patient and hear what Kaija Mae has to say."

"I'm trying," Jennifer sighed.

"Just listen, Jennifer. It'll make sense to you in time," Kaija Mae said. She patted Jennifer's small hands, but Jennifer was not comforted and pulled them away harshly. Nevertheless, Kaija Mae continued.

"Even though my soul was among those stolen before we could reach the other side of the veil, I hadn't actually died like the others had. So when the Trows dragged us to Trilleah and locked us away in the forest, my soul couldn't be rightfully held. I was very much alive—in the land of the dead."

"Oh, good grief," Jennifer mumbled. "That is supposed to make sense to me?" It seemed the more Kaija Mae tried to explain, the more frustrated Jennifer became. "I'm going to the bathroom," she snapped, and slid off of the bench. It was nearly comical as she stormed off, stomping to the back of the malt shop. Both Judah and Kaija Mae struggled to keep from laughing.

"Shall I wait for you to return, Jennifer?" Kaija Mae called after her, still sweet, kind, patient, and altogether lovely.

"Doesn't matter," Jennifer whined without turning around. "I don't have any idea how to make sense of what you're saying," and with that, she disappeared through the double swinging doors leading to the back of the shop.

Kaija Mae and Judah sat quietly and watched the doors swing back and forth, back and forth, until they stopped moving altogether and hung quietly on their posts. Kaija Mae looked down at her spoon, unsure of what to say next.

"I'm sorry," Judah said. "My sister has nearly had it with the entire thing. After her last experience in Trilleah, she says she's never returning to the land, and while Summer Solstice is coming quickly, I still cannot persuade her. The scars on her cheek are not helpful either. Every time Jennifer looks in the mirror she sees them; she is always scratching at them. They are just tiny scars, barely even noticeable really, but I'm afraid the marks we see on her cheek are only a fraction of the damage done to her soul."

"Have no concern for such things, Judah," Kaija Mae said. "It's not your job to convince Jennifer to travel to Trilleah. That is for her Shailma to do. Never try to do the job that only a Shailma has the authority to do."

Judah sighed loudly and rubbed his forehead. It was clear he was troubled by what had happened to his sister on the last visit to Trilleah. "Something happened that she hasn't been able to speak of," he said. "Whatever made those scars, she still hasn't said. They are so tiny that I can't even see them, but Jennifer knows they are there and only she knows how they got there."

"What do you mean?" Kaija Mae asked, somewhat puzzled, but then again, not as much as she probably should have been.

"The scars on her cheek, and if you remember, her lips were badly burned as well … she can't seem to remember what happened though." Again, Judah rubbed his forehead as if trying to remember what had been long forgotten. "She's tried to tell me many times, but every time she opens her mouth to speak about it, her lips start to burn all over again. She either stops talking altogether or says something that doesn't make any sense. It's like her tongue gets tied into knots when she tries to speak of what happened.

"I don't get it," Judah said. Anger was beginning to speckle his words, so Kaija Mae decided to change the subject without Judah noticing. After all, she was well aware of what had occurred between Jennifer and Miriam, but it wasn't her place to speak of it … at least, not yet. She was aware of all happenings in Trilleah, which was her purpose in visiting Westlock and the twins. Part of her reason for coming was to speak of Miriam with Judah and Bella, but now was not the time to do so. She hoped she'd have an opportunity soon, though, for it was a matter of great importance. Kaija Mae waited for a moment, watching Judah rub his forehead first with one hand and then with the other. Compassion filled her belly.

Finally, Kaija Mae asked, "Shall I continue without Jennifer, or do you think we should wait for her?"

"Continue," he said. "It'll probably be a while before she comes back." Judah rolled his eyes, but it was apparent that he was more concerned and saddened for his sister than he was frustrated with her.

"OK." Kaija Mae was busy folding and refolding her napkin. Judah would have chuckled and teased the beautiful girl if he wasn't so keen on finding out what she had to tell him. It seemed that she must have valuable information if she traveled all that way to get here. However, as he thought about it, Judah realized he had no idea where she had traveled *from*. He was about to ask this very question and opened his mouth, but before the words could be spit out, Kaija Mae stopped folding the napkin and pushed it aside. She bent forward, leaning on her elbows, and motioned for Judah to lean in closer as well. When he did, Kaija Mae looked Judah directly in the eye.

"Judah," she whispered, "I must beg of you to not return to Trilleah, but I fear you will not listen and will return anyway."

Judah was dumbfounded. He had no words to say. His mind formed none. He was without speech. Judah stared blankly across the table at this girl—a stranger—who'd come from somewhere he did not know to deliver a message that he didn't want to hear. After many moments, he finally found the words he'd been looking for.

"I must return," he whispered.

"That's what I thought you would say." She sighed and swiped the crinkled napkin back into her hands. Kaija Mae began tearing off small bits and piling one piece on top of another. Judah could only assume it was a nervous habit, because she was making a horrible mess on the table and didn't seem to notice.

If that's what she needs to do, so be it, he thought to himself. *I don't have to clean it up, I suppose; it makes no never mind to me.*

Another generous slice of silence lingered. Concerned that Jennifer would return any second now, Judah wanted to gather as much information from Kaija Mae as he could; information that would be helpful for him but not so great for his sister's peace-of-mind. Judah's words interrupted the silence.

"I HAVE TO return!" he repeated. "My mother is locked in the forest and for Jennifer's sake, I must do everything I can to break the curse keeping her there." His words were firm and he surprised even himself in how much he believed them. Judah realized just then that he would do whatever was asked of him to break the curse. He'd pay whatever price was charged to free the souls of those guarded by the Trows. After all, he never went alone. His Shailma always went with him.

"Kaija Mae, please. What have you come here to tell me? What do you know that I don't? How can you help?" There were more and more and more questions rolling off of his tongue.

Because Kaija Mae was now firmly convinced that Judah would not take her advice and stay out of Trilleah, she felt the time was right to begin teaching him all she knew about the cursed land of King Shrailzhar. If he insisted on returning, she'd make sure he had all the information he would need to keep himself—and his sister—as safe as possible.

"Judah," she whispered and leaned in closer. "I have secrets that I must share with you since you refuse to stay out of Trilleah … secrets that will keep you from being trapped by the snares of King Shrailzhar." Just as Judah was getting ready to listen with all of his might, the doors at the back swung open, and they caught sight of Jennifer trudging toward the table.

"I can't tell you right now. Jennifer must not know the things of which I must warn you." Kaija Mae spit the words out quickly before Jennifer could get too close. Then, she threw her head back and laughed as though she'd just told the most hilarious of stories. Judah forced a bit of a chuckle as well, although he was confused about Kaija Mae … and curious about her secrets … and more terrified to return to the Dark Land than he'd ever been before.

3

UNTOLD STORIES

"Oh, Kaija Mae," he said, trying to hide the seriousness of what had been their conversation—until Jennifer had returned from the bathroom and interrupted. "You made such a mess." Before Jennifer could sit back down, Judah stood up and stretched. "I suppose we should be getting to school now, Jelly Bean." That didn't sit well with his already grouchy sister at all, who immediately turned downright foul.

She swatted him on the shoulder and whined. "I thought we didn't have to go to school today."

"Oh, I suppose that's right," her brother teased. Judah wasn't all that good at hiding his emotions and right now, his emotions were an ugly mixture of tension and turmoil. He tried, nevertheless, to be lighthearted and jovial, or at least, convince his sister that he was. "Well, I'm not going, but you can do whatever you want."

His unamused sister wasted no time in snapping back at him. "I'm going home." And with that said, Jennifer swiped one last drip of chocolate from the side of her malt glass and licked it off of her finger. She turned and headed for the door, neither waiting for nor looking back at the others.

Judah and Kaija Mae were right behind her. They each caught the other's eye and without speaking any words, both knew that their conversation would be continued later. Judah hoped "later" would be soon, as his dread-filled curiosity had been frantically stirred and was now refusing to be settled. All types of thoughts and imaginations began popping into his mind. He hoped most of them would be proven wrong by the odd visitor, and he tried to dismiss them all for the time being. Of course, that was harder said than done and most of his wonderings refused to be dismissed.

This stranger kept claiming that she brought great truths, yet Judah thought she was making it very tough to pull the information … or secrets … or riddles … or whatever else she wanted to call them … out of her. He was getting frustrated and wondered why she couldn't just tell them what she knew. Why the secrets? Perhaps she knew nothing about anything, but then what would her reasons be for traveling to Westlock? It was mind-boggling, and Judah's mind was thoroughly boggled.

While Judah and Kaija Mae tried to keep up to Jennifer, she kept running ahead. The young girl reached the little yellow house on the corner of Fairview Lane and Mitchell Avenue long before her brother and Kaija Mae, but still there was not enough time to discuss whatever there was to discuss. Jennifer reached out and grabbed the old brass doorknob on the side door of the house. Before the door had time to swing open, Jennifer's voice rang out loud and clear, echoing through the old walls.

"Bellaaa," she hollered. Then louder. "BELLLAAA." Jennifer waited, but her patience had shriveled up a long time ago. She stomped into the house, determined to be the first to find her aunt and question her on this surprise visit from Kaija Mae.

Auntie Bella, who'd been in the farthest part of the back garden, reached the porch at the same time Judah and Kaija Mae did.

"What's going on in here?" she demanded, sounding slightly perturbed and slightly delighted at her ability to keep such a secret.

"That's what I am wondering," Jennifer demanded right back. "We seem to have a guest … but I guess you already knew that."

"Oh, is that what all this ruckus is about?" Bella smiled and looked at their grinning visitor, who was shrugging her shoulders as if she had no idea what Jennifer was rambling on about. "I see you found the twins," she said.

"I did," Kaija Mae replied, nodding at Judah.

"Why are you annoyed, J?" Bella asked.

"I am not annoyed," Jennifer snapped, "exactly."

Bella was amused and threw her head back in an attempt to show how outrageous she found the answer … and how amusing her flustered niece was.

"Ha ha ha," she mocked, then stopped her antics and looked right back to Jennifer. "Are you sure about that?" she asked, raising one eyebrow.

"I guess I'm a little annoyed." Jennifer put her hands on her hips, which only caused Bella to laugh for real this time. "Why didn't you tell us that Kaija Mae was coming … or *why* she was coming?" Jennifer looked at Kaija Mae and became angry all over again. "WHY ARE YOU HERE?" Jennifer demanded.

"Jennifer Lillian Elliot," Bella scolded. "That is no way to speak to our guest. Does it really matter whether I told you or not?" Bella asked, she too, becoming a bit annoyed with Jennifer. "If I'd have mentioned it, you would have asked a thousand questions to which I did not have the answers, and that would've perturbed you more. I suppose I chose to avoid your perturbedness for as long as possible."

Bella made a reasonable point, one to which Jennifer had no good argument, so she shrugged her shoulders and let the subject drop.

Kaija Mae and Judah, on the other hand, had moved into the kitchen and were busy eating some pastrami and pickle sandwiches that had been made and left sitting on the table. "I hope these are for us," Judah snickered as he filled his mouth and deliberately ignored his sister's antics.

"Of course, they are for you. Who else might they be for?" Bella said, entering the kitchen. "Although I was expecting you earlier."

"Ya, sorry about that," Kaija Mae apologized as she wiped a bit of mustard from the corner of her mouth. "The twins thought I needed to try the world's best malts … and I'm glad they did."

"They're pretty great, aren't they?" Bella agreed. She turned to her deeply annoyed niece and said, "Eat up, miss Jennifer. Then you and I need to go into town for a bit."

Jennifer grabbed a sandwich and glared at her aunt, who she thought was being much too bossy at the moment, but said nothing about it. If truth be told, she wanted to get Bella alone so she could ask those thousand questions now since she wasn't given the opportunity to ask them earlier.

"Whatever," she shrugged and poured herself some sweet tea. When Jennifer's ears heard that she'd been called "Miss Jennifer," it made her stomach queasy because that was what the black adders had called her back in the Fowler's Snare. She really couldn't tell if her memory recalled the name, or if she was reminded by the dark eyes that decided now would be an ideal time to show up and peer through her own. Jennifer jumped, startled by them, and spilled a bit of her tea. She didn't care.

It had been months since she'd seen the eyes. In fact, she hadn't seen them since her return from the last Solstice. Trilleah was the last place they had appeared to her, and Jennifer was convinced the eyes had stayed behind the gates of the Dark Land. Now it was evident that she'd been misled, and the eyes had been hiding all along … that is, until this very moment.

Why now? she wondered. *What do you want?* Of course, no reply came; not that she expected one.

It wasn't difficult for the others to notice that something had spooked Jennifer, since she'd jerked her body so hard that much of her sweet tea had slopped onto the floor.

"You OK, Jelly Bean?" Judah asked. He snickered at first, but when he looked at her face it was obvious something had happened of which he wasn't aware—something that should not be snickered at.

Bella, too, noticed something had come over Jennifer, and she put her hand on her niece's shoulder.

"J," she said gently, "are you alright?"

"I'm fine," Jennifer snapped.

Everything inside of the girl wanted to break down and start screaming. She wanted to tell them about the eyes that had been appearing for no understandable reason and that they had begged her not to reveal them to the others. She wanted to explain the unexplainable creature that kept showing up and glaring at her. Jennifer desperately wanted to tell them how sometimes the dark eyes appeared from outside of herself and peered into her soul through the windows of her own eyes, and how at other times they used her eyes to peer out from somewhere within. Jennifer decided there was no way to explain such a thing to make the others understand, so she didn't even try, lest they thought her to be crazy. After all, how does one explain something they cannot understand themselves?

Jennifer was not even sure whether there was one set of eyes that moved back and forth from the inside of her soul to the outside and back again, or if there were two entirely separate sets of eyes. As she watched and paid attention, it seemed very much like there was one pair of intruding eyes, and they were somehow using her own eyes as a portal back and forth between her two worlds.

Oh, indeed, how she wanted to explain—or at least try. If she could not understand such a thing herself, how would she be able to find the words to explain it to someone else? Every time she was close to opening her mouth to try, those eyes begged her not to. It was something that came with the eyes, perhaps. Not a voice particularly, but more like the eyes themselves could tell a story or put thoughts straight into Jennifer's soul; just one more thing Jennifer couldn't explain, so she never bothered to try.

They'll think you're crazy, she read in the eyes. *Do you know what they do to crazy people? Well? Do You?*

In fact, Jennifer DID know what they did to crazy people. One night last Halloween when Bella was out, the twins watched a movie—or at least part of a movie—about that very thing; a movie about crazy people. She wished she hadn't watched as much as she had, but it was too late now. She couldn't un-see what she had seen on the screen that night, and the eyes reminded her of something from that movie. Maybe the words she kept hearing were from the eyes themselves or maybe they were something she'd heard from the movie that had looped in her memories. It was all a mixed-up jumble in her mind now, and she couldn't seem to separate the two. Nevertheless, the fact was that she did know what happened to a person when they were found to be crazy, and so the secret of the eyes was safe; quite safe, indeed. Jennifer had no intention of letting the secret out.

Once in a while, she would begin to wonder to herself whether she might, in fact, be crazy … or at least going there. The thoughts would become so frightening that she'd have to force them from her mind completely and repeat under her breath over and over that she was not crazy at all. This, of course, only made her wonder all the more. Perhaps only crazy people walked around whispering to themselves under their breath that they were not crazy, which was the sign that they were, in fact, crazy.

"J," Bella said, with her hand still on her niece's shoulder, "you are in quite a foul mood." The hand went from gentle and concerned to heavy and frustrated. "Either tell us what's going on or go find something to do in your room for a while, because I'm tired of being snapped at for no reason whatsoever and I'm sure Kaija Mae is as well."

Jennifer said nothing. She only stepped over the spilled tea, set her glass on the table, and walked down the hall.

SLAM, went her bedroom door.

What has gotten into that one? Bella wondered.

If only she knew that something had, quite literally, gotten into her beloved niece, she would not have sent her down the hall to be alone in her room. But Bella had no way of knowing the truth, however, for Jennifer would not—could not—find the words to tell it. So for now, the truth would remain cooped up, locked somewhere in the deepest dungeons of Jennifer's frazzled mind ... somewhere between the two worlds in which she now found herself stuck.

4

TEARS MAY FALL

Inside her room with her door firmly closed, Jennifer grabbed the tattered red blanket in one hand and her favorite picture of Mamma and Daddy in the other. She plopped her weary self down on the floor beside her bed. There was just enough space between her bed and the wall to squeeze into. This was the one space where she felt safe and cozy and if someone—specifically Bella—popped her head inside the door to scold her, Jennifer could avoid being seen.

This was her favorite spot in the whole room and she sat here often, mostly when she felt the way she was feeling now. There were not the right words to describe how she felt sometimes. A weight of sadness would cover her from time to time, loneliness she supposed, but whatever label she put on it, it was burdensome.

"Mamma," she whispered to the beautiful woman in the picture, "sometimes I think we'll never break the curse of that hateful land. I'm scared, Mamma. I'm scared you'll be trapped there forever and ever. Oh, it must be dreadful there, Mamma."

She'd set the picture on the floor in front of her, as she often did, and pretended Mamma and Daddy were sitting here with her. When the loneliness became too burdensome for the young orphan to carry, and much too prickly for her to hold onto, Jennifer would sit right here in this spot with the red blanket and the picture and pretend they were all together … pretend they hadn't been in the terrible accident … pretend she didn't have to live each day without them … pretend her life was normal.

With her right hand, she weaved the tassels of the blanket through the fingers on her left hand, first one way, then back the other. It was such a habit by now that she didn't even think about it. Somehow feeling the tassels around her fingers eased her troubled soul.

"Mamma, the eyes are back," she sighed. "Daddy, I wonder if I might be crazy."

All the things the troubled little girl could tell no one else, she told her mamma and daddy while tucked away in this hidden space on the floor. She didn't expect them to answer; not even once. She did, however, know they heard every word she said and somehow, that made her feel better.

One time recently, there was a slight breeze that blew through her room and made the curtains flutter. Jennifer was sure it was the wind from outside that had come in through the open window, but when she got up a while later, she saw the window had been tightly closed. Ever since that day, she knew both Mamma and Daddy heard every word she said.

Each time she'd come and sit in this hidden corner of her room and set the picture of Mamma and Daddy across from her, every time she'd have these little conversations with them, she'd become more and more determined to return to the terrible land of Trilleah and collect enough clay tablets to free Mamma's soul. She hated the thought of it—Trilleah, that is—but a determination to break that dreadful curse crawled through her veins, causing her heart to beat faster and her lungs to breathe deeper. She knew it was something she had to do and nothing would stop her.

"It must be awful for you there, Mamma," she wept. The biggest, wettest tears forced themselves from Jennifer's eyes and rolled down her bony cheeks. They refused to fall to the floor but instead hung stubbornly off of her chin. The red blanket, though worn through in some places, could still soak up every tear. The number of tears that blanket had held over the years was countless.

That blanket held many memories and had seen a lot of pain. It had covered her daddy and brought healing when he was sick with a disease no doctor could name … or cure. It had brought Jennifer comfort night after night after night when her mamma and daddy had been taken from her. Now again, it wiped the river of tears that demanded to be released.

"Mamma, I will do anything, anything at all to break the curse of those miserable Trows." She'd have been surprised to hear Judah say the same words every night, but it would have surprised Judah, even more, to hear his sister mutter the promise. He was sure Jennifer would never return to Trilleah; that she had come to find enough peace about losing Mamma and Daddy, that their latest trip to the bitter land—the one that had burned her lips and scarred her cheek —would be her last.

He couldn't be more wrong; Judah didn't know that all the while Jennifer was growing stronger and stronger on the inside. Even though he was her twin, he couldn't have known that she and Simeon had been communicating daily and even though she could not seem to reveal what had occurred with Miriam, Simeon knew thoroughly. They'd spoken about it countless times.

Perhaps Miriam had been able to stop Jennifer from telling the other Travelers what had happened, what she'd done, and that she was a Reptilian Mindbender, but nothing could keep Simeon from knowing. Even Miriam could not control such things … those things that went on in her mind and the silent conversations between Jennifer and her Shailma. Simeon saw what Miriam had done; he'd heard the words she uttered that had sealed Jennifer's lips.

Jennifer was learning that it didn't matter if she couldn't tell Judah, Bella, or Kaija Mae, about such things. What *did* matter was that Simeon was aware. He saw what had happened; he knew. Her Shailma had told her that it had to happen—what Miriam did—so that this Mindbender's true identity, her real intentions, could be made known.

"Secrets have power only until their truth is revealed," Simeon told Jennifer in one of their many discussions. Now, the scared orphan girl was again pondering the meaning of his words when someone knocked on the door, pulling her back from that terrible memory of Miriam and her secrets, now revealed, if only to her.

"J," she heard Bella call.

"I guess she's going to be all lovely now," Jennifer whispered to the photograph still sitting on the floor.

"What," she answered flatly through the closed door.

"May I come in?" she heard.

"Hold on." Jennifer got up, kissed the picture of Mamma and Daddy, and set it carefully back on her dresser. She caught sight of herself in the mirror and looked at her sad reflection for a couple of seconds. "Oh dear," the tearful twin sighed and tried to wipe her face so Bella wouldn't know she'd been crying. Jennifer fluffed her hair a little and pulled a few strands toward her face, hoping it would help. It didn't.

"Come in," she sighed. The door squeaked open and Bella stepped through. Seeing Jennifer's puffy face, she set the back of her hand gently on the girl's cheek and sat down on the bed.

"What's wrong?" she asked. There was a sincerity in her words, Jennifer noticed. "You've been out of sorts today … so unlike yourself. What's going on with you?" Bella swept back the strands of hair Jennifer had pulled forward to hide her tear-stained cheeks.

"Nothing is wrong, Bella. I just don't understand why this stranger is here, why you didn't tell me, or why any of this is happening." Jennifer sat down beside her auntie on the unmade bed and sighed. She had to work hard to hold back the rest of the tears that hadn't had a chance to break free, but Jennifer had become a pro at such things. "And, Summer Solstice is coming."

"Uhhh, yes, that it is, I suppose. I should've known that would be upsetting you. I'd wondered if that was part of the problem, but you haven't said anything about it, so I'd almost wondered if you'd forgotten, or at least not noticed that it was so close!" Bella hardly shut her mouth from the last word when Jennifer's shot open, her voice a full octave higher than her last sentence.

"Forgotten? Really Auntie? Forgotten? Oh, Bella. I would LOVE to be able to forget such a thing, but Mamma is there and I will not forget; not until she's freed from that damn curse!"

"Jennifer Lillian," Bella said, but not as harshly this time as earlier in the kitchen. Jennifer knew her auntie wasn't upset, *just doing her job as the one in charge, I suppose,* she thought to herself.

"Sorry," Jennifer mumbled and looked down to watch her fingers wind the tassels from the red blanket around themselves. First one way, then the other … just like always.

There were no appropriate words for Bella to say, so she didn't bother to come up with any; after all, she understood far too well. Bella had lost her own mother when she was only four years old. Being so young, Bella did not remember her; not really. Oh, a few little things here and there that Molly had told her about, but they weren't her own memories.

Molly was fourteen when their mother had passed and so, even though they lived in foster homes for a few years, the sisters had been fortunate enough to stay together. As soon as Molly was old enough to get out, she did. She took Bella, and together, the sisters fended for themselves. They never had much, but they did alright.

What Jennifer had never understood was that while Molly was Bella's sister, her sweet mamma had raised little Bella like her own child since she was four years old. The bond between the sisters was unusually close and resembled more of a "mother-daughter" relationship than a "sisters" one.

Bella missed Molly dreadfully; now was not the time to discuss such things, however. The time for such conversations never seemed to be the right time, so those conversations were never had. Bella often wondered if knowing some of those things would have helped Jennifer, but it wasn't something one could know for sure. Bella had always believed that since Molly had raised her for so many years, it was now Bella's turn to do the same for the twins.

They still had very little money and were, by all standards, poor. However, they had the little yellow house that had belonged to

Molly and Theo, and neighbors and church folk helped out now and again. Bella never let on to the twins how poor they were, because she'd figured Jennifer and Judah had enough to worry about without adding money to the list. There was much the young twins didn't need to know, but in keeping so many secrets, Bella was becoming weary and burdened.

The silence blanketing the room had been cuddled up to long enough as the girls both were lost in their own thoughts.

"Well, J," Bella smiled. "Let's go into town, shall we?" She stood herself up and held out her hands for her niece to grab onto. Jennifer's hands found the bed instead, and she pushed herself up, taking a moment to lay the red blanket carefully over her pillow. The back of her sleeve came across her eyes and she pulled pieces of hair back over her face. Jennifer said no words but grabbed a sweater on her way out the door. Bella followed.

Judah and Kaija Mae were nowhere in sight. Jennifer said nothing about it, but she did wonder where the two had gone. *Probably to the basement,* she thought and left it at that for truly, she didn't care. Jennifer didn't care about much of anything right now since her mamma was heavy on her heart and Trilleah was tugging insistently at her mind.

The sandwiches were still sitting on the table, so Jennifer grabbed one on her way out the front door.

"I'll be right out," Bella shouted quickly before the screen door could slam shut. She grabbed a piece of plastic and covered the last few sandwiches, grabbed the keys, and dashed through the door shouting a "see you later" to the others, wherever they were.

Jennifer was waiting for Bella and in just a few moments, the two drove off in silence. Jennifer put her window down and let the warm summer air blow her hair. She hoped it would blow in some comfort and peace, but of course, summer air can do no such thing.

Back at the house, no peace was lingering either. Judah and Kaija Mae had wandered to the back garden, one of the most peaceful places Judah knew. But today there was no peace to be found among the yellow sunflowers or the violet lilies or the white daisies. Judah plucked a couple of small carrots from the ground, wiped most of the dirt onto his pants, and began munching.

With Kaija Mae rambling on about things in Trilleah, Judah was growing confident that he'd never find any peace again. While sometimes he was annoyed at what she'd say, in the very next moment he'd find himself being grateful for the information she was passing on to him. Some of it seemed of utmost importance while other parts appeared thoroughly useless.

Kaija Mae picked peas and cracked the shells open, popping the little green balls into her mouth. "I hope Bella doesn't mind us nibbling in her garden. There's nothing like fresh peas right off of the vine. It's been so long since I've tasted anything so wonderful."

"She doesn't mind," was all Judah could say.

What he *wanted* to say was, "Who cares about the stupid peas or the garden or the lovely weather you keep rambling on about."

What he *wanted* to say was, "Tell me all that you know, all that you came to tell me. Tell me how to defeat King Shrailzhar and how to break the curse. Show me how to free the souls of the Waiting Ones." What he *wanted* to scream from the top of his lungs was, "Help me … please help me keep Jennifer safe … I don't know how to keep her safe!"

Of course, the truth of it all was that he could not keep her safe. There was no power that he had or would get from any of Kaija Mae's ramblings that would enable him to do the one thing he so desperately wanted to do … he was powerless to keep his sister safe and way deep down in a place he dared not let his mind wander, Judah knew the sad truth.

5

DON'T BE FOOLED

Judah sat on the bench munching grime-smeared carrots and listening to the beautiful girl sitting in the dirt enjoying the fresh peas. This was the same bench where his daddy used to sit and talk to Mamma while she picked the peas and carrots. He pondered many such times, and while silent on the outside, Judah desperately searched for his Shailma on the inside.

Shemaiah, he cried, *this girl is driving me mad. I want to reach down her throat and pull out the words, whatever they are; she seems to be getting nowhere. Or, smack her on the back of the head ... maybe the words are stuck somewhere inside, and I could jar them loose. Surely she didn't travel here to pick peas and tell me the sun was especially hot today.* He rambled on and on hoping to hear something—anything—from his Shailma. If Kaija Mae wasn't going to give him answers, maybe Shemaiah would.

He didn't. What he did say only frustrated Judah further.

My boy, be patient. You must wait. You must be kind and gentle, for this girl has wisdom ... a wisdom which you need to acquire. The information she has, you must receive, for it's essential to staying safe in Trilleah. The upcoming journey will be unlike any other journey you've traveled thus far. If you hope to return to this garden, Kaija Mae's wisdom must become your own. Be patient a while longer. Soon she'll begin to speak, and when she does, your ears must be open. Listen carefully, Judah, even when you hear nothing. There's much to be heard in the silence.

In the very next moment, with Judah's ears in tune to Shemaiah and not the girl kneeling in the dirt picking peas, he nearly missed her words completely. It was only the sheer madness of those words that grabbed his attention.

"I am seventy-three years old," she said. "I've been in Trilleah for nearly sixty years."

He couldn't have heard her right; definitely not. Judah let the carrot fall from his fingers and back into the dirt. "Um ... what?"

She repeated her truth. "I am seventy-three years old." Kaija Mae stopped picking peas and watched him with a bit of a smirk as her words ricocheted around his mind. "I've been in Trilleah for almost sixty years, working to free the souls of the Waiting Ones. But it's you and your sister who will pay the final cost for their freedom. It is you two that we need."

"What do you mean, pay the cost? What's the cost?" he stammered. Judah couldn't begin to comprehend what Kaija Mae was saying. As he stared at this girl who had such great beauty, he could not force himself to believe she was telling the truth. If she wasn't telling the truth about something as simple as her age, how could he be confident she'd tell the truth about anything else? Was Kaija Mae trying to trick him? Test him maybe?

"Shemaiah," he mumbled under his breath. "This girl is crazy … a complete lunatic." Instead of Shemaiah responding, it was Kaija Mae who answered.

"I'm not crazy, Judah," she said. "I know this sounds insane, but I speak nothing but the truth. You must choose to believe me no matter how you feel about it."

"Can you hear my thoughts?" he asked. He'd barely whispered his question, yet she had answered him immediately.

"No, I just figured that since you're looking at me like I'm crazy, I thought I would assure you that I am not." Kaija Mae winked in jest at the stunned boy sitting on the garden bench. He turned pale and all movement left him. He sat motionless, unable to do much else other than stare at her wide-eyed. How could this be possible? He had admired her beauty and assumed her to be only slightly older than his aunt Bella.

"How?" Judah finally got his wits about him enough to ask the most obvious question. "How is that possible?"

"I didn't know either, at first. But after being there so long, it seems that if your soul is stolen—even if it's by mistake, you remain stuck at the very age you were when it was taken."

He had no words to reply with because he was stunned into silence. Was she serious? Undoubtedly, this was the most ridiculous thing he'd ever heard; in either of the worlds in which he'd been.

Kaija Mae waited briefly for a reply, but it was soon apparent that no reply was coming. "I'm not the only one, Judah. You see, in Trilleah, there is no time, not really. The only time that passes is during the two short periods of Solstice. Each is only as long as the sun is up, but when the sun sets and the Travelers pass back through the gates, time does not keep marching on like here. Time stops moving altogether until the next time the Solstice Gates are open. Every year that you grow older, I grow older by only two days."

Finally finding a voice, though a bit raspy from shock, Judah spoke. "We thought Trilleah disappeared when the Gates closed."

"Oh dear," Kaija Mae threw her head back and laughed. "No, certainly not." There was quiet for a minute except for the crack of a few pea pods, and then Kaija Mae laughed again. "You really thought that?"

"Yup. We had no way of knowing until now, I suppose,"

Judah said, finally standing up from the bench and grabbing a few peas himself. "You know," he said, "if you eat too many of those, you're going to regret it.

"What goes on in Trilleah when we're not there?" he continued, now genuinely intrigued by this one called Kaija Mae.

"Many things, I suppose; some of which don't matter at all … but some of which I came here to tell you about." She tossed the empty pods onto the dirt and wiped her hands on her pants. "King Shrailzhar sets out more traps, mostly. He changes the land as much as he can to try and confuse your maps. He knows you have them, but has no understanding of them. Also, Shrailzhar rides through the forest listening to the groaning of the Waiting Ones. It seems to feed him somehow. He delights in the horrible sounds. It's horribly appalling."

"Does he know you're there? Not trapped in the forest, I mean? Have you ever been seen by him?" Judah had become so full of questions he didn't know which to ask first. His Shailma assisted him, though.

Judah, do not ask so many questions that you don't hear what she came here to tell you. Just listen, my boy; just listen.

Kaija Mae dropped one last pea pod into the dirt and wiped her hands again, trying to get all the dirt off. She didn't get up from the garden floor but instead looked up at Judah, who'd sat back down on the bench.

"OK, Judah," she said. "Clearly, Shrailzhar knows about you and the other Travelers' comings and goings in his land. It took him a long time to figure out how you were getting in, but now that he has discovered the gates, he's planning a horrible trap for you all."

"Is that what happened last time?" Judah asked. He was suddenly more interested, now that this girl with dirt on her face had decided to start talking about the very thing she came to talk about.

"Yes, of course," she said. "That trap was minor compared to what's ahead tomorrow," she explained. "Don't worry, though. The Shailmas are prepared. They've been made aware."

"Aware of what?" he questioned.

"Aware of the traps, of course," she answered back.

Judah sighed, becoming deeply agitated. *Shemaiah, this is horribly frustrating, talking to this girl*, he thought as he sighed again.

"What is the trap, Kaija Mae?" he asked. "How do we avoid it?" Any patience he started this conversation with was quickly evaporating into thin air. "Help me," he whispered to his Shailma.

"Oh, right," she muttered. "You must forgive me, Judah. I am old and I forget things easily."

"That would be easier for me to remember if you *looked* old," he chuckled. Kaija Mae smiled.

"The king is planning a trap that will entice you to turn from the map and follow a different way. He's planting a false tablet in one of the underground caves."

Finally, Judah thought. *Now we're getting somewhere.*

"The caves will be on the map, but the path will not be drawn to them, for the map is far wiser than the king. You must … MUST … be careful to follow the map's path PRECISELY, Judah. Don't sway from it even the slightest step, for the trap will seem very enticing. Do not be fooled. Stick to the path EXACTLY as the map will show you."

It seemed rather silly that she'd come all this way to deliver that message. Didn't they always stick to the maps, after all? But just as Judah was thinking about such things, the old lady sitting in the dirt broke into his thoughts once more. It was becoming difficult for him to believe that she couldn't read his mind, since every thought Judah had, Kaija Mae answered even while it lingered in his head.

"This may sound silly and obvious, but there are some among the Travelers who should not be trusted. Certain ones will encourage you to follow deception rather than the path. One, in particular, may try and lead you directly into the caves. Not all the Travelers are truthful, Judah. Not all the Travelers have loved ones whose souls they desire to free. Some of the Travelers are traps themselves."

"What do you mean," he asked anxiously. "Who?"

"I cannot say for certain, because I don't know for certain," the old lady sighed. "I mustn't stir up fear, only caution."

"Then why would you say such a thing?" he asked. "Why are you giving me only part of the information?" Judah's voice was rising, and he was becoming overwhelmed with frustration, which was coming out as anger, although he didn't feel angry.

"How do you get out of Trilleah anyway, once the gates are closed?" He was beginning to wonder if it was, in fact, Kaija Mae who was the trap, and she'd come to try and frighten them off from returning. *Maybe if she can get my mind so confused and make me afraid, we won't return*, he thought.

"Judah, I know this is frustrating, and I understand that you could be confused and angry with me. It might even seem like I'm against you and the others, but you must trust me," Kaija Mae whispered, looking around as though there were others who may overhear the secrets that Judah was still waiting to hear himself.

How does she keep answering questions that I'm not asking? he asked Shemaiah. This was becoming alarming and Judah wished he could stop his thoughts, in case she was somehow able to hear them. But as anyone who has tried knows full well, it's impossible to stop thoughts. The more one thinks about not thinking, the more thoughts arise.

"Ask me what you are wondering," she said softly.

Judah looked her directly in the eyes and spoke firmly.

"Kaija Mae, how did you get out of Trilleah after the gates were closed?" Judah was getting frustrated at having to re-ask but he needed the answers so kept his feelings hidden.

"Good question, I suppose, although not one I might have asked," she replied. "You see, Judah, because the king thinks that I'm in the state of not quite dead but not fully alive, like the other souls trapped in Malleana Forest, he doesn't keep his eyes on me." Her hands were waving wildly in the air now. "I can come and go as I please, really," and then she thought about that for a moment and changed her statement. "Well, I can *kind of* come and go as I please."

"What do you mean?" Judah asked. Now he was beginning to feel angry; quite angry. "How? If you can come and go as you please, why do you go back at all?"

"First, what you need to accept as truth, Judah," Kaija Mae scolded, "is that you cannot understand such things. You must stop trying to figure out those things beyond yourself."

Oh, how this girl—this old woman—was getting on Judah's nerves. She went from making no sense to making less than no sense —if such a thing were possible, and scolding him in between, no less.

"I don't understand what?" he huffed. "You haven't told me anything to understand … or not understand … or whatever."

"Judah, calm down," she whispered, again looking around suspiciously. "Let me start over, and Judah, try to be patient and listen. The longer one is in Trilleah, the more one becomes aware of things that don't exist here in this world, only there in that one." Judah opened his mouth, but before any words could shoot out, Kaija Mae held up her finger as if to hush him.

"For example," she continued, "did you ever see such a thing as Living Maps? Or a Book of Truths … or Lies?

Now she waited for a response, but Judah only nodded and kept quiet. This conversation was seemingly going nowhere, but Shemaiah had instructed Judah to listen, so listen he did.

6

DIRT TRAILS

"No, of course, you've never heard of any of these things before Trilleah. They don't exist here. But now … now that you've seen them and know they are real, would you deny their existence?" Again, the stunned boy merely raised his eyebrows and shook his head.

"If you explained any of these things to your friends at school or one of your teachers, would they think you to be a bit off?"

"Probably," he replied.

"OK. Then you must understand, as I said earlier, that you cannot yet comprehend the things I am telling you. But," the old lady continued, "you must believe I tell the truth."

"Fine," he muttered.

"Now let me try and explain how I am allowed to come and go between here and Trilleah, whether the Solstice Gates are open or closed." She took a big breath, crinkled up her lips, and made her eyes grow large as if to indicate to Judah that he was not the only one frustrated with this situation.

"I don't like speaking of how I got to Trilleah in the first place, but I think it might be helpful for you to understand how I can exist there when the gates are closed." Kaija Mae began drawing lines in the dirt with her finger. It reminded Judah of watching the path draw itself on the Living Maps and for the briefest minute, he wondered if this girl, this old lady, had anything to do with that.

"You see, Judah, when I was a young girl something happened to me, my family, and thousands of others in my country." Her finger kept retracing the lines over and over again, going deeper and deeper into the dirt. She never looked up but watched her fingers tracing the lines as she recalled what was obviously a horribly painful memory.

"Hundreds in my village were killed—for no reason except they were born into a particular race." She paused, and her face looked as though she was trying to forget but was unable to erase the pictures lodged deep in her memory. "We were a small village and didn't have much, but that didn't matter. It wasn't what we had that these people wanted. The army came and threw torches into our homes and burned them to the ground." Kaija Mae stopped tracing the dirt lines and with one quick swipe of her hand, erased them all. "The entire village was destroyed in minutes … because of hatred."

She was quiet for a short time and Judah dared not push her to continue until she was ready. As they sat in silence, the old lady began tracing a new path in the dirt with her finger. After a few awkward moments, she continued with her story.

"Nearly everyone I knew was suddenly dead; bodies were strewn everywhere. That's when the Trows came and ravaged our burned-out village." Her voice lowered to barely more than a whisper as she continued. "They gathered up the souls of my village like kids gathering eggs at an Easter hunt; my parents, my cousins, neighbors, teachers, sisters, grandparents … everyone."

"The problem is that while I was left for dead, I actually wasn't. The Trows had no right to steal my soul, but somehow I got caught up with the others and was taken to Trilleah." More lines were traced into the dirt, more looks of painful memories spread across Kaija Mae's sorrowful face. The more she talked, the quieter her voice became and the older she looked.

"I don't understand how it happened. It shouldn't have happened, but it did. There was nothing I could do. I've been in Trilleah ever since the beginning of Malleana Forest, though I have no idea how long Trilleah existed before that. Perhaps it always existed," she said, hopelessness clinging to her words.

"Anyway," she murmured, "that's how I got there. Now, somehow … and I don't understand it … but because my soul was wrongfully taken I can survive there; but also I can come here. My Shailma, Shekinah, has shown me how. I was locked away in the forest like the rest, but the king couldn't hold me there because my soul still had life. He cannot keep me under the curse."

Judah finally spoke up. "I'm trying to understand, really I am, and I think I do a little bit more than before, but not as much as I'd like." He noticed the look that was coming at him from across the garden and quickly added, "though I do believe you, Kaija Mae."

"I know it's difficult, Judah. I can't stay here. I must remain in Trilleah, but I'm able to leave for small amounts of time and I can go anywhere I choose when I do leave. Think of it like this," she said, brightening up as though a light bulb just turned on in her thoughts. I'm in a type of prison, although I am allowed a pass now and then."

"Yes," Judah said, also brightening up a little. "That makes more sense." However, if either of them had thought about it for even the slightest moment, they'd have both realized it didn't make any sense whatsoever. But then again, since Shemaiah had taken Judah to Trilleah, things that had once made sense no longer did. Sense and nonsense weaved themselves together leaving Judah wondering if what he knew to be so, wasn't so at all.

"Are there more like you?" Judah asked. "Ones who can leave Trilleah, I mean."

"There are a few," she answered. "All those you met in the Labyrinth are like me. We were all taken at the same time, but not from the same village. Aviel is from my village I guess, although I didn't know him there."

"How were you caught in the Labyrinth then?" Again, some suspicion snuck into Judah's question. "If you are there all the time, didn't you know King Shrailzhar was setting the trap?"

"No, we don't know all he does there. It's a huge land and he has many, many warriors spread throughout. They're constantly setting traps for us. We don't have much freedom to roam around Trilleah." Then Kaija Mae became very sullen and whispered, "Judah, do you think the Labyrinth was for you and the other Travelers?"

"Wasn't it?" he asked.

"Oh no!" she said, still whispering. "It was set for us, those of us that are above the curse." Then she became quite loud. "He is ALWAYS setting traps for us. He hates that we can leave Trilleah even though …" her voice trailed off.

"Even though what?" he asked, but no answer came, only more lines trailing from her fingers through the dirt. He asked again, very concerned now. "Even though what, Kaija Mae?"

"Even though the only ones who can see us are those who have been to Trilleah; Travelers like you and Jennifer." Sadness crawled up and settled on her pale face. "That's why I had you order my malt earlier while I pretended to use the bathroom. I didn't want you or Jennifer to know that the waitress would not have been able to see me."

"What?" Judah's voice became loud. "Are you a ghost?"

"Judah, keep your voice down," she said. "You never know who may be listening, and no, I'm not a ghost. It's just the only way I'm allowed to leave Trilleah is all." She looked as though she might burst into tears, so Judah lowered his voice and moved from the bench to the dirt where she was. He sat directly across from her.

"I'm sorry," he shrugged. "I didn't know."

"It's a part of the curse that does affect me, I'm afraid," was all she said on the subject. "Anyway, because of it, King Shrailzhar is constantly trying to trap us, which is how we got locked into the Labyrinth. If you and the others had not come along, we'd have been stuck for sure," she said. "I can't figure it out, but it seems he needs us to be trapped so that we cannot gather the clay tablets and break the curse of the Waiting Ones. If we could, Trilleah would be destroyed along with the king. That's why we need the Travelers."

"Oh," Judah sighed. "As much as I hate to say this, it's making a sliver of sense." He shook his head, "I don't know how, but it is."

"While I'm glad this is making some sense to you, that is not the reason I am here. The reason I am here," Kaija Mae continued, "is because I must warn you about the traps being set right now in Trilleah … for Jennifer." At the name of his sister, Judah sat up and paid very close attention.

Since their parents had been taken from the twins, Judah felt it had become his responsibility to look after his sister. Sure, Bella did what she could, and being only a few years older than the twins, she was doing a good job of it. But in some sense, in the things that could not be seen, Judah believed it was passed on to him to keep a watch over Jennifer and keep her safe.

This was one of those "unseen times," so he determined to pay close attention to whatever words Kaija Mae might say. He straightened his back and moved closer. "Tell me about the traps," he said sternly, "and why they are set for Jennifer."

"I don't know exactly, but I did notice much new activity around Asphelia's Hollow since the last Solstice, and I've heard the armies of Shrailzhar chanting, "Jennifer must fall, never again to rise …" The armies mumble a lot, so I couldn't understand much of what they were saying, but that one phrase they repeated over and over—so many times that I did, finally, figure out those words."

"Jennifer's presence in Trilleah is necessary if the Waiting Ones are going to be freed." Kaija Mae held up her finger as if she knew Judah was about to interrupt. "I don't know why and the more we try to figure it out, the more confused we become. We don't seem to have any understanding of it." Kaija Mae stood up while she was talking, her words filled with sadness. "She is so young … so innocent … perhaps that's why. Maybe it's because she believes the unbelievable—those things that the others refuse to believe."

"She says she's not going back," Judah said. "I've tried to talk to her about it because, we too, know her presence is vital to breaking the curse. We don't know why, but everyone agrees that she must be there if the curse is ever to be broken and the souls of the Waiting Ones are ever to go free.”

“She will return,” was all that Kaija Mae said and somehow, Judah knew she was right.

7

LIES & DECEIT

Judah knew there wasn't much time left before his aunt Bella and Jennifer would be home again, so if there were any more shreds of information he hoped to get out of Kaija Mae, he'd have to dig it out of her quickly.

"You mentioned 'activity' around Asphelia's Hollow?" He waited until the old woman trapped in the skin of a beautiful young lady looked at him so that he'd know he had her attention. Finally, she did.

"Mhm," she mumbled.

"What kind of activity?" he prodded.

"I've been noticing a large group of Shrailzhar's army spending time there lately—doing much chanting. They march around the Hollow over and over again. I can't explain what it is they do, or how they set up traps because they don't use things that you'd expect, like wood or metal or things visible to the eye."

Once again, Judah became frustrated that her answers were unclear, but he was determined to understand as much as he could about the traps—and why the army was marching around their Hollow—since his sister seemed to be their target.

"If they don't use things I would know about or that I would be able to see, what do they use?" He moved back to the bench.

"They use lies and deceptions, of course," she said so matter-of-factly that Judah felt somehow her peculiar answer was supposed to make sense to him; as if he should have known such a thing. He never knew anything of the sort. The look on his face must have made that clear to Kaija Mae because, for once, she expanded her explanation without being asked.

"You think you see things that are not actually there, such as false passages in underground caves … or Labyrinths. Once you enter into such deceptions, you're trapped. You fade away along with the lie that you are stuck in."

"Oh," was the only thing Judah could utter because truly, this girl was spinning his mind inside out and back again. He wondered if she herself, was not real, and he still could not shake the idea that maybe she was the trap; one of many. "It doesn't make any sense … I don't know," he muttered, unaware that he'd said anything out loud.

"Don't know what?" she asked.

"I don't know how to make sense of such nonsense, I suppose," Judah replied. "None of what you say makes any sense."

"Remember how I told you right at the beginning that you would be unable to understand?" She didn't wait for him to answer. "It seems like you've forgotten that. It's not going to make sense to you here, Judah; it will only make sense to you there—in Trilleah."

"Oh, yes, I had forgotten," he scratched his head. "Well, it looks like you were right about that." He snickered and stood up. Kaija Mae held her hands toward him.

"Help an old lady up, will you?" she chuckled, although this was anything but funny to Judah. "Maybe this will help," she said as she stretched and groaned a little. "Remember when we were caught in the Labyrinth, and we finally found our way out?"

"Yes," Judah replied.

"Do you recall when we turned around to look at it, and it was no longer there?"

"Yes," he replied again.

"That was a trap, a lie, something we thought we saw which the map did not see. It was not real, but because we believed it was, it became real. By our believing the lie, it had all the power to trap us forever."

"Don't worry, Judah. Once you are back in Trilleah, since you, and likely Jennifer, stubbornly insist on returning, all that I am speaking to you now will indeed—and sadly—make sense to you then." Judah was about to say something but sneezed instead.

"Judah, remember that while it will make sense to you, it will not make sense to the others, so you must take charge and not let the others—any of them—enter into the traps I'm telling you about, no matter how tempting they may seem. No matter who tries to convince you."

"OK," was all that he could say because he didn't know what else to say. His mind was confused and no questions he could think of would make sense out of it all. Shattering his confusion, he heard car doors slam in front of the house and knew the girls were back. He hadn't gotten any of the information he felt he would need. He was disappointed and angry but said nothing more.

Judah led Kaija Mae through the gate and in the back door, entering the kitchen about the same time as Bella and Jennifer. It seemed Jennifer was in no better mood than when they had left. He looked at the clock on the wall and was surprised to see so much time had passed. It was nearly 6:00.

"It seems like you just left," he said.

"Well, to me," Bella snarled and looked at Jennifer instead of Judah, "it feels like we were gone a *very* long time." An annoyed look settled on her face.

"Not a good trip?" Kaija Mae asked.

"You could say that, right, J?" Bella said, still looking at the girl.

"I didn't want to go in the first place," Jennifer snapped.

"I'm done talking to you for now," Bella said calmly. It always amazed both Judah and Jennifer how Bella could force her words to sound calm even when they knew she was angry. Bella began unpacking the bags that had been set on the table. "Judah, help me please because Jennifer needs to be somewhere other than here."

Jennifer sighed dramatically, rolled her eyes, and disappeared into the living room to sulk. Within moments, the rocking chair began singing out its usual edgy tune.

"We should get to bed early this evening, as Trilleah will be screaming for our attention bright and early in the morning," Bella sighed. "I don't want to travel back to the horrible land; it seems that time goes so quickly between our trips."

"If we could find more than one tablet tomorrow, it would be worth the trip but," Judah paused, remembering all that Kaija Mae had told him about the traps, with clay tablets as their bait.

"But what?" His aunt stopped pulling things from the bags on the table and turned to look at him.

"But … we have so little time, and the land is so big. I'm always surprised we manage to find any of the tablets at all." He was proud of his quick recovery and glanced toward Kaija Mae, giving her a satisfied look.

He had covered his near-slip quite well, and Bella asked no more questions. He decided to be more careful in what he said from now on and determined to think before he spoke or just not speak at all. Bella changed the subject so he knew he'd avoided spilling any secrets … for now.

"Judah, would you set the table?"

"Mhm," he mumbled and began digging in the cupboard. Before long the table was set, and supper was thrown together.

"Jennifer," Bella hollered. "Come eat." The weary and heavy-laden girl appeared at the table and plopped down, still extraordinarily out of sorts but ready to devour her food.

As she picked up her fork, Kaija Mae interrupted. "May I say grace before we eat?" Every eye around the table looked up with embarrassed shock. They glanced at each other and then at their guest.

"Um, yes, of course," Bella nodded. Each one bowed their heads and folded their hands like one might see on a postcard or a wall hanging. Praying was not exactly something they'd done much of, so they were not too sure how to go about it.

"Dear Lord," Kaija Mae began. "Thank you for this meal, and for such dear friends. Help us in Trilleah and give us strength in our bones, peace in our bellies, wisdom in our minds, and keep our feet from wandering in a wrong direction. Amen."

"Amen," came an awkward chorus from the others, followed immediately by the sound of forks scraping on bowls and drinks being poured into glasses. The small group chattered about meaningless things, some more meaningless than others, but they were sure to eat every last bit of food that had been set on the table.

No words of Trilleah or Trows or Hollows or Shailmas were mentioned.

"Thanks, Auntie," Jennifer plopped a kiss on Bella's cheek and set her dishes in the sink before making her way down the hall.

"You're welcome. Don't stay up too late." She did not want to say any more and hoped Jennifer didn't ask why, lest it sent her spiraling right back into the terrible mood she'd just climbed out of. The truth was that Jennifer was very aware of the reason behind Bella's statement, and she was fully prepared to head back to Trilleah just as soon as Simeon gathered her up.

Judah did the same as his sister, but before he darted from the kitchen he turned and nodded at the guest sitting at their table.

"Good night, Kaija Mae," he said.

"Good night, Judah" she replied. No matter what words came out of this girl's mouth, they carried a peace that Judah had never experienced before. He decided he liked it—and her—very much.

As he wandered down the hall toward his room, Judah began to think of all the secrets he knew, most of which he wished he didn't know—secrets from Jennifer and secrets about her—secrets whispered to him from Kaija Mae and secrets about the strange old lady. They were all beginning to swirl together in his mind and become one big jumbled-up mess. *How am I ever going to keep everything straight?* he wondered. *How am I going to keep my tongue from slipping in Trilleah and keep so many secrets that are not meant to be told?*

He became tired thinking about it all and was quite happy to crawl into his bed. Judah tried to hush his mind, but when it refused to be hushed, he turned instead to thoughts of Shemaiah. He began to search for his Shailma and as usual, Shemaiah was quickly found.

I'm lonely, Judah thought. *I know Jennifer and Bella are here but still, I feel lonely for someone whom I can share MY secrets with. These burdens seem too heavy for me to carry alone.*

Judah, the Shailma reminded him, *I am always here for you, and while I already know all your secrets and even the deepest thoughts which stir in your mind, you can tell me anything. I will always listen and give you courage and strength ... and hope.*

Those words from Shemaiah whispered to Judah's mind were enough to calm him and within minutes, the boy was fast asleep.

Just across the hallway, however, was a girl who was not fast asleep even though she was miserably tired. Instead of crawling into her bed, Jennifer had found her place back on the floor between the bed and the dresser, with the tattered red blanket working its way around her fingers. Jennifer had gathered all the pictures of Mamma and Daddy from her dresser and set them on the floor in front of her.

The sad, tired girl looked weak and forlorn in the little corner beside her bed. She sighed because … well… because that was all she could do. The words of sadness had been said a thousand times before, and she could think of no new ones. That little orphan girl just sat and looked at the pictures scattered in front of her. She continued to twist the blanket around her fingers; first one way and then the other.

Jennifer leaned her head against the side of the bed and let her eyes fall shut, knowing that when they opened next, it would be Summer Solstice and time to return to Trilleah. Her eyes grew damp, but she was asleep before the first tear had a chance to fall.

As she drifted off, however, she felt something touch her head —a hand perhaps. It was gentle and filled her with a deep and sudden peace. She smiled a little and knew Simeon had come to guard her while she slept and keep her mind stable.

Back in the kitchen, Kaija Mae and Bella had cleaned up the table and were sipping tea and chattering about unimportant things. That changed immediately when Kaija Mae finally blurted out, "Tomorrow will be a most important trip to Trilleah."

"Of course," Bella said, looking a bit confused. "They're all important trips to Trilleah."

"That is true. However, tomorrow will be a little more so, and you must keep your eye on Jennifer," Kaija Mae replied. She was not very forthcoming with information which, Bella thought, she seemed to have plenty of.

"Kaija Mae, why do you say such things?" Bella spouted. "If you have knowledge that I should be aware of, please don't make me drag it from you. Just tell me what I need to know." Bella poured herself a little more tea but offered Kaija Mae none.

"I've seen the armies of Shrailzhar marching around Asphelia's Hollow. They are looking for Jennifer." Kaija Mae gave Bella a bit of a sour look and poured her own tea. "I don't know their plans or what kind of traps they are setting, exactly."

"Why do you say they are looking for Jennifer, then?" Bella asked. "Maybe they're trying to get into the Hollow or, more likely they are trying to destroy it or steal back the clay tablets."

"They were chanting Jennifer's name. That's what makes me believe they are targeting her." Kaija Mae was becoming frustrated; perhaps because she, too, was exhausted. After all, she had traveled from Trilleah just this very morning. Perhaps her frustration was because she had been answering questions all day; questions from an angry Jennifer, questions from a confused and protective Judah, and now questions from a perturbed Auntie Bella.

Perhaps she was frustrated because she was seventy-three years old and tired in her old bones.

Regardless of the reasons, Kaija Mae felt a lot of feelings; none of them were good ones. "Bella, I don't know the reasons for what goes on in Trilleah. I only hear what I hear and see what I see and nothing more. I made the trip here to warn you about the traps being set by the king to get rid of Jennifer, but I don't know the specifics of those traps, only that they are being set right outside Asphelia's Hollow.

Finishing her last mouthful of tea, the old lady stood, suddenly remembering that Bella had no idea she was so very old.

Setting her cup beside the sink, Kaija Mae turned and said, "I'm sorry that I don't have more details for you. I tried to get as much information as I could, but the armies and King Shrailzhar are very sly. They know I can travel here and tell you what's going on there, and I think they hope to give me enough information to come and scare Jennifer into not returning but not so much information as to give away his secrets and plans.

"They are going to try and deceive Jennifer, without a doubt, and I feel that some within your very own Hollow will be used to achieve that goal. Be careful, Bella. Watch Jennifer and do not let her wander off, even for a moment."

Bella sat there, not sure what to say and a bit dumb-founded by Kaija Mae's strict warning. Nevertheless, she took the warning with utmost seriousness.

"Oh dear," was all she could mutter. "Oh dear, oh dear," Bella sighed and began running a sink of hot water to wash up the dishes before she, too, headed off to bed for what she was sure would be a deeply disturbed sleep.

8

UTTERLY INCONSOLABLE

As was expected, Bella had a restless sleep that night. She went to bed plenty early without a doubt, and perhaps it might have been that she had the breathing sounds of Kaija Mae hovering in the room—something she wasn't used to. The most likely reason for her troubled sleep, however, was the disturbing dream that kept repeating itself; over and over and over again it played.

Particular dreams had been playing off and on in her sleep for many nights now, but it was tonight's dream that was the most disturbing by far.

Molly and Theo bombarded her dreams, and it was so real—they seemed so real, so alive—that Bella found it difficult once she woke to make herself believe it was just another dream.

"My darling twins," Molly would wail. Bella could see her sitting in the rocking chair in their living room and hear the recurring squeal from its old tired-out legs. Almost as if it played a sad, eerie song, Bella could hear her older sister and the rocking chair singing together in perfect harmony, warning of pending doom; wailing as though it had already come.

In her dream—or whatever it was—Bella went to Molly and put her hands on the inconsolable mother's arms, trying to comfort her. Molly would not be comforted. Instead, she turned and grabbed Bella's face between her icy hands and begged, "Sweet Bella, do not let my twins back to the dreaded land which they are so determined to come to. It's treacherous and unsafe; they will suffer considerable and unrepairable damage."

Then, in the repetitive dream, Theo would burst into the room and take Molly's small hands in his big burly ones, get down on one knee so he could look her straight in the eye, and calmly say the same thing he had said the night before … and the night before that … and the night before that.

"Molly, you know Bella must bring them. It's the only way, my love. It's the only way."

And once again, Molly would burst into deep, painful wailings and sobs, covering her face, but unable to stifle her screams. What was so horribly eerie and what made Bella cringe every time, was that the groans and sobs coming from Molly were painfully familiar. They were the same groans and sobs that were heard in

Malleana Forest. There could be no mistaking one for the other; they were undoubtedly the same. Theo continued to console his undone, broken wife, but as before, she was utterly inconsolable.

Night after night for the past week or so, Bella had this same dream over and over and over again. The first night she awoke, shaking because it seemed so real, as though Molly and Theo had truly come to her. But each night, as she'd awaken from the same dream, Bella would be a little more disturbed because it seemed a little more real than the night before.

It was as though Bella was somehow outside of herself, somehow hovering above her sleeping self, watching Molly and Theo play out the same scene time after time. It was like she was watching a movie on the big screen, hoping for a different ending, but each time seeing the same one—each time powerless to stop it from coming.

Tonight, however, it shook Bella as she slept. She sat up, startled more than once on this particular night; sure she'd felt Molly touching her arm. Tonight, she awoke and wanted to begin calling to her sister, but instead heard the deep, peaceful breaths of Kaija Mae a few feet away. Someone was most definitely touching her arm. She squinted, trying to see into the dark, but her eyes were unable to squint hard enough to make the darkness fade.

Bella fought sleep, not wanting to watch the same episode of this horrible program she was unable to turn off. However, a very narrow part of her did want to return to sleep so that she could hear, see, feel her big sister one more time. Oh, how she missed Molly and Theo. Of course, while the dreams made Bella so terrified for the twins that her stomach ached, it also made her that much more determined to return to the deplorable land and break every curse that held her there.

In a half-sleepy consciousness, she tried focusing on the clock beside her bed which flashed 4:58 in neon green. *Hmm,* was the only thought her mind had. She would have had many more thoughts if she wasn't too tired to think them. Bella drifted back into her unconsciousness, that place where all of one's imaginings and fears and thoughts mingle into one and become dreams … or nightmares.

Again in that place, she saw Molly and heard her wails intertwining with the squeals from the rocker. Again, it upset her and shook her from the inside and again, Theo came and tried—without success—to console her broken-hearted sister. Again, Bella was awakened enough to be annoyed at the constant disturbance. Again, she glanced toward the neon lights. Now they shouted to her 6:17. The sounds of Kaija Mae's peaceful sleep lingered in the air poking fun at Bella, making her envious of the quiet rest this near stranger had found.

The sun was finally beginning to peek through the window, so Bella pondered her choices. Get up now and enjoy a little while of peace and quiet before the rest woke … before they were whisked away to Trilleah where it was certain no peace would be found … or fall back asleep one last time. If she knew that the second option would not be disturbed by Molly and Theo, she'd have chosen that one. However, it was less than probable that falling back asleep would bring any peace at all.

As she was pondering such things, Bella drifted back to sleep without intending to. This time, however, was far different than the many times before. Oh yes, Molly and Theo were there waiting for her. This time, however, her sister was neither wailing nor rocking nor begging Bella to keep the twins out of Trilleah and Theo had no need to try to calm his wife.

Not at all.

This time as Bella's mind drifted into dreamland, she wandered into a space so calm, so lighthearted and peaceful, that it reminded her of the Chamber of Rest back in Asphelia's Hollow. The walls were a brilliant emerald green, but the color was so pure that it was transparent. She could see straight through it. The light that came from it was brilliant but not so much as to burn her eyes.

The room was so similar to the Chamber of Rest that she wondered—even in her sleep—if she'd somehow been transported there without knowing it. She might have believed that to be true if there were not a few significant differences.

First, the room was not a room at all but more like an uninterrupted space; a space so big that it didn't seem to have a beginning nor an end. The transparent emerald walls were not closing her in, but instead, allowed her far more space than she felt comfortable with. There was no ceiling, no top at all to this particular space, so when Bella looked up, her eyes were unable to find anything to limit her view. It felt like she was looking into forever; eternity perhaps. She could not comprehend even slightly what she was seeing, but as she tried, a familiar voice grabbed her attention.

"It's unfathomable, isn't it?"

Bella looked around but could see no one to whom the voice might belong. She recognized it, though. She knew instantly that it belonged to Molly. She knew her sister must be somewhere in this infinite space, but where? She continued searching but in a place that has no beginning and no end, it's hard to know where to start looking.

"I'm here, Bella, all around you. Your eyes cannot see me because it is my spirit that is here—in the moment. My dear sister, if you can find all the tablets and break the curse, this is where you will free me to dwell for all time." Bella was still searching for her sister, but instead, she found Theo. He was a far distance off but moving toward her. He wasn't walking, but it looked as though he was drifting, suspended somehow within the space. It made no sense to her, yet Bella kept looking. Her eyes had no desire to look anywhere else; not now or ever.

"How are you here, Theo?" Bella asked. "How can I see you but not Molly?"

"My soul was not captured by the Trows, so I'm not trapped by the curse in Malleana's Forest," he said. "This is where I dwell now."

"Ah, yes," she replied. Some things were beginning to make sense, but as dreams go, sense is not part of their illusions.

As Bella opened her mouth to say something else, she suddenly found herself in a much different place, a place that wreaked of terror and trouble; a place without light of any kind. But then, light was not needed to feel the evil that lingered there. Her skin felt crawly both on the outside and the inside. She shuddered, and it seemed to go on forever. One shudder followed by another so quickly that her body was in constant motion, even though she tried to force it to be still.

She could hear what sounded like large teeth gnashing at her, and while she couldn't see clearly what—or whom—they belonged to, she distinctly sensed they wanted her destroyed. Bella tried to escape into her own skin to avoid them. They felt close to her on every side. She could feel their hot breath and smell the sulfur that hurled itself from their nostrils. Bella recognized this heat encasing her had no explanation; no words would be able to describe its intensity; she felt it, nonetheless.

Bella's ears were pierced with the sounds of horrible wailing and screaming from a great distance away, and while she was in this place, she was deeply thankful for the darkness that covered her. Even her deepest curiosities did not want to see what her ears were hearing and her skin was feeling—or from where that fierce heat was coming. Yes, blackness was to be hoped for here in this place, but there was no darkness deep enough to cover her.

How did she possibly go from a place of such brilliant light—full of peace and rest—to a place as opposite as one could get? The void of anything peaceful or sound or restful was so heavy and painful here that Bella wanted to join the wailing and start screaming herself. But then in the distance and in a voice so weak and broken that it was barely recognizable as her own sister's, she heard these terrorizing words.

"This is where I am now, and this is where I shall remain for all eternity unless I'm freed from the curse of the Trows."

Bella was so broken that she was convinced her soul had been destroyed at that moment. She doubled over in a deep anguish which consumed her entirely. She wanted to find her sister and pull her out this very instant but in such thick darkness, Bella couldn't even find herself. She had to get out of this place before it destroyed her and she was of no help to anyone. Pure evil reigned here; it was not only present inside of this space but it was the space itself.

Bella was so distraught that she tried to force herself to wake up, but she could not. She wanted to run but was unable to move, feeling as though her feet and hands were bound. She felt someone shaking her and she woke slightly. Bella squinted and rubbed her eyes, which felt damp to her hands. When she could focus enough to see, although a bit blurry-eyed just yet, she saw Kaija Mae.

"Bella, wake up," the girl was whispering. "What's wrong? What is wrong?" Kaija Mae repeated over and over. When she noticed that Bella was waking, Kaija Mae wiped pieces of blond hair away from Bella's wet face and whispered, "You were having a nightmare."

"Oh dear," Bella sat up. "You have no idea!" She grabbed Kaija Mae and pulled her close, wailing and sobbing uncontrollably.

"I have a slight idea because you were hysterical." Kaija Mae sat herself down on the bed next to Bella and pulled back slightly, loosening Bella's grip. "Tell me what you saw," she pleaded.

"I need a minute to sort it out," Bella said and wiggled her left hand free to wipe her eyes. "Was I crying?" she asked.

"I wouldn't use the word crying … exactly," Kaija Mae said. More like you were going mad, wailing and flailing in your bed. I had to struggle to keep you from throwing yourself to the floor. It looked like you were caught in some sort of trap and were fighting to escape. You woke both the twins, in fact, so I sent them to the kitchen to make us all breakfast." While Kaija Mae told her these things, Bella stared blankly, remembering the feelings of being bound in the eternal darkness. She shuddered … repeatedly.

"It seemed so real. So real," Bella mumbled flatly, her thoughts here, there, and everywhere. "But it couldn't be," she winced. "It just couldn't be." Her wrists hurt dreadfully, and as she grabbed them, her eyes glanced down. She was disturbed to see the thick, deep gashes all around them. Unmistakably, whatever had bound her within the nightmarish blackness had literally dug into them, leaving wretched, open wounds. She covered them quickly to keep Kaija Mae's eyes from noticing, but Bella knew in an instant that the nightmare was real … very real indeed.

Kaija Mae was curious at Bella's oddness and asked again to share the nightmare, but again, Bella shook her head and kept her wrists hidden.

"Maybe in a while when you are a bit more awake." Kaija Mae wiped Bella's sweating forehead and stood up. "I'll go help the twins and let you get your wits about you. You'll be alright if I go down the hallway?" It seemed a silly question, but Bella knew she was shaking and must have looked a terrible mess. If Kaija Mae described her actions accurately, and Bella believed that she had, then the question was a reasonable one.

"Yes, thank you, Kaija Mae," she said clutching one hand in the other underneath the blankets, trying to make the shaking stop. "I'll be there in a few minutes." As Kaija Mae headed toward the door, Bella stopped her.

"I'm glad you're here," she whispered.

"So am I, Bella … So am I."

And with that, Kaija Mae stepped into the hallway and headed toward the kitchen, leaving Bella to herself.

9

TOO MUCH INFORMATION

As Kaija Mae entered the kitchen, it was obvious that Jennifer was still tired. The sight of her dozing at the kitchen table made Kaija Mae giggle, so she quickly covered her mouth to keep a loud burst of laughter from escaping. Jennifer, after all, seemed unpredictable in her emotions since Kaija Mae had arrived. Judah heard her giggles and turned around. They both stood there for a moment while Jennifer's head bobbed this way and then wobbled that way as the poor girl was losing the fight to stay awake.

Judah, on the other hand, was putting together an elaborate breakfast for the four of them. He had made a pitcher of orange juice and had a growing stack of toast started. Eggs were sizzling in a frying pan on the stove, which looked about done, as well.

"I feel bad disturbing her," Kaija Mae whispered. "She looks dreadfully tired."

"I don't," Judah laughed and rubbed his hands together as he skulked close to his sister. "JENNIFER!" he hollered. The poor girl jumped sky high and nearly fell off of the chair. Judah, of course, laughed so hard he almost fell to the floor himself.

"Judah!" Kaija Mae said, pretending to be perturbed but again stifling a laugh, in case it hurt Jennifer's feelings. "That wasn't nice at all."

"It wasn't meant to be nice … it was meant to be funny, and funny it was," he said, still laughing and holding his sides.

"Well, your eggs are burning, which isn't funny at all," Kaija Mae pointed out. She had to admit the whole thing was amusing, but now Jennifer appeared to be a bit … no, a whole bunch … on the grumpy side. That was never amusing.

The sleepy girl didn't say a word. She stood up and stretched long and hard. Then she calmly walked over to her brother, kicked him hard in the shin, and continued straightaway into the living room where the rocking chair soon began to sing its usual tune.

"Now *that* was funny," she shouted back and chuckled.

Judah was hopping up and down on one foot while rubbing the stinging shin in his hands. "Jennifer," he screeched, "you best watch yourself!" He pulled his pant leg up to reveal a throbbing red spot. "That's gonna bruise."

Kaija Mae was giggling now, and shaking her head. "Oh, you two make me laugh," she said. They were having quite the fun when suddenly Bella walked into the kitchen. The look on her face put an immediate end to any sort of fun and the air became thick with tension.

"What's the matter, Auntie?" Judah asked. There was a genuine concern in his voice that couldn't be missed, and it brought Jennifer rushing back the kitchen.

"Nothing to worry about," she replied, although the look on her face told another story altogether. Usually, Bella would have smiled and messed up Judah's already messy hair, but her lack of either was a sure sign that something was dreadfully wrong.

"Auntie, you look awful!" Jennifer gasped as she dug plates out of the cupboard and began setting the table. All the while, she kept a close eye on her aunt. Clearly, the look on Bella's face when she'd entered the kitchen abruptly ended all shenanigans the twins were playing, and they were immediately forgotten. Suddenly, all attention had turned to Bella.

"Auntie," Jennifer asked. "What happened?"

"Oh, I had some dreams last night that kept me from sleeping too well," Bella said. "I'm just tired, is all." But it was clear that it was more than just a dream or two. Bella, who was usually fashionable and beautiful was now frumpy and mismatched. Nothing was in place with her this morning, at least it seemed that way to the twins.

To make matters more confusing, Bella had a large sweater with unnecessarily long sleeves that had bunched up around her wrists and slipped halfway over her hands. It was a beautiful sunny morning which called for short-sleeves; something was not making sense.

"Aren't you hot?" Judah asked, since he too, had noticed the inappropriately warm sweater.

"I'm just a bit under the weather and have a chill is all. Stop your worrying—all of you." Bella was sure not her usual self; that much was clear.

Kaija Mae, of course, knew that the "few dreams" Bella was referring to were very different from what she was letting on about to the twins. The "few dreams" were in reality, many dark "night terrors," which explained the black circles under Bella's eyes and the redness in her eyes. They did not, however, explain the dreadfully warm sweater.

The odd visitor caught a glance of Bella, and their eyes locked together for a brief moment, although Bella looked away before the twins had a chance to notice.

"Thank you," Bella said as Judah slid a couple of slightly burnt eggs onto her plate. Jennifer set a high stack of buttered toast on the table. "This looks great," Bella said. She tried, unsuccessfully, to sound delighted.

"I'm surprised you can see it," Jennifer mumbled, "since your eyes are so swollen." She seemed angry, but it behooved Bella as to why that would be.

"I'm just tired, J," was all Bella replied. She hid both hands under the table and gently rubbed her wrists, which were throbbing. She hoped the bleeding had stopped but would keep this horrible sweater on just in case. Two cut-up wrists were not something Bella wanted to try and explain to the twins, although she decided that when an opportunity presented itself, she would tell Kaija Mae every detail of the dreams and reveal her wrists.

It was difficult trying to eat breakfast while making sure her sweater sleeves didn't slide above the fresh wounds, but Bella managed to do just that. What she did not manage quite as well, was to pay attention to the conversation around the table. More than once, someone was talking to her or asked a simple question to which she failed to respond … or, at least, failed to respond to appropriately.

Kaija Mae had asked Bella something about her garden and apologized for eating so many of the peas; Bella replied with, "It's a beautiful day, for sure."

Another comment from Judah went something like, "Auntie, pass the milk," but poor preoccupied Bella responded with, "Oh … no, thank you I'm fine."

Yes, it was crystal clear that Bella was significantly distracted this morning. The twins and Kaija Mae did a fair amount of exchanging confused looks, shoulder shrugging, and whispering. Bella was, of course, unaware of any such happenings.

She did, however, notice the blood that was beginning to soak through her sweater and excused herself before anyone else noticed. She was dreadfully afraid that one of the twins might ask her about the nightmares or what the shouting was that had been coming from her room earlier that had woken them both.

"I'm still feeling a little ill, I suppose," Bella said as she darted from the table and down the hall. Once she reached the bathroom, she pulled up her sleeves slowly, revealing more blood than she'd expected. It looked as though Bella had slashed her wrists to bits, and she certainly did not wish for the twins—or anyone else for that matter—to see such a horrible sight.

Bella ran cold water over the wounds, washing off most of the dried blood and letting the coolness of the water calm the stinging. She noticed both wrists had begun to bruise a little. She slumped down onto the cool floor and searched for her Shailma. He was easily found this morning.

I'm here, Bella. I am here, is what she heard straightaway.

Where were you last night when I was having such disturbing dreams?

The same place as you were, Shura responded. The answer was unhelpful, but the conversation continued for a time. When Bella had settled slightly and calmed down, and once her wrists quit bleeding, she opened the door and headed back toward the kitchen. She found Kaija Mae was gone and asked the twins about it.

"She said to tell you goodbye and that she had to go, but we'd see her later this morning," Judah answered.

"She's rather strange," Jennifer commented.

"More than you even know," Judah responded, laughing. *If you only knew that the beautiful Miss Kaija Mae was seventy-three years old, you'd be downright befuddled,* he thought to himself. Judah wondered if Bella knew Kaija Mae's age or for how long she had been in Trilleah.

Judah wondered if his auntie knew that the other group of Travelers had also been there since the beginning of the forest. *She'll know soon enough, I suppose,* he thought to himself.

"Well drat," Bella said. "I had hoped we'd all go to Trilleah together, like last time when Matt was here." As soon as the words had tootled from her mouth, Bella wished she could suck them right back in. She'd been determined not to speak of Trilleah this morning, lest it stirred up Jennifer and caused a change in her mood. *Keep a better guard over your tongue,* Bella scolded herself.

Jennifer noticed the uncomfortable quiet around the kitchen table and broke the awkward silence. "It's OK, Auntie," she said. "I'm coming to Trilleah with you and Judah this morning, whenever the Shailmas come for us." The young girl seemed a little perturbed that they hadn't come already. A broad smirk slid across her face and for the first time, Jennifer gave strength to her auntie rather than the other way around.

It would not be long now, however, for the Shailmas had already gathered some of the others. Miriam and Matt were already in the Dark Land but hadn't yet been able to get into Asphelia's Hollow. The armies of Shrailzhar had indeed surrounded it; the way inside was blocked.

All they could do was hide behind a large tree and wait for the rest to arrive. Their minds were set on watching for the others to warn them about the trap before anyone was caught in it. Soon enough … soon enough.

Back in the kitchen of their little yellow house, however, the three remained—impatiently waiting for what was entirely out of their control. Each quietly wondered why they were not yet in Trilleah and each silently searched for their Shailmas.

As the three of them cleaned up breakfast, Bella told the twins only the smallest bits about Molly calling to her from the darkness. She described the space as best she could without giving too much detail and said, "A good reminder of why we must return to Trilleah, I suppose."

While Bella tried to share only the tiniest amount of the nightmare as possible, the twins gathered most of the dishes. They clanged and rattled as they were piled in the sink, which was filling with warm, bubbly water. Neither Judah nor Jennifer asked many questions, but while Bella shared bits and pieces of the nightmare, only those things she thought would give the twins enough to explain away her wails from earlier this morning, Jennifer excused herself.

"Perhaps that was too much information," Bella whispered to Judah.

"Way too much information, Bella, way too much," Judah replied. Both Judah and Bella hoped that it wasn't so much information that Jennifer would now change her mind and refuse to return to the Dark Land.

10

AND AGAIN

Jennifer escaped into the bathroom. She did not want to hear any more about Bella's nightmares. Also, she wanted to look at the scars on her cheek one last time before heading back to Trilleah. The scars were so tiny that no one else would even notice them. But she knew they were there, and she remembered how they got there. "What atrocities could possibly happen this trip," she asked the pale reflection staring back at her. Oh, if she only knew.

She rubbed the scars carefully and dabbed some cream on them. Jennifer turned on the water to wash her hands and noticed a small bit of blood on the tap and another few drips in the sink. She promptly returned to the kitchen to share her findings and get to the bottom of it. She knew Bella was the one in the bathroom before her and wondered what her auntie was hiding.

"Who's bleeding?" she asked, even before she reached the kitchen.

"Huh?" Judah asked.

"Who's bleeding?" she repeated. "There's blood in the sink, and it's not mine."

Bella's stomach did a quick flip-flop as she realized she'd forgotten to double check the sink before she left the bathroom. "Oh, it's mine," she said quickly. "I had a nosebleed earlier and forgot to wash the sink out, I guess." She crossed her fingers in hopes that her lame excuses would appease the curiosity of her nosey niece.

"Oh," Jennifer mumbled and turned to go back down the hallway.

"Where are you going when there are dishes to be washed and dried, young lady?" Bella asked.

"Ugh," was all Jennifer said and turned, dragging her feet back to the kitchen. She grabbed a towel but rather than pick up a wet dish, she whipped her brother, causing him to throw a handful of bubbles at her. Normally, this would be the start of some messy shenanigans, but this morning Bella was in no mood for such shenanigans.

"Stop," she reprimanded. "We need to finish this. Any minute now the Shailmas are going to come." Bella poured herself the last drop of coffee and set the coffee pot in the sink. "For once, I'd rather not return to a mess."

With that, she walked out of the kitchen and down the hall to her room. The twins looked at each other, both disturbed by Bella's strange behavior this morning, but neither said a word. Often, as twins go, words aren't required. Each knows full well what the other is thinking. They raised their eyebrows at each other, shrugged their shoulders, and finished the dishes.

Down the hall and behind a closed door, Bella flopped down on her bed. She had painfully throbbing wrists, a terrible headache, and her eyes were swollen and stinging.

"I look a mess," she said to herself. "It might be OK to tell Pierce or Kaija Mae what happened once I get to Trilleah—if I ever get there."

"Shura," she said aloud. "What is the holdup this morning on this day of Solstice?" As Bella had learned a long time ago, when one speaks to their Shailma, they must hush and wait for an answer with great patience, since a Shailma will not often interrupt. She remained quiet, listening carefully with her heart. She didn't have to wait long. In only a few seconds, an answer came to her heart.

Sweet Bella, came the calm voice of Shura. *The land is very perilous and shakeable this morning because Asphelia's Hollow has been discovered by the armies of Shrailzhar.*

"So we won't be going then?" she asked. Bella certainly wouldn't be disappointed to stay out of a land that was perilous and shakeable.

Oh yes, we will be going soon. Some are already there; they're safe. Shura had answered the question before Bella had a chance to ask it.

However, as safe as they are now, it's not those who the armies are after.

"Oh dear," was all Bella could say. "Oh dear."

Don't fret, Bella. You will be going soon.

"But will we be safe?" Bella asked again, really wanting to avoid anything that would put Jennifer or Judah at too high a risk. Shura's answer gave hope, but then again, not so much as to calm Bella's disturbed heart.

You and the others will be just as safe in Trilleah on this Summer Solstice as you are on any other Solstice journey, my dear one.

"Oh dear," Bella sighed loudly again. There was not much else to say. She went back into the bathroom and ran warm water; hot really; as hot as she could stand it. She held a cloth under the stream—soaking it thoroughly—then pressed it gently against her eyes. Bella was a dreadful sight. She didn't want to arrive in Trilleah looking so dreadful because, well, because Matt would be there. She didn't want him to see her looking so terrible. After all, Bella found Matt to be quite dreamy and hoped he thought the same about her.

As her eyes were covered by the soothing warmth of the cloth, Bella felt herself be whisked away by her Shailma. The cloth fell to the floor, but she kept her eyes closed tight. She dreaded the sting she was sure would return if she opened them.

Up out of the bathroom, out of the little yellow house on the corner of Mitchell Avenue and Fairview Lane, and through whatever curtained portals the path to Trilleah took, Bella went. She hung on to Shura with some regret that another journey had begun but a sliver of hope that Shura had come for her. At this moment, at least, while Bella could feel her Shailma with her hands and see with her eyes, if she chose to open them that is, she felt safe. As long as Shura was with her, Bella was brave and confident; not because she believed in herself, but because she believed in the Shailmas.

If Bella could have anticipated even slightly what lay ahead for her and the others in Trilleah on this dreadful day, she would have begged Shura to take her anywhere but to the Dark Land.

Shura approached the Solstice gates. The closer they came, the more vividly Bella recalled the last trip. She remembered the slimy trap that awaited them and how it was necessary that they all came plowing through the gates together. With the gates now in sight, Bella felt alone. She looked all around, straining her eyes this way and that, hoping to see someone—anyone—near her.

There was no one; just her and Shura racing toward the gate together. She saw it was open, and she strained her stinging eyes, looking for anything suspicious or out of the ordinary. She saw nothing to alarm her presently. However, the overwhelming loneliness of the moment alarmed her plenty enough. *Where are the others?* she wondered.

Some are already inside the gates, as I told you earlier, came the reply of Shura. She wasn't looking for an answer but was glad to have one, nonetheless. *Your new friends Kaija Mae and the others are, of course, inside as well.*

Where are the twins? was the question Bella was most curious about.

They're not yet on their way to Trilleah, but they will be ... soon enough, Shura replied. Bella had a thousand more questions, maybe more, but they were upon the gates now, and all questions seemed to fall out of her mind as they passed through and into the tragically Dark Land. Bella could feel the heartbeat of the land and its air choked her slightly.

They did not go to the middle of the forest to where the Shailmas usually delivered their Travelers. Instead, Shura flew right past most of Malleana, hovering close to the top of the forest, close enough for Bella's stomach to churn as she heard the moans of the Waiting Ones.

"I'm back, Molly," she whispered.

As she said her sister's name, the terrors of last night came rushing back. That place of such great and eternal darkness filled her mind and the dreadful sound of those gnashing teeth seemed so close that Bella jolted her body, trying to get away. As she did, her wrists twisted, causing flashes of pain to shoot up her arms.

"Shura," she cried and dug her fingers tighter into his back.

I'm here, was all he said but it was enough to calm her slightly, enough to keep from breaking into a full force frenzy. She buried her face in Shura's back, pinched her eyes shut, and began humming a tune. She didn't know where the tune came from since she was not much of a musician, but it didn't matter where it was coming from. Somehow it was calming her and as long as the tune kept coming to her mind, she would keep humming it.

As quickly as the tune had begun, it ended. The anguished young Bella found herself kneeling behind a large burning bush, looking toward the rock covering Asphelia's Hollow. She was confused and began turning her head this way and that, wondering what it was she was supposed to be seeing. Maybe something … maybe nothing. She really didn't know.

Rather than finding anything in particular to see, she heard someone calling her name; a familiar someone.

"Bella, over here," she heard. "Over here, Bella," she heard again. She was looking, but her eyes were so sore and swollen she was having some trouble focusing. Finally, just to her left and back a bit, she spotted a marvelous sight.

"Matt," she whispered.

It was then, as she looked at Matt and wondered how to get to him, that someone else caught her eye. It was someone she'd hoped would not be here at all, but there she was, halfway between herself and Matt.

"Drat," Bella said probably a touch too loudly. Miriam was also on her knees, watching something going on outside of the Hollow, not seeming even to notice that Bella had been deposited among them.

Now, Bella had no idea what had gone on between Miriam and Jennifer during their last journey, but she knew that something had, and it was not anything good. There was no doubt about it, since back home—after they'd been returned to Westlock, Jennifer had tried and tried and tried again to talk to Bella about Miriam. Every time she tried, however, something odd would happen—and not always the same odd something, either. Jennifer would begin coughing uncontrollably … or the words that did come from her lips would be jumbled and make no sense … or her tongue would swell up, making it impossible for her to say any words at all.

One time, in particular, the poor girl's throat began to close off and even getting breath became troublesome. Eventually, Jennifer stopped trying to tell anyone about Miriam. All she could do was point to the scars on her cheek and shrug her shoulders.

At first, Bella thought that maybe Jennifer was being silly or putting on such antics for attention so that she wouldn't be expected to return to Trilleah. After a while, however, Bella began to notice other things … things that made her aware Jennifer was being attacked by some painful ailment every time Miriam's name was mentioned. Yes; something had gone on between her niece and Miriam, but Bella had no idea what that something could have been.

Now, back in Trilleah and seeing Miriam again, Bella's soul was stirred up like a raging fire. An uncontrollable uneasiness crept over her from the outside, and a troubling amount of doubt poured into Bella's insides like hot tea filling a cold mug. She wanted to explode.

Sweat began pouring down Bella's face and her clothes started feeling sticky and damp. Surely it was not that hot in this Dark Land. She'd been here many times before during the Summer Solstice and not once had she noticed such extreme heat, even when she wore the horribly thick cloak. This heat was coming from somewhere else entirely.

The burning bushes, maybe? she wondered. Bella held her hands out toward the bushes like one might do if they were chilly and trying to get warm. She did expect a certain amount of heat to come from the bush and was surprised to find none whatsoever. She wondered if she could put her hands directly into the middle of the burning bush or even grab onto it, but she was already in enough pain and decided to keep her hands away just in case.

Instead, Bella looked around as far as her head would turn one way before turning it as far as it would go the other way. She wasn't sure what she was expecting to find. *A fire-spewing dragon, perhaps?* A ridiculous list of possibilities paraded through her mind, poking fun at her.

None of the exaggerated ideas from the parade of silliness came into her vision, but there was something causing the extreme heat to build up and pour down her face. Small droplets were hanging from her chin and running down the back of her neck. It tickled and caused her to shiver repeatedly. She raised her right arm and dragged it across her forehead, wiping a good amount of the dampness from her face.

It's from anxiousness, came an uninvited thought to her swirling mind.

"What?" she asked out loud.

The extreme heat, came the quick reply of Shura. *It's from deep anxiousness.*

Am I more anxious this trip than the other trips? she asked. Without waiting for an answer, Bella asked a list of other questions without waiting for replies to any of them. They were more like reasonings than questions but nevertheless, they rattled around in her mind. As the list grew and rattled and bumped together, the more anxious she became. The more anxious she became, the more sweat gathered, now dripping from her chin.

Of course, I'm anxious ... and scared ... and angry ... and disappointed ... and perturbed that Miriam is right beside me yet doesn't even seem to notice I've been deposited here ... and frustrated that Matt is behind me, but I can't get to him. And where are the twins and when should I expect them? And how can we get to the Hollow, if in fact, we are going to be getting to the Hollow at all?

Bella probably would have gone on and on and on if Shura did not interrupt.

Bella, he spoke firmly in her mind. *Slow down your thoughts and take control of your mind this instant.* The firmness she felt startled her, and she realized how crazy she had let her thoughts become.

Honestly, Shura, she said to him, *I don't know how you put up with me.*

Never mind about such things, he replied. *Bella, control your mind and your thoughts lest they control you. One will most certainly be in control; it's up to you which that will be at any given time.*

Neither Bella—nor any of the Travelers for that matter—liked being lectured or spoken to harshly by their Shailmas. However, every Traveler knew full well that the Shailmas were much wiser than themselves, so when scolding came, they listened, whether they liked it or not.

All the words of the Shailmas were for the Travelers' own good; for their safety and direction. The magnificently wise creatures who were nearly always unseen to the human eye, never made a joke or laid down a pun or participated in foolishness of any sort. They were always serious, always compassionate, always firm, always wise.

Yes, it was a sensible Traveler who paid attention to every word their Shailma whispered, and Bella was most certainly paying attention now.

NOT SO

For just a small stitch of time, Bella had forgotten about Miriam, forgotten about Matt, forgotten that she was crouched down behind a burning bush instead of safely in the Hollow which was, of course, where she longed to be. But now as her knees and calves were beginning to cramp, she was brought back to the moment. Bella knew she'd have to change her position in short order. Otherwise, when she finally did have to move, she'd be unable to do so. Her legs were not trustworthy at the moment, and if she had to go quickly, they would undoubtedly fail her.

Slowly, slowly, slowly, Bella sat on her bum and straightened out her legs, one at a time, until the blood began flowing back into them. She wiggled her feet back and forth and rubbed her calves, trying to make her fingers reach down to her toes. "Mmmmm," she sighed under her breath. The stretching felt wonderful and Bella allowed herself a few seconds to hold the stretch out, enjoying the pull on her cramped muscles.

She liked it so much, in fact, that she forgot—for a second—to keep an eye on Miriam. As she felt the muscles in her legs stretch out and gain feeling, Bella glanced over toward where she'd seen the strange, black-haired girl, but she couldn't find Miriam anywhere.

Bella let go of her toes and turned back to see if Matt, too, had gone. He hadn't, and was still in the same place where she'd first seen him. When he noticed her looking at him, he again waved his hands, frantically motioning her to come back to where he was crouching. There did seem to be more room where he was, and it would be quite nice to be able to whisper to him while they waited for —well—whatever it was they were waiting for.

Bella crouched again and slowly moved one foot a small bit, transferring the weight onto that foot to move the other. It was slow going—slow indeed—and as Bella kept one eye on Matt and one eye on the army, she was beginning to panic. Although she knew none of these feelings would do her any good, she seemed powerless to stop any of them. The words of Shura came rushing back, filling her mind with tenacity to follow his direction … and her body with strength to keep going.

Little by little, Bella inched her way to Matt, choosing to think good thoughts, powerful thoughts, rich thoughts. Every time a fearful thought would come to her mind, she'd replace it with a calm one. By the time she reached the handsome young man, Bella had become empowered with inner strength and a driving force to carry on no matter what may come upon her this journey. It was a good thing, too, because Matt—who was usually the one who was fearless and strong—was anything but fearless and strong now.

"How long have you been here?" Bella asked him. He looked rather pale, she thought.

"I don't even know; a long time," he answered. "I'm not sure what the army is doing, but they aren't marching," he said. "They were when I first arrived—marching, that is—but they stopped a while ago. Now I cannot figure out what they are doing," he sighed. "I don't know how we can get in and …" his voice trailed off.

"And what?" Bella asked. He didn't reply. "Matt … and what?" she prodded.

"If we can't get into the Hollow to get our cloaks and the Living Maps, how can we possibly be safe out here in Trilleah? How will we have any idea where to look for a tablet?" He was indeed pale and his voice raspy. "We can't, Bella, we just cannot do this. What if we need the Book of Truths? Or the Book of Lies?" he continued after a short pause. It seemed to Bella that he'd been out here too long letting his thoughts carry him away to places that were not good to visit; it appeared that his mind had decided to camp in those exact places.

"Matt," she said sternly. "You mustn't allow your thoughts to go wild. What you allow your mind to focus on will direct your emotion, and I see yours has fallen into the ditch."

He moved his eyes from the army to Bella; he was looking at her like she had two heads. "What?" he asked.

"How long have you been here, watching the army and thinking such terrible thoughts?" Bella asked for the second time.

"Since dawn, I suppose," Matt said, his eyes back on the armies. "A couple of hours, at least."

"How long has Miriam been here?" she asked, suddenly curious about a possible connection between the odd girl and the army and Matt's thoughts.

"Oh, I suppose she's been here almost as long as I have," he answered without moving his eyes from the army.

"Hmm," Bella said and began tapping her lip. "Curious, indeed. Well, no matter. If the Shailmas brought us to Trilleah, then there must be a way into the Hollow, and I believe they'll help us, and I believe that somehow, even though the sunlight hours are ticking by quickly, we will retrieve another tablet." The rambling girl continued to tap her lip even as she spoke, making Matt wonder what was wrong with her. She wasn't normally the one who was strong and confident and trusting.

Sure, the group thought she was all of those things and more, but Matt knew she was not. He knew that Pierce was usually the one helping Bella to have confidence, but now, without Pierce or anyone else for that matter, Matt was intrigued with where Bella was finding her strength. He had no way, at least not yet, of knowing that she'd been visited by Kaija Mae and had a great deal of information that Matt did not have.

"Matt, the Shailmas know much more than us. They're here even when we are not; they know what is happening. The army's movements and traps and marching aren't a surprise to the Shailmas." She made some good points, he supposed. The more she spoke, the more his heart was helped. His emotions were settling down a little.

"Thanks, Bella," he muttered.

Bella looked back to where Miriam had been crouching but still didn't see her. "Where's Miriam?" she asked. Matt looked around but when he couldn't find her, he shrugged.

"I don't know," he muttered.

"Odd," they said at the same time. Both Bella and Matt turned their heads this way and that, searching for the dark-haired girl but could not see her anywhere.

"She couldn't just disappear," Matt whined. "She's been here for hours. It makes no sense that she'd not be here now."

"I don't trust her," Bella said. "There's something about her that set me off from the first time she appeared in the forest. I'll never forget the secretive argument she and Pierce had in one of the dark passageways and what she said." She had Matt's full attention now, which was precisely what she was looking for.

"What argument? What did she say?" he asked.

Even though the two had been whispering quietly, Bella raised her voice now and spoke in an odd tone, one that was intended to mimic the argument she'd heard in the passageway earlier. *"… if you were to listen to me as you have been instructed from the start, I would not have to be here at all …"* Bella recounted in a mocking tone. "Pierce said he didn't ask her to come, and that was her response." I've been curious about it ever since that day but haven't had a chance to ask Pierce about it.

"I think that she had something to do with Jennifer's …" Bella didn't get to finish this sentence because as the words were pouring from her mouth, she spotted Miriam.

"Matt," she said. He looked at her and saw her eyes were looking over his shoulder. He turned to see what Bella saw, since she had suddenly gone noticeably pale.

Matt didn't need to turn his head very far before his eye caught sight of the black hair of the missing girl. Standing directly behind him, was Miriam. He jumped a little in surprise and blurted out, "How did you get there?"

"It doesn't matter, does it?" she stated, her voice cold and her eyes icy. "I am here, and that's what matters." The next question out of her mouth caused Bella's blood to freeze up and her heart to skip many beats. "Where are those beloved twins of yours, Bella?" The question sounded like a wolf asking for directions to the sheep pasture. "Those precious ones who are going to save us all and break the dreadful curse?"

The hair on the back of Matt's neck stood up. He quickly butted in and answered the question, attempting to rescue Bella.

"They'll be here shortly; no need to worry."

"Who's worried?" Miriam snarled. "Certainly not me." For a moment, Bella thought she saw Miriam's eyes turn black, but when she blinked and looked again, the color had returned.

Can't be, Bella thought. *It just cannot be.* She couldn't have been more wrong, for it could be and, in fact, it was exactly so.

12

FLIGHT OF SAVAGES

Bella's skin crawled, almost literally it seemed, and caused her to itch here and scratch there. There was something so eerie and unexplainable about Miriam that Bella couldn't figure out, but it overwhelmed her with uneasiness. *Wolf in sheep's clothing,* was the only thought that kept spinning in her mind. She wasn't sure what such a thought meant exactly, but those words kept running through her mind as if stuck in a loop.

Miriam had become silent since asking about the twins, and the three of them stood awkwardly hovering, watching their beloved Hollow. Were they ever going to get inside? Did the Shailmas bring them here just to shiver out in the forest, ducking behind burning bushes and watching the dreaded army? The daylight hours were ticking away, causing them much concern. Bella again felt her skin begin to dampen with anxious sweat. Her hands were clammy and her skin sticky. The girl was deeply troubled.

Just as she was about to open her mouth and voice her concerns, the words of Shura returned. *Control your mind, Bella, or it will control you.* She pondered it for a moment and realized that yes, one or the other is always in control, and it was her who could choose which it would be at any given moment in time.

Unfortunately, she had very limited time to consider it right now, or to control her mind, or to give a voice to whatever words were heaping upon her tongue. In that instant, the largest—colossal really—creature appeared overhead, swooping down upon the army. It was blacker than black, if such a thing were possible, and the wingspan of this beast had to be wider than their entire house back in Westlock. It was so unbelievably enormous that as its wings stretched wide, gliding on the stale air of Trilleah, it blocked out the entire sky. It caused the land to grow dark—blindingly dark—but only for a moment.

Bella didn't know which to keep her eyes on, the beast or the army … or Miriam.

"What," Matt muttered almost silently but loud enough for the girls to hear. Bella pictured him the same as she imagined she looked right now; eyes big as saucers and jaw dropped wide open. She reached back and grabbed his hand. It was clear that the beast was not for the army and as it swooped down, the army stopped all activity and fell face down to the ground on their bellies. Not one within that army of hundreds moved; not even a twitch or a sneeze or a flutter. It was as though the entire army fell dead under the presence of the flying beast. With any luck, they had.

As the three of them crouched down in silence, watching the army cower in fear of whatever creature this was, a loud sound echoed from somewhere behind them. Neither Matt nor Bella—not even Miriam—wanted to turn and look, so none did. Bella squeezed Matt's hand and Matt wondered if they were going to be plucked up one by one by this gigantic beast and taken away for good.

Miriam wondered nothing of the sort for she knew exactly what this was. It was her who had called for them. However, she'd called for the savages of the air to come and remove the army, not the Travelers, but she was the only one who knew such secrets. While Miriam had a great desire to end all future journeys by the Travelers, it was not this tiny group of two that she cared to get rid of. She didn't care about Matt's presence in Trilleah, nor Bella's. Not in the least. However, to lure the presence of the ones she did need to stop, both Matt and Bella were required. They were the bait; Asphelia's Hollow the lair. Miriam awaited the arrival of her prey.

The ones she cared about removing had not yet entered Trilleah, and Miriam feared that while the army of Shrailzhar surrounded the Hollow, the guests she was waiting for may not show up. She was going to make sure they did.

The three of them who were here, crouching in the bushes, plugged their ears to keep whatever hideous sound that was barreling down behind them from utterly deafening their ears. Never had they heard a sound so loud. Still, none turned to look toward what was causing it, nor did they need to. In only a few seconds, the carriers of the noise passed overhead, allowing every Traveler's eye to see a most disturbing sight.

Above them flew another army, only this army was some sort of flying savages, much larger than the one that had already swooped down. There were hundreds of them, so it seemed anyway, and as they flapped their wings, the sound exploded around the Travelers. It felt like the whole land of Trilleah would surely be blown apart by the screaming hubbub.

The Travelers tried to make the ruckus as painless as possible. They shoved their fingers in their ears. They cupped their hands over their ears. They even tried to close their eyes, although that was a rather absurd way to keep the pandemonium out.

They closed their eyes only briefly, however, for when they realized the creatures were not here for them, the sights they were seeing were far too compelling to block out. The beasts were flying overhead, and once they reached the Hollow, they would swoop down, wings outstretched, and grab large numbers of the army in their talons. Those talons looked razor-sharp, and it was doubtless that as they plucked up one after another of the army, those talons were causing extreme damage, despite the solid metal armor that covered each member of the dreadful army of Shrailzhar.

The whole thing seemed completely unreal, and Bella slowly reached back looking for Matt's other hand, but instead, he quickly found hers. Watching the dreadful scene became strenuous; while Bella desperately wanted to shut her eyes and block it out, she couldn't make herself look away.

The entire time all the swooping and diving and grabbing of this one or that one from Shrailzhar's army was going on, the sky was dark … absolutely dark … dark dark. With more flying beasts than their eyes could take in at one time, and with their wingspans being collectively larger than the entire sky, it made the sun impossible to force even a flit of its rays onto the land.

Every once in a while, when there was a gap in the flying formation of savages, a tiny sliver of light would peek through, but it certainly was not often, neither would it last long when it did happen. Those few glimmers of light here and there allowed the crouching Travelers to see just enough to wish they couldn't see anything at all.

With a short time passing, the bedlam fell quiet, and the marching army of Shrailzhar had dwindled down to only a very few. Those that did remain, waited, still lying face down and motionless, until there was not even one of the beasts of the air remaining. When the last one had gotten bored with the game and left, flapping its astounding wings and stirring up the air something fierce, the few army individuals that remained crawled away on their bellies; wounded, bleeding, and desperate for safety.

They chanted, although, with so few members remaining, the chants were low and powerless. The army was no longer even a tiny bit intimidating; they were downright laughable. While Bella did not care or even wonder about Miriam, she knew that the time was now to get to the Hollow. The thought of the army returning struck Bella, and she whispered to Matt with no care of whether Miriam heard or not. "We must get to the Hollow before they return."

"RUN!" Matt hollered, and run they did. The three of them jumped to their feet and ran as fast as they could move. They jumped over and darted around whatever pieces of armor had been left strewn behind, and thoughts of whatever traps may be laying in wait didn't cross their minds. Within seconds, they reached the boulder covering the Hollow, and Matt stood with one arm on the stone, and one arm outstretched, hurrying the girls inside.

It took no time to tumble in since no one cared about making a gracious entrance. Bella plunged in first with Miriam following close behind. The instant Miriam was inside, Matt jumped in behind her, and within a moment all three were sprawled on the floor, trying to catch their breath. They were holding back both tears of fear and snickers of relief. A plethora of opposing emotions swarmed both in and among the three of them.

They were in no hurry to get off the dirt floor, as the extreme anxiousness from outside overwhelmed them inside. The three laid there being deeply thankful for whatever those beasts were that had shown up, and even more grateful that they had gone again, taking the army of Shrailzhar with them. It didn't cross the minds of either Bella or Matt that it was Miriam who'd beckoned the help of the flying beasts; why would it? After all, how could they know such a thing? Miriam played along well, so she didn't give the secret away.

Someone laughed just inside one of the passageways, and quicker than a wink, the three Travelers who'd been sprawled on the floor were standing upright, shoulder to shoulder. Well, more like shoulder to elbow, since Matt was indeed a fair bit taller than either of the girls.

"Who is that?" Bella asked nervously. Up until now, no one other than the Travelers had ever entered Asphelia's Hollow, but then again, up until now, the army of Shrailzhar had left it alone. So with voices and laughter coming from the passageway to the kitchen, nothing would have been a surprise to the three standing there trembling. All at once, the Travelers wondered if they would have been better off to stay outside.

"I … I don't know," Matt stuttered. More voices lingered in the air and filled their ears. Suddenly, out stepped Kaija Mae, Aviel, and Tahlia. There were a couple of others as well, but their names had been misplaced in the minds of the Travelers.

As soon as Kaija Mae spotted the wide-eyed Travelers, she giggled and fluttered over to them, extending hugs to all. "Oh, my dear, I am so glad you made it. I was beginning to worry and was just telling Tahlia and the others how wonderful you are, Bella."

"Uh, thank you … I think," Bella responded. Everyone in the Hollow was confused, yet at the same time, relieved to see the others.

"Where are Judah and Jennifer?" Kaija Mae inquired. She motioned everyone to the table to join her in whatever concoction it was that she had made. "Want some?" she asked.

Some said, "No, thank you," others sat down at the eating stump and took chunks of what was on the plate. It looked rather questionable, although questionable things sometimes turn out to be the most wonderful things of all. This was one of the questionable things which neither Bella nor Miriam decided to take a chance on. Matt, on the other hand, dug right in.

"Mmmm," he mumbled and nodded to Kaija Mae.

"Now, about those twins," Kaija Mae said. "Are they coming? They didn't decide at the last minute to stay back in Westlock, did they?" This one seemed to have a few too many questions about the twins, and Bella became more suspicious.

"They'll be here as soon as the Shailmas bring them, I suppose," Bella answered. She opened her mouth to say more but was interrupted by a clattering behind her. She spun on her heels to see both Pierce and Sam make a not-so-grand entrance into the Hollow. "Yeah," Bella squealed and ran over to help the boys to their feet.

"Oh my, Sam," she said. "You just keep growing and growing." As Sam pulled himself upright, it was clear that he was well over six feet tall now, and he towered above Bella. The usual greetings were handed out; many hellos and hugs were exchanged within the Hollow.

The noise and chit-chat hullabaloo in the Eating Chamber was loud and rambunctious. It all promptly ceased as a sight none had witnessed before was now witnessed by all. From thin air, without a peep or a clatter or a stirring or a whisper, Judah and Jennifer appeared from out of nowhere in the midst of them all. Down through the roof of the Hollow they came, riding in on the backs of their Shailmas ... and every eye saw it.

13

POWER OF TRUTH

The twins had been delivered straight to the Eating Chamber in Asphelia's Hollow and were now standing among the others. The Travelers were surprised—of course—but the twins were even more surprised. Never had anyone been delivered directly to the Hollow's belly, but here they were … seen by everyone … as plain as day.

The Travelers stared at the twins. The twins stared at the Travelers. Like deer in headlights, Judah and Jennifer became uncomfortable with all the eyes that were focused on them. Finally, partly because he wasn't sure what to say and partly because the awkward silence was getting annoying, Judah opened his mouth.

"That was easy enough, I suppose." Laughter broke out among everyone in the Eating Chamber, and the greetings began.

"JUDAH!" Matt shouted. "JENNIFER!" he hollered, giving

her a bear-sized hug and a kiss on the forehead. "That was the most unlikely entrance to the Hollow—or to Trilleah for that matter—that I've ever seen."

Yes, everyone was glad to see everyone else, everyone except for Miriam and Jennifer, that is. As the girls' eyes met, tension filled the room. Everyone noticed. It was impossible not to notice. The temperature in the warm underground Hollow dropped, and a cold breeze blew in from the windowless walls.

A yellow haze spread over the whites of Miriam's eyes, and Jennifer was sure she saw that hellish, forked-tongue slip out for a second. The hair on Jennifer's neck stood up and she felt as though something had been lifted up from around her feet, pulled up over her head, and tied at the top.

Instantly, she was overcome—completely claustrophobic and unable to breathe. Jennifer panicked, grabbing her throat and gasping for breath while Bella, Matt, and the others rushed to her, trying to stop whatever it was that was happening to her. All the while, Miriam continued to glare at her with those hazed, yellow eyes.

"J, calm yourself this instant," Bella demanded and began rubbing her back.

Kaija Mae put her hands on Jennifer's face and lifted it toward her own, whispering, "Look at me. Jennifer, look at me." Finally, Jennifer did look, her own eyes meeting Kaija Mae's. As soon as they did, Jennifer began to calm down. Her breathing slowed and she stopped shaking.

Kaija Mae continued to hold Jennifer's face between her hands and kept staring into her eyes until the small, frazzled girl returned to normal. All Kaija Mae had actually done was to block the view of Miriam, but Jennifer and the other Travelers were unaware of that and wondered what special powers Kaija Mae was hiding.

Now, as Kaija Mae slowly took her hands from Jennifer's cheeks, Bella stepped in and held tightly to her niece. Kaija Mae stepped back and again, unnoticed by anyone else, moved to where Miriam was. Miriam's eyes had returned to their normal color, and her tongue wrapped itself up and was put away for a later time.

Ever so quietly, although it wouldn't have mattered, since the entire group of Travelers had moved to surround Jennifer and were all talking at once, Kaija Mae glared at Miriam and grabbed her wrist so she couldn't move away.

"Miriam, I warned you before the Travelers came this morning." Kaija Mae glanced toward the Travelers and found their attention still fixed on Jennifer, so she turned back to the Reptilian Mindbender. "You stay away from Jennifer. Don't you dare pull tricks of any sort, or you will have to deal with me. Do you hear me?" Kaija Mae jerked on Miriam's arm, demanding a response. When none came, she continued her rant.

"The others may be unaware that there's a Reptilian Mindbender among us, and you may have cursed Jennifer's tongue to be unable to speak of it, but I know, and you cannot curse MY tongue. Now, stay away from Jennifer … Miriam."

"Fine!" Miriam seethed loudly. "But only for a time, for it is well within my legal rights here in Trilleah to bend minds and twist words and there will come a day when I—and all of Trilleah—will win this war. The cursed souls shall be mine for eternity ... Kaija Mae."

"Perhaps ..." Kaija Mae whispered through gritted teeth. "Perhaps you believe such lies and perhaps a time will come when you get to walk in your full powers briefly, but that day is NOT today, so back off and stay away from Jennifer and the others."

"Do not forget, Miriam, who *I am* and what *MY* legal rights are here in Trilleah." And with that final statement, Kaija Mae harshly released Miriam's arm, spun on her heel, and stomped back to Jennifer.

"Looks like we all made it back," Matt was saying as Kaija Mae wandered over. He was standing awkwardly close to Jennifer and was keeping himself near to her for a purpose. Neither he, nor anyone else knew what had happened between Jennifer and Miriam last time they traveled through the land, nor did he know what had happened just now between the two girls. What Matt *did* know, however, was that something had indeed happened. There was no doubt about that.

He determined in his heart to keep close to the fragile, young girl and do his best to keep her safe from Miriam or any others who might try do her harm. He felt it was his duty to make sure no wrongdoing came to her and that she leave Trilleah at sunset just as safe and sound as when she'd arrived.

Of course, if he'd used his head and thought about it even for a moment, Matt would have realized that none of the Travelers left Trilleah the same way they came—ever. There was always something that went on, always some element of change that dug in and refused to let them leave in the same state in which they'd arrived. But he did not think it through, and he'd felt responsible for Jennifer from the first day she was brought to the Dark Land; maybe even a little before that. Judah and Bella had talked about her so much during their journeys that Matt felt like he knew her before he ever really did.

Regardless, Matt determined in his own heart to do his best to keep her safe. He didn't notice that Sam was also very close to Jennifer and, of course, he had no way of knowing that Sam was thinking the same thoughts. Perhaps it wasn't their own thoughts at all that were hum-drumming around in their minds. Perhaps it was the Shailmas planting such thoughts into the minds of the two young men. Perhaps they had become so accustomed to the voices of their Shailmas that those thoughts were becoming as common and regular as their own thoughts. Perhaps … but then again … perhaps not. It was impossible to know. Either way, whose ever thoughts they were, both Sam and Matt were determined to stand guard over Jennifer.

The tiny Eating Chamber was full and felt crowded with all of them mulling around. Aviel had moved beside Judah, and the two of them were having a rather loud and rambunctious discussion, the way boys often do. Bella had begun chatting with Kaija Mae, and all seemed well—or as well as things could seem in Trilleah.

There was no time to waste, however, as much of the time had already been wasted. The sun was inching its way through the dim sky and once again, Bella feared the group may not have time to find any tablets in the land while still saving enough time to get out before the sun set and the gates closed themselves off. It seemed they never had much time to spare; it also seemed that with each journey, they escaped with a little less time remaining than the journey before it. One of these times, they may not escape at all.

"OK," she bellowed. Bella had a tone to her voice that always demanded attention without ever stirring up resentment with the others. Jennifer often thought of it as a gift and was regularly surprised that no one ever got annoyed with her bossy auntie.

"We cannot stand around jibber-jabbering," she said. "So much time has already passed. We must hurry now." Heads nodded and a few "mhms," echoed here and there throughout the tiny Chamber.

"What do you want us to do, Bella?" Miriam asked. "I think you know best, so if you just tell us what to do to get prepared, we can get moving."

Everyone glared at the girl doing the talking. The words were coming out of her mouth alright, but the Travelers were all outraged about it. This attitude and these words were not coming from the Miriam any of them knew. She'd rarely say such things to Bella or anyone for that matter, so rather than putting the Travelers at ease like Miriam had hoped, it put them on guard all the more. They shifted their gaze from Miriam back to Bella and waited quietly for her response. They didn't have to wait long since Bella replied immediately.

"OK. Um … thank you, Miriam," she said. "We will need both the Book of Truths and the Book of Lies today so, Sam, I'm putting you in charge of those. Please don't forget, because I feel that we will need them both." Sam nodded and moved toward the basket which held the two books.

"Of course, we will need to pack a lunch with plenty of morango juice so …" Bella looked around the room deciding which of the Travelers to put in charge of that project. "Kaija Mae, do you know how to make morango juice?" she asked. Kaija Mae nodded her head, so Bella smiled and said, "OK, perfect. You, Judah, and Jennifer head to the kitchen and make the juice—we will need a good amount of it—and a large lunch as well, please."

"Yes Ma'am," said Kaija Mae, who promptly took Jennifer's hand. The girls disappeared into the passageway with Judah following close behind. Bella looked around the room at who was still waiting for instructions.

She didn't know what to say to Miriam, but as long as she was not near Jennifer, it seemed any job would suffice. She considered getting her to help Pierce choose maps but quickly decided against that. In fact, everything she thought of to get Miriam to do, she immediately decided against for one reason or another. Without wasting more time, Bella assigned this job to one and that job to another, until everyone was preparing for the journey.

Bella hoped they'd all return soon since she was getting anxious about where the sun was already hanging in the gloomy sky. For herself, she gathered this item and that one, not knowing for certain what they might need. She listened carefully to her Shailma but also packed a few other things that caught her eye, just in case.

Sam had gathered the Book of Truths and the Book of Lies and had returned to the eating stump. While he waited, he sat down and began looking through the books, releasing thoughtful sighs of "hmm," and "really?" as he flipped through the pages. Every now and again he'd say, "Bella, did you know that …"

Each time, Bella would raise her finger, cutting him off and saying, "not now, Sam."

Sam thought there were a few times when Bella might have wanted to pay attention and listen to what he was reading in the books. However, he knew better than to harp and hound on Bella when she had made her point. Instead, Sam decided to read as much from the books as he had time for before they left the Hollow.

He tried to remember as many details as he could, thinking it might come in handy later on today, or even possibly for another journey altogether. Either way, he felt it a wise idea to try to store the words from the pages somewhere in his mind, just in case. There was so much to remember that he asked his Shailma to guide his eyes and let his brain pick out what would be the most valuable to know.

As Sam skimmed page after page after page after page, he wondered out loud, but not loud enough for anyone to hear, why nobody had read the books before now. "Knowing that would have saved us much trouble," he muttered. And then again, "If I knew that was a lie, I'd have not been worried at all."

Yes, the great wisdom from these books could have saved much difficulty and trepidation on their earlier travels. Sam determined to memorize every page in the books which, of course, would be an altogether impossible task. Nevertheless, he had resolved to do his best and tuned out everything around him to focus on the words in the books.

Bella had completed gathering the necessary—and not so necessary—items and was now crouching by Pierce, gazing over his shoulder at the Living Maps. She was discussing (rather bossily) with him which maps they should bring. The choices for today's journey seemed far more complicated than those of past journeys.

Miriam had moved closer to the maps as well, and from the constant movement of her lips, it seemed she was mumbling something under her breath. It was so quiet, however, that nobody would be able to hear her. It did catch Sam's attention, though, and he was so intrigued by watching her that he forgot what he was doing. He stopped reading the books and turned his attention to the mumbling Miriam.

If he would have realized that this was exactly what she wanted him to do—the very reason for her mumbling—he'd have been much more stubborn and read the books faster. He did not realize, nor did he have any way to realize, that she was a Mindbender or that Mindbenders are unable to bend the minds of those who know the truth. She had to get those books from him, and if she couldn't get them from him, she could at least distract him from reading what was inside of them.

There was only one thing that would block Miriam's ability to bend the Travelers' minds, and that was the knowledge of the words written in the Book of Truths and the Book of Lies. Truth always exposes lies, and lies are always revealed in the realm of truth.

Always.

No exception.

Not even one.

PAY ATTENTION

"*Aha!*" Pierce shouted, throwing his hands into the air as if he'd just scored the winning point in some important tennis match. Bella, who'd been crouching close behind, was startled something silly. He nearly hit her in the nose. Bella jumped to her feet and smacked Pierce on the back.

"Pierce!" she shouted. "You scared me half to death."

He chuckled, apologized, and held out the map that was in his hands. "Look at this." He sounded so excited that Bella forgot at once that she was annoyed with him. Sam, too, was enticed by his excitement and jumped up. He moved close to Pierce and Bella—and the map—to find out what the excitement was all about. As he did, Sam forgot all about the Book of Truths and the Book of Lies that he'd been reading through. They both lay opened … and unwatched on the eating stump. Unwatched by Sam, that is. Miriam's eyes had been on them ever since Sam had dug them out of their basket a while earlier. Now, there they laid, unnoticed and unattended by anyone at all. She was torn, however, between going to the books or moving toward the maps to see what the fuss was over. She needed to be in both places, but of course, she could not be. Reptilian Mindbenders have certain powers, to be sure, but being in two places at once was not among them. She could only choose one way to move, so she chose to go after the books; keeping the truth hidden would be far more damaging, after all.

Her feet were swift and in a jiffy, the Book of Truths was tucked under one arm and the Book of Lies stuffed beneath the other. She exited quickly into the darkest passageway … the one nobody ever entered. "I'll figure out the maps later," she mumbled to herself. "For now, I must get rid of these troublesome books."

None of the three Travelers jumping and squealing over the maps noticed that Miriam had gone. They didn't see that the books had been taken, or that the other Travelers were beginning to return. What Pierce had discovered on the Living Maps was so exciting that it took all of their attention, so they noticed nothing else at all.

"What's going on?" Judah hollered at the top of his voice. Startled—but only slightly this time—Bella and Sam spun around. Their faces were beaming and Judah repeated his question. "What …

is … going … on?" he asked again slowly. "What are you all so happy about?"

"Surely not that we've returned with lunch," Kaija Mae teased. "I mean, I'm a great cook, but nothing here is quite that exciting." She giggled and playfully stuck her elbow into the ribs of Jennifer, who was not playful at the moment, and gave Kaija Mae an annoyed look. Sadly, this was becoming her most familiar look of all.

"Oh, it's just a little something Pierce spotted on one of the maps, is all," Bella giggled, finally answering Judah's question and ignoring both Jennifer and Kaija Mae altogether. It was clear that she wasn't about to offer any further details on the maps, so Judah again asked a most obvious question.

"Well … what did you find?"

Finally, it was Pierce who spoke up, and it was about time, too. Everyone was getting thoroughly annoyed with Bella's lack of straightforward answers.

"I saw that the army are silent. There's no marching, no chanting, nothing at all. It seems they've been almost entirely taken out by … by … well, by whatever those flying savages were that carried them away earlier. It appears the army of Shrailzhar is no longer a threat."

"Oh," was the only thing that came in response to what Pierce had apparently thought much more exciting. Eventually, as those lingering in the Eating Chamber thought about this discovery, another question arose, this time asked by Jennifer.

"Shouldn't we be concerned about whatever those flying devils were who took the army? Won't they be looking for us as well? If they wiped out most of Shrailzhar's army in mere seconds, we sure won't be a challenge for them. They'll wipe us out completely … in seconds." It seemed a valid question, as no one knew what those flying savages were; valid enough that the celebration ended abruptly.

"I suppose we do need to consider that," Bella said. She wrinkled up her nose and looked at Pierce, who looked right back and shrugged his shoulders.

"Maybe," Jennifer suggested, "they weren't looking for the army at all. Maybe …" and here she paused, whether to think carefully about what should come from her mouth next, or perhaps to ponder the question before it was even asked. "Maybe they were coming for us …"

"Regardless of what we should wonder about or be concerned about or not concerned about, we need to get going," Bella said. She looked around the Eating Chamber and saw that everyone had returned. Even Miriam was there, although, Bella never realized that there'd been a few brief moments when Miriam wasn't there. "I'm sure that if those flying beasts were coming for us, the maps would show it," Bella said. "So far they haven't, so we will believe they were sent, somehow, for the army."

Pierce folded the maps, stuffed them in his pocket, and threw his cloak over his shoulders, buttoning it up tightly. Together, the Travelers moved to the hooks on the wall, grabbing their cloaks and doing the same as Pierce. Jennifer, Judah, and Kaija Mae divided up the containers of food and shoved them all into the carrying pockets inside of their cloaks. Everything, that is, except the morango juice, which they didn't particularly want to spill.

There were three large jugs with lids screwed on tightly, and handles. Kaija Mae handed one to Judah and one to Jennifer, and she picked up the third jug herself. "I guess we're ready," she announced with a woeful sigh. Judah reached over and took the jug from his sister, leaving her hands empty.

"Ready," came the voices ringing out one by one and all at the same time; all but Sam, whose voice rang out something altogether different.

"I'm not ready …" he shouted. "The books are … they're gone …"

"What?" Bella shrieked, hurrying toward the eating stump.

She knelt down and crawled all around the stump. "Did someone pick them up?" she asked. Nobody admitted to doing so. "Sam, didn't you have them out?"

"I did, Bella," he answered. "I had them right here on the eating stump. I was reading them both." Sam was so upset that he looked rather foolish. He had reason to be upset, though, as Bella and the others seemed to be cross with him, even though he was not the one who was responsible for the missing books.

"Well," Pierce said, "we will have to go without them."

"Pierce, no." Bella cried. "I have a strong feeling that we'll need both those books today," she said, getting more worked up.

"We have no option, Bella," he argued back. "We must get going, or we might as well head straight back home again."

She knew he was right, but her stomach churned and grew increasingly distressed. She was convinced that at least one situation was going to arise during today's journey where they would need the Book of Truths or the Book of Lies. They had no other option than to leave without the books, however, so Bella pulled her cloak on, put her head down, and quietly mumbled, "Let's go." She sounded defeated, and they hadn't even left the Hollow yet.

One by one the cloaked Travelers stepped up and out of Asphelia's Hollow and into the dreary land. They didn't know where they were heading or what may lie before them. They were putting their trust in Pierce and Bella, who'd chosen the maps for today's journey.

They were each on their very highest alert, trying to be aware of their surroundings but knowing that their surroundings would likely change before they came back this way. Hopefully, that would be long before the sun nestled its way back down into hiding.

The Travelers were now becoming a small army of their own. They were growing in numbers, but also in knowledge of the land and wisdom of what it took to travel through it. Trust in each other was important but not unquestionably necessary, but trust in their Shailmas was both important *and* necessary. They each had to trust their own Shailma to see what their eyes could not, and hear what their ears were deafened to, and direct them accordingly. With each new journey, this trust in the Shailmas was getting stronger and more valuable and much, much more crucial.

"We've come this way before," Sam said to Matt. "Doesn't it seem familiar?"

"A little, I suppose," Matt replied. "Then again, this entire land looks the same after a while, so I really can't say if we've been down this path before."

"I suppose you're right," Sam said.

They hadn't gone far at all—or at least not far enough—before some of the traps laid out by the army were felt. They were still deep in the Forest of Waiting Ones, and it was disturbing to hear the deep moaning and see how much the forest had grown since the Winter Solstice.

Jennifer's mind was unchallenged at the moment, and so it began to wonder about many things. *If we do find all the tablets, how is the curse broken? Do all these moaning souls have Shailmas? How do we get them out of Trilleah? If we break the curse, do the Waiting Ones return to where they were when the Trows stole their souls or do they go straight to Heaven? Will they all go to Heaven? Does everyone go to Heaven? Will I go to Heaven? This is such a dreadful land. I want to go home.*

Question after question after question popped itself into her mind, each rolling around searching for answers but finding none.

Jennifer paid no attention to her feet or the path. Furthermore, she felt that she had no need to pay attention to her feet or the path because she was tucked so neatly in the middle of the Travelers; somewhere between Matt and Sam, who had both grown taller since the last visit to the dreadful land. She felt safe.

Jennifer could not have been more wrong and should have known better than to listen to her feelings, for rarely did they tell her the truth; especially in Trilleah, where everything was shaken and upside down and mixed up and turned around. In Trilleah, feelings should never be trusted.

Yes; Jennifer should have been paying attention to the path.

DARK SECRETS

Ling Shrailzhar's traps had not *all* been set since the army had been scooped up and taken away before the final traps could be put into place. But many of them had been set; not in the dirt where they could easily be seen. Not in Asphelia's Hollow, for the army could not get inside, but around … here and there. Some were in the air and others rode on the wind and still others had been carried into place by Wintbuhs and Flaybins—those creatures unseen by the eye and unheard by the ear, but present, nevertheless.

Yes, the traps were set. Deception would be their lair and lies, their bait.

Little by little the Travelers made their way through the forest, trying hard to tune out horrifying moans and distracting groans of the Waiting Ones. It seemed that with each new Solstice, the groans were louder … deeper somehow … more painful. As they wafted into the ears of the Travelers, the sounds coming from the souls were oppressive and agonizing. With no words to explain such an oddity, no one bothered to try. They felt it, though. They felt the sounds deep in their bellies; rumblings beneath their skin.

Bella and Pierce, who led the way, were moving quickly and getting far ahead of the others. Some straggled far behind. Neither was good.

"Can you go any faster?" Matt whispered to Jennifer.

"I'll try," she replied.

"They must be hurrying to get out of the forest," Sam added. "At least I hope that's why they're going so fast." He looked down at Jennifer, who had to take twice as many steps as either of the long-legged boys, just to keep up. "I'll have to put you on my shoulders and carry you soon," he said and patted her on the back.

Jennifer knew he was only teasing, but her thoughts were not laughable.

If they don't slow down, you'll have to do just that. We've been gone less than ten minutes and I'm already tired; my legs are aching. She said nothing but kept putting one foot in front of the other and began to focus on her steps across the rugged ground.

Suddenly, and without warning, Pierce and Bella stopped. They did not slow down to a stop, they just stopped. Completely. Rather than everyone else taking the chance to catch up with them, they each stopped too. Everyone. Even the stragglers who didn't seem to be paying any attention stopped. There was dead silence—except for the groans and wailings of the Waiting Ones.

The sudden silence in the land magnified those deplorable moans and groans a million times. It seemed like those sounds were bouncing off of every tree in the forest, getting louder and deeper with every tick-tock of time.

All that the Travelers wanted to do was get through the forest and out the other side. But for reasons known only to Pierce and Bella, they'd stopped and now stood motionless right in the heart of Malleana Forest. Dreadful … purely dreadful.

From where the next sound came, no one knew. It was so powerful and startling that for the first time that the Travelers knew of, the Waiting Ones turned silent. Not a sound came from them. Not a groan or a moan or a whisper or a peep. Nothing.

The ground beneath their feet shook; not a shake like an earthquake, but a shake as if afraid. Perhaps it was more like an ongoing shudder of terror. It was the same kind of shake of which the Travelers themselves were doing. It was as if the land itself was afraid of whatever was making such a horrendous sound.

It was incomprehensible … completely unbearable … a sound so loud it caused every single one of them to press their hands over their ears and try to block out some of it—any of it. It forced them to the ground; every Traveler bent low, squatting with their face down, hiding as though the sound was pushing them into the dirt.

The sound caused their eyes to water and their brains to pound. If they could have dug holes in the dirt and climbed in to get away from the dreadful racket, they would have gladly done so. The sound was like ten thousand screams of death, magnified ten thousand times more. It was piercing and lasted a very long time, or so it seemed.

It was as though the land was trying to tuck itself away and hide, afraid of whatever was producing the sound, or perhaps afraid of the sound itself. Even the trees in the forest seemed to crouch down a little; to bend as low as they could without snapping in two.

The ground continued to shake; the sound continued to screech. Where there had not been even a wisp of a breeze, now out of nowhere, a miserable wind picked up and howled. It blew through the trees of the forest and surrounded the Travelers. The wind shrieked, but it was not nearly loud enough to block out the other noise.

The Travelers were so afraid that none even had a thought. If there was any thought at all, it was fear, and it consumed them thoroughly. They appropriately assumed their fate was sealed, and this was the end; that whatever creature was making such a howl would quickly present itself and stop their breath.

The Travelers were trying to dig into the dirt, begging to be swallowed up by the ground. But then, just as suddenly as the great wind came and the unbearable sound appeared, both were gone. The wind stopped and the sound silenced. In an instant. No explanation … no warning … just gone.

For the longest time, no one moved. No one stood up, or made a sound, or formed a thought. Even the moans of the forest did not return for a moment or two. But then, one by one, and then two by two, and then all at once, the trees began their wailing and moaning once again.

The Travelers peeled their hands away from their ears, cramped from being pressed so hard for so long. They began to lift their heads and open their eyes and found the land had grown dark; pitch black dark, as though the sun had been switched off and the moon was not yet hanging in the sky.

Some of the Travelers felt their eyes just to make sure they were indeed open. The ground had stopped shaking but the Travelers had not. One asked another if it was black, for they each wondered if they'd been blinded.

Their feet shook and their knees wobbled as they stood. Their hands reached out in front of them, trying to find other Travelers. Jennifer felt one hand on her left and one hand on her right.

"Jennifer," she heard faintly.

"I'm here," Jennifer replied.

"We must find the others," were their whispers back and forth.

Matt and Sam had each found a hand of Jennifer, and they held on tightly, her tiny hands gripped by their large ones.

"Don't be afraid, Jenny," Sam said. But even as her ears soaked in the boy's words, her hands felt both Sam's and Matt's hands shaking terribly.

Ya right, she thought. *I WILL be afraid, thank you very much.* And afraid she was.

The Travelers had no option but to call out to each other, even though they knew they should remain quiet. The only other sounds heard in the land were the groans of the Waiting Ones and a dim hum that had started right after the horrible noise had ended. It seemed like it was left over from the noise.

"Pierce," Bella called out. "Do you hear a hum?" She'd found his arm in the dark and was holding tightly to it. They remained where they had stopped, waiting for the others to catch up. In complete darkness, that was a difficult task.

"I do," he answered. "I'm not sure if it's an actual hum in the air or a buzzing left over in my ears."

"Good thought," Bella said. She listened harder, trying to figure it out. It seemed like the sound was coming from both within her head and from the air. "Odd," she muttered.

"Matt … Kaija Mae … Judah," she called out probably a bit too loudly.

"We are here," said someone, although Bella couldn't recognize who was who from whispering voices muffled by cloak hoods.

"Take your hoods down; I can't hear you," Bella whispered loudly.

Yes, of course, Matt thought. *We don't need to be covered when it's so black. Nothing will be able to see us; that's for sure.* He pulled his hood down and so did everyone else, all thinking the same thoughts of how silly it was to be hiding in their hoods when the darkness hid them so perfectly already.

Quickly, Matt and Sam, with Jennifer still tucked between them, arrived at the spot where Bella and Pierce stood waiting.

"Ouch," a voice said.

"Oh, sorry," came another.

"You kicked my shin," whined Pierce, annoyed.

"I said sorry," Sam shot back. "I couldn't exactly see your shin—or any of you for that matter." Sam chuckled and leaned down to where he imagined Jennifer's ear may be and whispered, "If I could have seen his shin, I'd have kicked it harder."

"I wonder where the others are." Bella said and called out, quieter this time. "Judah, where are you? Kaija Mae? Aviel? Tahlia!"

As she listened for the others and tried to tune out the annoying hum, she heard the sweetest sound she could imagine. Singing. It was Kaija Mae, no doubt, since she was nearly always singing. There was power in whatever it was that she sang, even though the words were unrecognizable to any of them.

It was Kaija Mae's singing that had stirred Jennifer when she had gotten attacked in the caves. It was her singing that calmed

Jennifer down back at their house, just before arriving at Trilleah. Yes, there was no doubt that Kaija Mae's song was the sweetest of all sounds; both powerful and peaceful … both in Westlock and Trilleah.

Just as the singing came close to the others already gathered and holding on to one another, an itty bitty light escaped from the sun. So slight, it was nearly unnoticed. However, when a space is so completely void of any light, it only takes the smallest flicker of the smallest flame to divide the darkness. Something had most assuredly broken through the darkness but was so tiny, and it had such a large space to occupy, that it was thin; very thin.

The Travelers could see one another's shadows, which was more than they could see two seconds earlier. For that, they were thankful. At least they would not need to hold onto one another, although nobody stopped holding onto anybody else.

With the hum of the land, and Kaija Mae's singing, and the groaning of the Waiting Ones, the sounds were beginning to mix themselves together. It was a wonder that when Judah quietly whispered, "Look!" anyone heard him at all.

"Look at what?" Jennifer asked.

"The sun," he replied.

Now, it was still very dark, so it was unnoticeable. But if one could have noticed, they'd have seen every head tilt up toward the sun —or where the sun seemed to be hiding away behind something they couldn't quite make out.

Many sounds slipped from the mouths of the Travelers and drifted into the warm air as they all saw the same thing. The sun was not refusing to shine, nor had it been moved or hidden or fallen from its place in the sky. There was something draped over it; a shield of some sort … or a blanket perhaps.

The Travelers were gawking, wide-eyed, trying to figure out what was hanging over the sun and blocking its light. Finally, after many guesses and numerous, "No, I don't think that's it," responses, Miriam spoke up.

"It's a veil," she stated flatly.

Now, it seemed to the others that Miriam had made more of an announcement than a guess; like she knew for a fact that it was a veil covering the sun. But how would she know? How could she know? Was she not simply a Traveler like the rest of them; albeit a million times more annoying?

Jennifer knew Miriam was something other than a Traveler, but she dared not open her mouth. Every time she had tried in the past, small but horribly painful boils would cover her lips and tongue, making it impossible to speak. She didn't even try to reveal the Reptilian's secret. Jennifer looked at Kaija Mae, but it was still too dark for her to notice the desperate look in Jennifer's eyes.

Kaija Mae was the only other Traveler who knew of Miriam's secret, but she chose not to mention it; not yet. She knew it would cause chaos if the Travelers knew of the Reptilian Mindbender's true identity—as well as her own—so she kept quiet, since there was no way to give up Miriam's identity without also revealing her own. Instead, she joined in the discussion of the veil and distracted the Travelers from their own curious thoughts.

The truth would come out eventually and reveal the dark secrets; surely it would. It would have to. But now, in the near-dark with traps set all around the land, was not that time.

It would reveal itself in due time … dark secrets always do.

16

WHERE NO LIGHT SHINES

"A veil?" came the angry echoes of Bella, Pierce, and Judah.

"Why would the sun be veiled?" one asked.

"Who would … how could they … it can't be possible to veil the sun … can it?" asked another.

"Surely even King Shrailzhar is not powerful enough to accomplish such a thing," spouted yet one more.

Then Jennifer spoke up, asking the one question that was on everyone's mind. Boldly, she turned her eyes away from the veiled sun and laid them directly on Miriam.

"How did YOU know it was a veil?" she demanded.

Without hesitating even for a second, Miriam replied. "It's obvious." Her answers never seemed to make complete sense, but rarely did anyone question her on such nonsense. From the first moment Bella had laid eyes on the girl in Malleana Forest, to the argument she'd overheard between her and Pierce in the darkest Hollow passageway, to this very second, she knew something was odd … very odd … unexplainably odd … about Miriam.

Bella hadn't yet been able to put it into words or make any sense of what that oddness was specifically, but with everything that came out of Miriam's mouth, Bella was more and more and more convinced that she was not one of them. There was something no good about that one, and even though Bella couldn't determine what that no good something was, she knew it was there.

As they stood staring into the sky at something they were sure they did not want to see, a shriek from Jennifer brought their attention —and their eyes—straight back to the land. An anguished high pitched "OUCH!" shot from the girl who was still being held onto by Matt and Sam, followed by a loud thud.

Jennifer had slumped hard to the ground. She looked as though she'd been thrown down violently. She yanked her hands away from the two boys and rubbed her knees.

Sam looked at Matt and Matt looked back at Sam. The boys looked this way and that, up into the sky and then behind them. Every which way they could strain their necks to look, well, that's precisely where they looked. Finally, seeing nothing of any notable value, they knelt down beside Jennifer.

"What happened?" Sam shrieked.

"I have no idea," she squealed. Her voice sounded angry, but her face—what could be seen of it in the dimness of midday—looked terrified. "I was standing between you and Matt looking at the sun like everyone else. It felt like something sharp grabbed my shoulders and tried to pick me up." At that thought, Jennifer reached up with one hand and began rubbing her shoulders.

"You and Matt were holding my hands, so whatever it was that was trying to grab me, let go and threw me down." Jennifer didn't seem all that upset. Well, not as upset as the others thought she should be if what she was telling them was what had happened. Perhaps she was a bit shaken up, and that caused her emotions to be a bit wobbly. The others thought she should be much more upset if such a thing as she was describing was the thing that she believed to have happened. It seemed odd, to be sure.

"My feet left the ground," she said, her voice getting higher, now sounding more perturbed than frightened. "Did neither of you feel that?" she asked the boys. They both looked at her and then at each other, and back again to Jennifer.

"Nope," Sam said.

"I didn't notice anything," Matt said.

Some of them began wondering if Jennifer's overactive imagination was getting the best of the poor girl. After all, she had been through a great amount of trauma here in the land—more so than any of the rest. Perhaps she was beginning to experience things that were not really happening. Maybe her imagination was getting confused with reality because indeed, reality in Trilleah seemed dreadfully similar to outrageous imaginations from back home.

Upon closer investigation, however, it did look like her cloak had been torn up a bit at both shoulders; sliced right through in fact! Jennifer was rubbing her knees from tumbling onto them, but her shoulders stung a decent amount as well. It didn't seem to the onlookers like she was bleeding. However, with the veiled sun offering barely enough light to Jennifer's eyes, it would be hard to see any blood on the dingy cloak.

Matt and Sam took Jennifer's hands in theirs and helped her up. She did not let go of either one of them once she was upright, and they continued to hold firmly to hers.

"We haven't moved in a very long time and now, with the veiled sun—or whatever it is—it will be impossible to tell how much of the day we have left," Bella said. She sounded far too worried for anyone's liking. They all allowed panic to set in.

"Jennifer, are you OK to walk?" Bella asked.

"Oh, of course, Auntie," Jennifer replied.

"Then we should continue, I guess," Bella sighed. "We must hurry and get into the caves." She took Pierce's arm and they began trudging along a path that none of them could see; one foot in front of another; one step at a time.

As they walked blindly, trying to be quick but forced to be slow, Bella dug around inside her cloak looking for something she'd stuck in the carrying pocket at the last minute, just before they left the Hollow.

"Aha," she whispered to Pierce.

"Aha what?" he echoed.

"I grabbed this last minute," she said excitedly. "I didn't know why and thought I was being silly, being it was the middle of the summer day and all, but now I know. I love when things that make no sense suddenly make perfect sense." She thrust her hand out of the cloak, and a small bit of light came with it.

"A flashlight," Pierce chuckled a little. "Yup, I can see why you'd wonder about bringing that." He took the small flashlight from Bella.

"Do you have any more?" he asked. He was waving the flashlight around, this way and that, looking for something undetermined. He hoped he didn't find anything with the small ray of light but thought it best to look anyway, just to be sure.

"Where did you get that?" came a few voices from the back of the parade of Travelers.

"Jennifer, does he have a flashlight?" Judah asked. He was quite a distance behind his sister, holding onto Kaija Mae. Miriam was even farther back, just behind Aviel, Tahlia, and the other Travelers they'd met up with in the Labyrinth. As usual, she lagged far behind.

"I think so," Jennifer answered. "Bella, where did you get the light?"

"Oh, in my pocket," her aunt whispered back.

It's quite the thing, when an entire land is so quiet except for a dull hum, how loudly one can whisper and still consider it a whisper. There is a fine line between a loud whisper and a hushed holler. Bella seemed to master that line and even though everyone could hear her well, she was still safely on the side of a whisper.

"The Carphlour Caves are just ahead," Pierce said. "I hope this light is enough to read the maps because the land has changed since we left the Hollow. I'm sure of it."

"I can't recall what it showed exactly anyway, even if the land had not changed," Bella added.

"Are you sure they are just ahead?" Matt asked. "It seems like we haven't been walking long enough to be close to the caves already."

"From my calculations," Pierce continued, "the caves should be about four hundred yards ahead and to the left a few steps."

"OK," Bella replied. "We trust you."

It was interesting how the Travelers were talking quietly to one another, but their voices caught the wings of the air just right, so that every word between the two drifted back and were deposited in the ears of the Travelers behind them; all the way back to Miriam— the very one from whom they wished to keep their words from reaching.

There were many things—countless things—that were far from the Traveler's understanding, but what was very evident within their realm of understanding, was that Miriam was not one of them.

17

DARK CAVES ON DARK DAYS

Sure enough, another few steps and the path veered slightly to the left and then, viola!

Pierce waved the light ahead to try to find the entrance to the largest of the Carphlour Caves. Bella and Pierce ducked inside and waved each Traveler through until everyone was tucked safely inside the dark cavern.

"That wasn't too bad so far," Judah announced.

"Speak for yourself," Jennifer snapped. Her knees were a bit stiff, and her shoulders throbbed. She let go of the boys' hands, feeling only a little safer inside the caves and reached up to touch her shoulders as best as she could through the thick cloak. "Ouch," she grimaced as her fingers felt the rips in the cloak.

Bella took the flashlight from Pierce who, of course, gave her a bit of a huff, and shone it on Jennifer.

"J," she said. "Lemme see." She shone the light on Jennifer's cloak and saw it had been shredded to bits on both shoulders. There was absolutely no doubt the far-fetched story Jennifer had told was the truth.

"What in the world," Bella demanded. "Jennifer, didn't you feel something on your shoulders?"

"Your cloak is destroyed," Sam wailed.

None of their comments were making Jennifer feel any better whatsoever, and a horrified look crossed her face.

"I already told you I felt something grab my shoulders!" She was angry now, which momentarily replaced the fear she was carrying. "I was lifted right off the ground, but when my hands were held by Matt and Sam, whatever had me by the shoulders tugged hard and then flung me to the ground." She raised her voice now, aware that the story she'd told just a few minutes earlier was apparently not believed. Why would she make up something so outrageous?

"I ALREADY TOLD YOU THAT!"

"Oh, mercy," Kaija Mae shrieked. "Let's get that cloak off and see if it got through to your skin or if it's just the cloak that's torn up." She began helping Jennifer take off the cloak, while Pierce and Matt started laying out the maps. They all needed the flashlight, but instead of Bella handing it to Pierce, she kept its tiny beam directed on Jennifer's shoulders and told Pierce to find a lantern.

Bella began snapping orders around the group of nervous Travelers. They had all gathered to see what Jennifer's shoulders would reveal, which was understandable, but Bella knew Jennifer well enough to know that the young girl would not appreciate such an audience. Besides, there were other things that needed to be done. Surrounding Jennifer was, for most of the others, a waste of time.

"Sam, can you get out the food? And bring some morango juice to Jennifer."

"Yes Ma'am," Sam answered. He wanted very much to stay close to Jennifer, to see if her shoulders were marked up, but also because he felt responsible and even obligated to keep her safe. It disturbed him greatly that neither he nor Matt did a good job of that, even while they had held the girl by the hands.

It was the two of them whom Jennifer had been counting on at the very moment she had this terrible experience. It was the two of them who were protecting her when the … the … whatever it was … had grabbed her and hurled her to the ground. Both Sam and Matt felt an enormous weight of failure sitting heavy on their shoulders.

While the boys were busy feeling responsible for the situation Jennifer was in, Kaija Mae quietly walked over and spoke softly to them.

"Thank you, Matthew. Thank you, Samuel."

"For what?" the surprised boys said at once.

"For looking after Jennifer, of course." The boys both looked up at her in shock, knowing they had done a terrible job of the one thing she was thanking them for.

"If you had not held her by the hands and had her tucked between the two of you, she'd have been snatched up by whatever it was that tried taking her." The boys didn't seem convinced, so Kaija Mae tried again. "Whatever grabbed her could not take her because of the two of you.

"Thank you," she said again, putting one hand on each of their shoulders. Kaija Mae smiled and returned to where Bella and Jennifer were still squatting on the floor inspecting both the cloak and Jennifer's shoulders.

It was dim in the cave, and the only light they had was small. Pierce was unable to find the lantern, so the small light was all they had. But if she held it right, Bella found it would bounce off of the rocks in the caves and throw sufficient light around to let Sam see what he was doing with the lunch, as well as allow Kaija Mae and Bella to get a decent look at Jennifer's shoulders. There were some marks to be sure, but they were more like yellow bruising, not the gashes they had expected to find.

"Girls, I hate to break up your tea party over there," Pierce mumbled, "but I need some more light to read these maps. If Jennifer's going to make it through that tragedy," he mocked, "would I be able to have some light? The maps are rather important."

"Oh dear," Bella said. "Pierce, I'm sorry." She helped Jennifer get her cloak back on before taking the light to Pierce. "Sorry. I didn't consider reading the maps; I was busy thinking about Jennifer. She seems OK ... for now."

Pierce took the light from Bella and looked up at her. "For now?" he asked. "What do you mean, 'for now?'"

"Her shoulders seem fine, bruised is all, and her knees are scraped up from falling—or being dropped—but that's not what I meant."

While the conversation continued in hushed tones and quiet whispers, both Pierce and Bella kept their eyes on the map, which was springing to life. Some deep valleys dug themselves down while the Malleana Forest sprung up ... groans included. Hundreds of huge flying savages began to appear, some here, some there. There was no rhyme nor reason to where they were appearing ... no indication of where they were coming from ... or where they were going.

"I just meant that it seems as though Jennifer is going to be targeted from the beginning to the end of this journey." She knelt down and leaned in close to Pierce. With everyone preoccupied with lunch, or Jennifer, or this and that, Bella was relieved to have a chance to give him some information.

"Pierce," she whispered, "Kaija Mae came to visit us in Westlock and brought a warning that the land is filled with traps." He chuckled one of those uncomfortable, not sure what to say, sort of chuckles.

"Oh, sweet Bella, the land is always full of traps. That's why we need the maps." She was leaned in so close to Pierce that he could smell her scent; a bit of her hair brushed against his ear. He wanted to lean over and kiss her, but knew better than to do something as stupid as that. Instead, he moved his head a tad closer to her, pretending to be listening carefully to her words.

"I realize that, but she said the army had discovered Asphelia's Hollow and had set traps right there … specifically for Jennifer."

"What? Why?" Pierce took his eyes from the maps now so he could look into Bella's face. He may have had a rough way about him, a grouchy and hard shell, but he did have a space in his heart where Bella had moved into and now fully occupied. Besides having his heart completely overtaken, he also had a compassion for the girl and felt responsible for her, probably because it was the two of them who'd been coming to Trilleah longer than anyone else.

Bella and Pierce had made the first journey together, although much less dangerous and frightful than this one, and they had built a bond that existed between none of the other Travelers. Pierce turned his eyes back to the maps, which appeared to be finished laying out the land. With the dim light, it was hard to see, and Pierce was hoping they didn't miss any important pieces of information because of it.

"Do you think the sun will shine again while we are here?" came a question from behind the two. Bella was startled and spun around. Miriam. Oh, how her very presence made Bella's stomach twist and her skin crawl. Why was she so interested? Surely she already had the answer, since she was the one who knew why it had stopped shining in the first place, so it seemed.

"I hope so," was all Bella could force herself to say. She hoped Miriam didn't overhear the words she'd just shared with Pierce, but there was no way to know for sure.

Miriam glanced over the shoulders of Pierce and Bella and peered down at the map. Pierce tried to puff up his shoulders to try to block her view, but she moved to the left and kept her eyes focused.

"How are Jennifer's shoulders, Bella?" Miriam asked. Bella couldn't decide if the girl was concerned, or if she was nosey.

Of course, what Miriam was really doing was trying to see the map. Since Bella's eyes were set on the map, and because she refused to look at Miriam, and because it was quite dim in the cave, Bella didn't know that the girl was making distracting conversation so that she could study the map herself. Miriam didn't know what she was looking for, but was certain she'd know it when she saw it.

18

KEEP WATCH

"Food's ready," Sam reminded the others. He startled nearly everyone in the cave since it had been almost silent for quite a few moments, except for the whispering that had been going on back and forth between Miriam and Bella.

"Oh, right," Bella said. "How much of the morango juice has Jennifer had?"

"A lot," Matt answered. "Probably more than she needed, but better too much than not enough, right?"

You see, morango juice, although perhaps an odd sort of name, is filled with many things: bitter roots and sour herbs, both excellent for healing wounds, and also a sweet leaf from the rooma tree, which was the only thing that made the drink … well, drinkable. Without the rooma leaves, the drink was so awful it would have made the one drinking spit it out immediately, disabling any healing abilities. But the rooma leaves gave it a sweet taste, although still quite tangy, enough to make it acceptable enough to the tongue and warm in the belly.

If it was heated, the morango juice would make the tongue tingle in a delightful manner. Unfortunately, there was no way to keep the juice warm on such a journey, nor did they have a way to heat it in the Dark Land. No, they'd have to drink it cold, which was not completely terrible, just not tingly.

Bella loved when she'd bring something along on one of these journeys that she didn't know they'd need but would most surely become a very necessary element somewhere along the trip. She loved it because it always reminded her that her Shailma spoke to her even when she didn't necessarily know it was him she had heard. Now, with the small light and the morango juice both making themselves useful, Bella was pleasantly thrilled with herself.

Shura would somehow deposit thoughts in her mind, the tiniest of thoughts, really, and she'd act upon them without ever stopping to think where the thought had come from. She never considered that perhaps Shura had planted them, or that the thoughts somehow mingled among her own thoughts or ideas. Nevertheless, Bella knew that neither the light nor the morango juice was completely her idea. Furthermore, she was thoroughly grateful that she hadn't questioned either one of the thoughts, as she sometimes did, which often led her to ignore them altogether.

Bella was saddened, however, that it seemed far too often the necessary items, such as the morango juice, was required solely for Jennifer; the weakest one, the smallest of them all, the very one whom Bella had tried to leave out of Trilleah altogether. For reasons they didn't understand, Jennifer was the one who was needed more than any other in the Dark Land. It was Jennifer who was necessary on each journey, on each day of Solstice, to eventually break the curse.

"Pierce," Bella put her hand on his shoulder, "have some food."

Yes, Miriam thought, overhearing Bella's whispers. *Have some food. I'll gladly give up any food and your stupid morango juice if I can be alone with the maps—even for a minute.* That was the only way she could get the information she required and certainly, if she was to change the maps in any way, both Pierce and Bella would have to stop paying such close attention to them, and maybe, discredit the maps completely.

"Drat," Miriam said when she saw Pierce fold up the map and shove it in his pocket. She meant to keep her frustration inside her head, but the word slipped out.

"Drat what, Miriam?" Bella questioned accusingly.

"Nothing," the angry Miriam spouted back.

"Pierce, why did you close all the maps up?" Bella asked. She seemed genuinely clueless as to why Miriam had been there, hovering over her shoulder for the last few minutes. "The path has not

been drawn yet. Now we'll have to lay it out and wait all over again."
Pierce handed Bella the flashlight and at the same time, gave her a look which Bella interpreted well.

The look said, "I had my reasons which I will tell you later but for now, hush." Bella hushed. She'd been around Pierce long enough to read his looks well and while she trusted him, there was a teensy shred of something that shot through her mind every once in awhile that wobbled that trust … just a little.

The shred of mistrust would pass through her mind so quickly that she never considered why. It came and went so fast it was almost as if it was never there at all. However, the fact was that the teensy shred of mistrust had been there, and maybe Bella should have pondered it more deeply. Then again, maybe not.

The whole bunch of them ate every last morsel of food and guzzled back two of the three jugs of juice. They would have finished the third off as well, but Bella wouldn't allow it.

Unfortunately, she had a feeling in her belly that caused her to want to save some of the juice for a later time, for somewhere down the road that they were about to set their feet upon. She crossed her fingers and hoped she was wrong. *Better safe than sorry,* she supposed.

Pierce barely ate anything and had the maps laid out again, this time with his back to the wall and the map facing the Travelers. He'd never read them like this before but felt he needed to stay aware of where certain Travelers were in the cave—Miriam in particular—and this was the best way to do that.

He felt it necessary to keep the map away from her eyes, although Pierce didn't have any particular reason as to why he felt this way. Nevertheless, he knew it didn't matter if he had all the reasons why to do something or not to do something. If Pierce felt it in his belly, that was enough reason for him.

"Bella," he called across the cave. He waited until she looked over at him before motioning for her to come over to where he was. She whispered something to Kaija Mae before rushing to Pierce.

"What do you need?" she asked.

"I need you to stand here with me and look at the maps—or pretend to look at the maps." She looked at him curiously.

"Why would I pretend?"

"Well," he whispered, "I have a feeling that Miriam wants to see them for purposes that would not benefit any of us, or our journey, or the Waiting Ones. I want you to look as though you're looking at the maps but somehow keep your eyes on her."

"Of course, she wants to see ..." An enormous rant was building in Bella's belly and she wanted to let it all overflow and spew out onto Pierce, who she was sure knew more about Miriam than he was saying, but she decided now was not the time. She let her sentence dwindle off without finishing it. "Yes, I can do that," was all she ended up saying.

So, as Pierce shuffled the maps around one more time, searching for the flying savages that were hiding somewhere in the land, Judah and Jennifer tucked the food containers one inside another inside another again until there was only one container left. Kaija Mae sang quietly but loud enough for all to hear; Matt, Aviel, and the others did whatever else there was to do before heading out of the cave and into the open land.

Bella kept her head down pretending to watch the map, but truthfully, she had both eyes on Miriam.

She watched the strange girl carefully and wondered about her, pondered over her, and asked Shura about her. No thoughts came to her mind, no good thoughts that is, but flutterings did dance around in her belly; many of them. There were so many, in fact, that Bella's tummy felt full and an ache filled her from the inside and seeped through her skin, climbing through to the outside. She wanted to look away but couldn't. She dared not to. There was something about this one that could not be figured out, at least by Bella. The longer she watched her, the more uneasy she became and the more ache filled her up.

Keep alert, she heard Shura whisper. *Keep watch of that one ... very close watch.*

Bella's concentration was disturbed and she was glad for that.

"Ready," she heard Pierce's voice loud and clear.

"I didn't even get to look at the maps," Bella said, finally letting her eyes wander away from the mysterious Miriam. She looked at Pierce, who had already folded up the maps and tucked them away.

"You didn't need to," he said while giving her the most unusual smile. Any smile on Pierce's face was unusual because smiles didn't seem to belong there—like they were uncomfortable being there. "I saw all that was needed to be seen; the maps drew the paths plainly."

"But I would've liked to see it also," Bella argued. Again that teensy flash of doubt shot through her mind like a bolt of lightning and her trust was shaken even more.

"I know, but we couldn't risk Miriam being unwatched." Pierce's awkward smile faded and was replaced with his normal scowl. "Bella," he said, "you trust me, don't you?"

"Of course," she sputtered. Bella never really questioned it until now, but as he asked the question, she realized maybe he wasn't quite as trustworthy as she had thought. I mean, thinking about it now, he did seem a bit shaky. He *had* asked her to keep a watch on Miriam, which appeared to be a good idea at the time but now, since his question, she wondered if maybe he was the one she should have been watching.

"Was there a reason you wanted me to watch Miriam?" she asked in a teasing voice, even though she was fully serious. "Were you trying to distract Miriam from seeing the map … or me?" Again, she disguised the true curiousness of her question with a tone of flirty teasing, but the moment the words left her lips, her curiosity grew.

Perhaps it was Miriam who'd been watching Bella, distracting her, keeping her eyes off of the map rather than the other way around. The private argument she'd heard between Pierce and Miriam popped up in her mind and suddenly, Bella was unsure what—or who—to trust.

Pierce had been the only one to see the maps and watch the paths be drawn. *Had he arranged for everyone to be busy and have Miriam watch Bella and Bella watch Miriam, casting doubt into both the girls' minds about the other so that he alone could read the maps?* This was getting curiouser and curiouser by the moment. Her mind was spinning with so many dreadful thoughts. There was no time for such confusion, but then again, time was all she had.

Bella shook her head. *Good grief, Bella,* she reprimanded herself. *You're not thinking straight.* She scratched her head, smiled at Pierce, and put the silliness out of her mind—for now—and promised herself she'd consult Shura about it later. Later, when she was safely back in her little yellow house, she'd ponder what may or may not be the truth of the matter.

For now, they had to get going. She decided to put all her trust in the one who'd read the maps and chose to be fully confident in her Shailma to let her know if he was leading them down a path of danger or destruction.

"Let's go," she said sternly.

Pierce stepped out first and was disappointed to see the sun was still covered. Even more of its light had been concealed, making it tough to see where to go—even with the itty bitty white beam coming from the flashlight.

"You couldn't have grabbed a bigger light?" he asked Bella.

"Or more of them?" Matt teased.

One by one they exited the cave, Pierce not moving down the path until the last Traveler was out. Then, standing together in one large group, he laid down a few rules.

"OK," he said firmly. "It's dark, and I don't want to lose anyone and we don't have time to look for you if you do get lost." There were a few "mhm's" and whatnot, but nobody replied.It seemed he was wasting valuable time pointing out obvious things and nobody had a shred of patience left. The dark was overwhelming them. The land was treacherous enough in the light, but in the dark? It seemed like another land altogether, one that was impassable.

Bella spoke up. "Everyone get in groups of two … and keep track of one another." The Travelers moved quickly to whoever happened to be the closest to them. They linked arms and held on tight.

"Jennifer, I want you in between Judah and Matt," Pierce commanded. "I want you directly behind Bella and me," he added. While Jennifer felt protected by most of the Travelers, the feeling was overshadowed by her stinging shoulders and bruised knees. The need for her to walk between Judah and Matt made her uneasy, although there were not two people she would rather have been tucked between.

She knew Judah would do anything to keep her safe, even put himself into harm's way if necessary; and Matt—well, she enjoyed any reason to be close to the tall, handsome, young man.

"Ready?" Pierce asked.

"Ready," came overlapping voices.

Jennifer was not ready, but the time had come and ready or not, the dark journey was about to begin.

19

RUMBLINGS

Each one stepped out of the cave in the order Pierce had directed them. First, Pierce and Bella followed closely by Jennifer, who was comfortably sandwiched between Judah and Matt. Sam and Kaija Mae were directly behind them and at the end of the short parade was Miriam, Tahlia, Aviel, and the others.

As they stepped out, each, in turn, noticed—in fact, it could not go unnoticed—that the land had changed significantly since they'd gone into the Carphlour Caves and not for the better, either. The sun was still veiled and even though it was Miriam who had pointed that out earlier, and even though it had made them all angry that it was her who did so, not one of them could argue that she had spoken the truth.

Until now, the sun was something their eyes had not been able to see directly because it was too powerful to gaze upon, even though it wasn't generous on giving light. But today? Today they could stare right into the middle of it … and they did. As each Traveler looked, and all in their own time, it was obvious that it had been veiled. It was undeniable, even by those who'd want to deny Miriam's statement.

They could all see that something had been laid over the sun, draped almost entirely overtop of it. Like someone—or something—wanted to block out its light altogether. But who? And even more importantly, why? Trilleah was a horrible land to be sure, but never had any of them wished to wander along the bitterly dangerous ground without light. Yet here they were, doing exactly that.

As she stared up at the darkened sun hanging above, it reminded Jennifer of when she was younger and her mom would hang a cloth over the lamp in her bedroom to dim its light. All those times when she could not sleep because it was too dark, but turning on the lamp caused the room to be too light, that's what her mamma would do.

It seemed now, in Trilleah, that someone had done a similar thing and had hung something over the sun to mask the light that usually came from it—even if it was only a small bit of light. Oh, there was a teensy sliver of light here and a very tiny slice there, but not enough for the Travelers to see their way through the land.

It's bad enough that when we can see, so much of what our eyes find is questionable and confusing. How are we supposed to find our way with even that gone? Jennifer pondered. But then, another thought, a rather odd one to be sure, popped into her mind and made the first thought seem less annoying. *Maybe the darkness will keep us from seeing what is not there in the first place. Maybe darkness will let us see only what is truth.*

Her mind, confused and tired as it was, waffled back and forth between opposing ideas, not sure where they came from or where they needed to go; certainly, they could not both remain in her mind at the same time.

"I wonder if Miriam didn't know any more than the rest of us," Judah whispered to Jennifer.

"What are you talking about?" she asked.

"About the sun … when she said it was veiled." Jennifer was slightly unhappy that Judah had disrupted her thoughts, but then again, she was relieved to have something else to think about.

"Oh, that," Jennifer answered. She began rattling on about other things regarding Miriam, but Judah suddenly seemed uninterested in the conversation and entirely taken with something else. Jennifer didn't care even slightly and continued speaking her thoughts out loud. Sometimes forcing her thoughts to get in line so she could march them out in proper order helped them to make more sense. "It looks that way to me too; just as Miriam said," Jennifer mumbled.

"Yes, Jelly Bean," Judah answered, still not even glancing back toward the sun.

"Oh, never mind," she grunted. Sometimes when she would talk in that tone, or act like her feelings had been hurt, her brother would huff and turn his attention fully toward her to appease her. This was not one of those times, and he kept his attention fixed on something else; something of which Jennifer was still unaware.

She never bothered to look around much because she was far too busy talking to herself. The more she had a conversation with herself, the angrier she became.

Now, it shouldn't need to be said, but it would do a girl good to pay attention in a land such as this one; especially in such a land that is nearly dark and filled with traps. Although, while Bella and Judah and Kaija Mae knew it was filled with traps—set for Jennifer— Jennifer herself was unaware of such things.

It was not particularly in her best interest to know these things since her presence was absolutely necessary on this journey … and every journey that was yet to come. The very reason Kaija Mae had made the trip to see Judah and Bella was so that THEY knew about the traps. It was THEIR jobs to keep Jennifer safe as they journeyed through Trilleah searching for the tablets.

That was precisely what Judah was doing—or trying to do. His sister did not make the task any easier. Nevertheless, Judah was doing his best to pay attention to all things surrounding them, or so he thought. They journeyed on, not noticing some things that deserved to be noticed and paying attention to other things that mattered not.

"Is anyone else noticing that rumbling?" Bella asked.

"Rumbling?" Kaija Mae repeated.

"Rumbling," some of the Travelers kept saying, as if repeating the word over and over might somehow make those who had not noticed suddenly do so.

"I did," Judah muttered. He gripped his sister's hand tighter.

"It's been doing that since we left the caves," Pierce added.

"What is it?" Jennifer asked, still unable to decide what kind of rumbling the others were noticing.

"Rumbling like a hungry belly," Bella explained. "It feels like the land itself is rumbling … but that makes no sense."

"Yes, because everything in this ridiculous land makes sense, I suppose!" Jennifer snapped. "Judah," she whispered and wiggled her fingers. "I can't feel my hand."

"Oh, sorry," he said and loosened his grip, but only slightly and not nearly enough.

"I don't know," Kaija Mae joined the conversation. "I've never noticed the land rumbling before, and indeed, I do hope it's the land because I don't want to think what else it could be," she added. As soon as the words were out, she wished they weren't.

Tahlia spoke up from the back of the line of Travelers. She had been quiet until now.

"I've been in a couple of earthquakes, but this feels nothing like that sort. What's that over there?" she asked. The question was silly, of course, since wherever "there" was, none of the rest of them knew. In such a dreary darkness it was impossible to see where Tahlia may have been looking or pointing if indeed, she was pointing anywhere at all. The Travelers had no idea which direction they should be looking, so some looked this way and others looked that way; some looked no way at all.

It took only a few more steps, though, and suddenly everyone noticed what Tahlia must have been looking at. Just ahead there was a great deal of light coming from some burning bushes; an entire row of them, in fact. How did they not see these from far off, since they were exceedingly bright?

"I don't recall seeing burning bushes on the maps," Pierce whispered quietly enough for only Bella to hear and indeed, she was the only one who did.

"Are you sure this is the right way?" Bella asked. "Because there's no doubt those are burning bushes."

"I am a hundred percent sure." Pierce never appreciated much when another questioned him. Not even if it was Bella.

"Maybe the map doesn't show every detail," Bella reasoned. "Or maybe because it's so dark out here, the land supplied them for light." Bella listed as many reasons as she could come up with as to why there could be burning bushes here when they weren't on the map, although even as she popped off reason after reason, in her heart she knew none of them were right.

"What are those?" Jennifer's innocent question interrupted the hushed conversation between Bella and Pierce.

"What are what?" Matt asked.

"Those things on fire, of course," she huffed.

"Jennifer, those are burning bushes," Sam said. "We've seen them before, don't you remember?"

Everyone seemed to agree with Sam; everyone that is, except for Jennifer.

"I know what burning bushes are and of course, I remember seeing them; many times." Without any hesitation, she continued. "But these things are certainly not burning bushes." She sounded a bit perturbed but, of course, it's often difficult to tell with Jennifer, especially in the dark, and even more especially in Trilleah, if she is perturbed or not perturbed.

A debate broke out between Jennifer and the rest of the Travelers. Jennifer stuck to her conviction that these things, while indeed bushes that were burning, were not burning bushes. Everyone else tried to convince her that they were. Now she unmistakably went from being perturbed, to annoyed, to downright angry.

"If these are burning bushes," she demanded, "then someone, please tell me why they're not attached to the ground. Do bushes not grow in the ground, because these certainly aren't."

There was silence, except for the continual rumbling of the land, as every Traveler looked more carefully at what Jennifer had already seen. Indeed, the burning things were not bushes at all. They were hovering just above the ground. Jennifer was right.

"Maybe they're a different type of burning bush?" Sam offered. Inside, he knew differently; he knew they were impostors. But he didn't want the others to know that he was afraid.

"Pierce, are you sure this is the right way?" Miriam snarled from the back of the group. It wasn't that she cared, since she knew the land well. She only wished to plant doubt in the others' minds about Pierce … and the maps.

He answered with a simple, "Yup," but the tone in that one word spoke loud and clear. Pierce was not about to admit anything to her. Whether he was going the wrong way, whether he took a wrong turn or not, he was certainly not about to admit it; not to Miriam.

In fact, the bushes—or whatever these things were that were giving them reasonable amounts of light—had tricked them into believing they were on a path that they were, in fact, not on. These things had lured them straight off of the path and Pierce had indeed led them the wrong way … and all at once, he knew it.

As the Travelers argued among themselves as to whether they were on the right path, words from the Book of Truths rushed into Sam's mind. A simple statement he'd noticed while reading the book back in the Hollow barged into his brain and without even thinking, he blurted it out.

"Not every light that catches the eye is to be followed, but only that which is planted firmly in the soil of integrity and rooted in the ground of truth."

About six voices responded to Sam, and they all had the same tone of confusion.

"What?" Pierce asked loudly.

"Huh?" Jennifer shrieked.

These were not words that sounded like anything Sam might say, not even a little.

"I read it in the Book of Truths earlier this morning," Sam explained. He sounded bewildered and repeated the phrase. He was quite surprised that he'd remembered the words, but sure enough, they came out the second time the same as the first, like he'd spent a good long while memorizing them.

"Not every light that stirs the eye is to be followed, but only that which is planted firmly in the soil of integrity and rooted in the ground of truth."

These burning imposters were not planted in soil of any kind. They had no roots and had led them down a path that was not intended to be walked on.

"We have to go back," Pierce hollered. They all stopped suddenly; it seemed that while they did need to turn back, there was no way they could. These burning imposters moved toward the Travelers and entrapped them, virtually imprisoning them in a circle of fire with no way to escape.

They rose up tall and broad, the small balls of fire stretching high into pillars of fire hovering and intermingling around them.

"I'm sorry," Pierce cried. "I thought they were to help us. I didn't realize I was following the light rather than the path. I forgot to trust the maps and followed these stupid lies instead." He was nearly screaming now just to be heard over the raging sounds that were coming from the pillars of fire.

Inside of each pillar, thirteen in all, there seemed to be shadows—willowy black centers—and it seemed to Jennifer, at least, that these willowy centers were weak. Perhaps she was just strong. Either way, as she watched the dark shadows inside each pillar, Jennifer knew they were watching her right back. She knew they were there for her, not for the others, and she wondered about this.

Simeon, show me what to do, she screamed inside her head. As she did, her mind filled with peace; her fears vanished. Jennifer felt empowered to take control of these things that were trying so hard to intimidate her. That was it. They were mere intimidation and had no power of their own whatsoever.

Jennifer wiggled her hand away from Matt's. She reached up and felt around until her fingers laid hold of the locket that hung around her neck and for a moment, considered her mamma. She let her hand wrap tightly around the locket, taking a deep breath and shouted the words Simeon had told her to say.

"MOVE OUT OF OUR WAY … STEP BACK AT ONCE!"

Most certainly, she startled the other Travelers far more than she startled the fiery pillars; they only seemed to mock the small girl.

Matt grabbed her hand back in his own. Both he and Judah yanked on her arms, pulling her back a few steps. The boys moved together, making a wall in front of the crazed girl in a useless effort to protect her—or perhaps to protect themselves. She was unsure of which it was.

"JENNIFER!" Sam shouted. He remembered a second truth from the Book of Truths and blurted it out.

"Every untruth can be overcome by truth; both cannot live in the same space at the same time," were the words he hollered.

The Travelers were confused about these random, senseless words spilling from Sam's mouth; but not Jennifer. She knew exactly what those words meant and the power they held and how to use them to her advantage.

"Simeon," she whispered. "Give me courage."

20

BETWEEN TRUTH & LIES

While the land of Trilleah may have been covered in darkness because of the veil draped over the sun, where the Travelers stood right then was unusually bright; thirteen pillars of fire tend to cause such a brightness. In fact, fire rages much brighter in the dark.

Oddly, while the fire itself was giving the Travelers a generous amount of light—which fire is expected to do—the pillars of fire were not producing any amount of heat. One would expect heat, though, would they not?

Being encircled by a great fire should make one quite hot … unpleasantly hot … uncomfortably hot. There was none of that here, though. This, Jennifer found odd.

Somewhere within the oddness of it all, it began to make sense; the burning bushes that were not burning bushes, a raging fire that gave off no heat, and Sam's words of untruth and truth all began to twist themselves together into a perfect braid of sense in Jennifer's mind. Or maybe Simeon was whispering sensical thoughts to her soul. Either way, sense was being made of all the nonsense.

Jennifer grinned for a second, envisioning this vision of Simeon winding nonsensical thoughts together; pulling one strand from over here and adding another from over there to make a braid of perfect and complete sense. She'd forgotten that she was surrounded by others who were still filled with panic. They hadn't been given the understanding of truth that she had. They were still believing the lies that their eyes were telling them. They remained deeply afraid.

When she chuckled, Jennifer didn't expect anyone else to notice. They noticed anyway.

"JENNIFER," Sam hollered above the loud hiss and steady crackling of the towering pillars of bright reds and oranges.

"Oh," she said as she was suddenly brought back to the seriousness of the situation.

Without any fear left, not even in one cell or the tiniest corner of her heart, Jennifer wiggled both her hands away from the boys who had been holding them tightly. She raised them high in front of her and with the very loudest voice she'd ever been able to force from her small lungs, she screamed.

"I DO NOT KNOW WHAT YOU ARE, BUT YOU ARE NOT FIRE … AND YOU ARE NOT TRUTH."

Her voice cracked, not because she was afraid, but because she was shouting so loudly that her voice couldn't bear it. Now that Jennifer had everyone's attention—both the Travelers and the thirteen pillars of fire—she could shout a little less loudly.

"You are nothing more than a baker's dozen of harmless, bent up, broken down sticks masking yourselves to be something that you are not." Jennifer began laughing, since her eyes had been opened to see what was surrounding her and the others; she found it to be amusing.

While the rest continued to see enormous towers of raging flames, which could quickly consume the entire group of Travelers with only a breath of wind, Jennifer's eyes saw something altogether different.

The truth was nothing more than blowing dust and a few scrawny sticks that the land had propped up. Each stick was in a costume of fire, like at Halloween. The blazing crackles were nothing more than bits of orange-colored dirt and dust being blown around. Somehow, what Jennifer saw made her laugh and laugh. The silliness of it caused her to giggle uncontrollably and her eyes to water. The costumed twigs seemed to take offense at her laughter and roared and raged with as much ferociousness as they could stir up.

The other Travelers did not know whether to look at her or the fire pillars; both were equally outrageous.

"She's gone mad," Sam shouted to Matt. Judah stepped toward his sister and tried to grab her; it seemed any moment she might collapse into the dirt and be consumed by the raging pillars.

Before Judah could reach her, she held her arm out and gained a small amount of control over her herself. "No no Sam," she shouted back through her laughing. "Don't you see it?"

"The pillars of fire?" he asked, sounding confused. Of course, he saw them, how could he not see them? They were ginormous and towering straight above the Travelers. How could anyone miss them? It seemed to Sam that Jennifer was not seeing them at all. Otherwise, she would absolutely, most certainly, and without a doubt, *not* be laughing.

"Sam, it's fine. They are not what they appear." Nobody seemed to be counting her words to be right. Finally, Jennifer was able to stop laughing. She held her arms up high and again shouted, a little less loudly this time. "Oh, you silly sticks, I reveal your true identity and remove all the power from your lies by speaking the truth. You are NOT fire, there is NO fire in you, you hold NO danger, and indeed NO power at all."

She chuckled, trying to keep her voice firm. "Truth overpowers lies, and I have spoken truth." Right then she remembered word-for-word what Sam had shouted moments ago and she, in turn, shouted the words to the lies still waving their phony fierceness above them.

"Every untruth can be overcome by truth; both cannot live in the same space at the same time. So in the power of Truth, I demand all lies and all untruth be gone. Now sticks, find your places back on the ground and DO NOT BOTHER US AGAIN."

Instantly, what had appeared to be fires vanished and the thirteen sticks were revealed to the eyes of all Travelers as those twigs fell back into the dirt of the land. The Travelers stood in the open air again, in complete silence. Jennifer felt uncomfortable; she knew all the eyes were looking at her, but she joined her hands back with Judah and Matt and whispered in a croaky voice, "OK, let's go."

"What … was … THAT?" came the questions. Jennifer did not wish to explain what her eyes had seen for often, such explanations are long and complicated. Usually, they make very little sense—if any sense at all—to the listener. They didn't have time for such explanations, but it was clear that nobody was going to be moving in any direction at all until she said something.

"I have never known fires not to be hot," she sighed. She had recalled a time not so long ago when she and Judah had been playing with a fire in their backyard. Bella had made one for them, and they were having loads of fun throwing in their papers from the school year they had just finished. Every summer they performed this end of school ritual, getting rid of all their homework and tests and papers from the year before.

This particular time, however, Judah had gotten a little too close to the fire. As boys tend to do, he "pushed the limits," as her father used to say. He'd held on to a burning stack of papers a little too long, and the fire crept up and burned his thumb badly. Surely, if that tiny little flame had caused such damage to her brother's thumb, these enormous pillars of raging infernos would have done far greater damage from the sheer heat they'd have spewed out. That thought brought her right back to her explanation.

"Those fires were so massive that our skin should have melted off of our bodies, or at least caused us a lot of pain. I felt no heat at all." She talked quickly, leaving no room for questions.

"Simeon showed me that they were not what we were seeing, so when Sam hollered about the truth and untruth not being able to dwell in the same space at the same time, I realized that I had the truth, and they were the lies." She looked around, wondering why nobody was trying to interrupt her with endless questions.

Jennifer looked into the eyes of the Travelers and saw they were listening, but fear still held them tightly, so she continued.

"I thought that if I spoke the truth, the untruths would have to leave since they can't both share the same space … and they did."

Now she was finished with her explanation. Still, not one question was asked, so she stepped upon the opportunity to ask one of her own. "Can we get going?" The staring eyes were getting a bit annoying, after all, and there was nothing else to explain.

"Uh …" Pierce stammered; Bella elbowed him in the ribs.

"Pierce," she whispered "which direction?"

"Uh …" he said again and blinked hard, looking down at the harmless and scrawny sticks now laying in the dirt. "This way," he finally said and took a few steps in that direction.

"OK," Bella said. "This way everyone."

One by one, the Travelers stepped into a disorderly sort of line and in silence—except for the grumblings which the land was still rattling, and the groaning of the forest—and followed Pierce. There was no talking because the Travelers were so dumbfounded by what they'd just seen. They'd been surrounded by fire and then in an instant, they were not. Jennifer had commanded the fire—and it listened to her. The land had obeyed the smallest one among them.

As bewildered as each of them was, the whole situation made some sort of twisted-up sense. After going a reasonably long distance, someone finally said something worth saying.

"Sam," said Kaija Mae from somewhere in the back, "it's brilliant that you knew that piece from the Book of Truths." Some chatter followed and then Kaija Mae asked a reasonable question, but one without any acceptable answers. "Where is the book now? Surely you brought it …"

"I planned on bringing it. In fact, it was the only job Bella assigned me back in the Hollow."

"And you left it behind?" Jennifer asked. "Seems like it would have been a wonderful thing to bring," she said.

"Seems like it was a brilliant idea that he read it and memorized some of it, don't you think?" Matt asked. He was always the defender of all. Matt was not one to ever speak harshly to someone—or about someone. He always stood up for anyone that may have been an underdog and right now, he felt that Sam was unfairly attacked, and came to his aid. Matt didn't need to, though. Sam was capable of looking after himself and began to do just that.

"I do think it would have been a fantastic idea—one of the best ideas—to have brought the Book of Truths *and* the Book of Lies, which is why I had them both out on the eating stump," Sam explained.

"While I was waiting for everyone else to gather their list of things, I laid both of the books open and read a great deal of them. For a reason I didn't know at the time, but I most certainly know now, I thought it would be a good idea to read as much from each book as I could.

"Someone needed a quick bit of help, so I moved away from the eating stump for a moment but," he waited for a couple of seconds before finishing off the end of his explaining. "When I returned to grab the books, they were gone." He expected many questions now and was not disappointed.

"What do you mean, gone?" Jennifer asked.

"I mean gone, as in they were there … and then they were not there," he replied. When questions to which he had no answers kept on being asked, he finally had enough and said impatiently, "I'm glad

I read what I did and even more glad that what I did read stuck in my head."

"Yes," Jennifer said. "If you hadn't, we would still be trapped in that circle of fi … her word trickled off, for while she was about to say "circle of fire," she realized they'd never been in a circle of fire. She didn't know what else to call them.

"Circle of lies, you mean," Bella said.

"Yes … circle of lies," Jennifer agreed.

"Well, no matter. We're back on the path and no more distractions will interfere. We are well on the way to the clay tablet." Pierce rambled on, and Sam was happy to let him do so. After all, he had no idea where the books had gone, and wondering about it was not going to do any good. Sam knew that it was his Shailma who'd caused him to read the parts that would be necessary for the journey and he whispered a quiet, "Thank you."

Suddenly, an interesting thought came to Sam, and he couldn't determine if it was a thought of his own making or a thought deposited by his Shailma. It was a brilliant thought, and no matter where it had come from, he would carry it. Sam decided to speak the idea out loud and see what the others thought about it.

"It seems a good idea," Sam began, "that I should take the books home with me until Winter Solstice and memorize as much as I can." The others may not have known, but Sam had a unique ability to remember things; surely this ability would come in useful for such a task as this one. "We did not need the books themselves out here, after all, we only needed the truth inside of the books to defeat that lie."

"That is a brilliant idea, Sam," Bella answered, and Matt wholeheartedly agreed. As they were discussing it, a voice came from the back of the group and reminded them of a severe fault in their plan.

"We don't know where the books are."

"Right, good point," Sam grunted. "We've got to search the Hollow when we get back and …" He was interrupted by Judah, who spotted something to the west and wanted everyone else to take note of it as well.

"Um, I'm sorry to cut you off, Sam, and yes we must find the books. But for now, look to the west; something's stirring there."

Every head turned to the west.

Every face disappeared into the cloak hoods.

Silence was all that was heard.

21

WHAT LIES BENEATH

A pain pierced through Jennifer's hands, first one, and then the other, as Judah and Matt each tightened their grips. She sent both her elbows—at the same time—into their ribs, and they both let a little pressure off; enough to let some blood flow through her veins again.

"Sorry, Jelly Bean," Judah whispered. All this happened without taking even one eye off of what was hovering in the sky to the west. It was hard to see what was coming at them, or if it was coming at them at all, since it was so dim in the land. But there was no doubt that something was there.

"We will never find that tablet," Bella sighed.

Maybe it was because Bella was always at the front of the group, but she didn't seem to realize that even the slightest whisper could be heard all the way to the back. Peculiar sound waves were hiding in the air here in Trilleah that delighted in picking up whispers that were meant to remain unheard and carry them along, depositing their echoes into every ear along the path. Sometimes Jennifer wondered if theirs were the only ears to hear or if there were other unseen ears, hiding in the air, that heard their whispers as well. She recalled her first trip to Trilleah when Simeon had warned her gravely to keep her words quiet. It was then that he'd told her of listening ears in the air. Jennifer was about to warn her auntie, but Pierce spoke up instead.

"Bella," he said sharply. "You can't think that way."

Hmm, that was odd. Usually, it was Bella who was giving the lectures or consoling disappointed hearts. To hear Pierce do it sounded awkward and unnatural. Although, Pierce was awkward and unnatural most of the time, so this was nothing unusual.

Nevertheless, Bella's words found agreement in every heart. Surely, they wouldn't find a tablet here today. How could they? The journey had already been much too difficult, and their feet had barely made an indent on the path. Many sighs escaped and wafted into the air. Disappointment from one found frustration from another and soon the air was filled with a mixture of oppression.

"OK, this is silly," Kaija Mae said softly. "We can do this. If we stick together and everyone uses what they have, we can do this." She tried to be encouraging, but her words were full of the same doubtful echoes that everyone else's hearts were drowning in.

"What's that?" Jennifer squeaked. This time, it was her tiny hands who squeezed the boys' big hands tighter. Whatever had been hovering in the air was now climbing higher and higher into the dark sky. They had drifted so high, in fact, that they were nothing more than teeny tiny dots getting lost in the shadows of what little light the sun was casting.

With everyone gawking toward the sun trying desperately to keep watch on the odd things, they lost sight of them. So, with all eyes staring directly into the veiled sun, it made the brightness of it nearly blinding as the veil was suddenly pulled away.

In an instant, whatever had been laid over the sun keeping the bright rays from getting through, was removed. They assumed it was the flying savages who'd unveiled the sun, which raised their curiosity even more as to what those flying things were and why they had removed the veil. They still were unsure whether the flying savages were for them … or against them.

The Travelers rubbed their eyes and squinted, trying to find any sign of the flying creatures. While they were too high in the sky to spot, a few eyes did see something else; a large banner or covering of some sort was floating to the ground just a few hundred yards away.

"THE VEIL," Sam shouted.

"Shh," came the other voices.

"But the veil has come down," he repeated, not much quieter than the first time.

"Yes, yes it has," Kaija Mae squealed. She sounded excited.

"Let's go see it." Sam shrieked as his feet left the trail—which was now very visible to the Travelers in the sunlight. He headed toward whatever it was that had settled on the ground just a short distance away.

"Sam," Pierce whispered loudly. Sam didn't stop.

"Samuel!"

Sam stopped. He turned to look at Pierce and had a defiant gleam in his eye.

Pierce spoke sharply. "We don't know if this is a trap and we do not have the time for you to be caught in it if it is."

"What if it's not a trap?" Sam asked. "What if whatever those things were that pulled off the veil did it for us?" That seemed to be exactly what had happened. It did seem possible that it was not a trap but rather, whatever had removed the veil may be helping the Travelers. It seemed unlikely, but not impossible.

It felt necessary to find out, but how? If something in this land was on their side, they needed to know … didn't they?

If they moved toward the veil and it was a trap, the Travelers would be caught—all of them. On the other hand, if the savages that had pulled it off had done so to help the Travelers, they might find the veil itself to be helpful on their journey. Maybe that was why the flying things had waited until the Travelers were close enough before tearing it off; so they could retrieve it. Maybe the veil would be a necessary item to finish the journey … maybe not.

So many "maybes" and "what-if's" swirled in their minds. Some were spoken, others were kept quiet. The truth was, however, that time was quickly moving, and perhaps the distractions of all such things were themselves the very trap King Shrailzhar and his wicked army had set. Distraction can sometimes be the most trapping trap of all.

"Oh dear," Bella sighed. "What to do, what to do." What she, Jennifer, and everyone else were thinking, was the same thing. *Send Miriam to retrieve the veil.* If it did turn out to be a trap, she could get caught in it; they'd all know it was a trap, and they could carry on their way while getting rid of the unwanted companion. It seemed like a brilliant plan with no possible way to lose.

But how does one pull off such a plan without letting the bait know that they are, in fact, the bait? No, it wasn't going to work to use Miriam without her knowing. While it may have been a lovely idea, it was neither decent nor workable.

"I think we should keep going," Miriam said. It was as if she knew what the rest were thinking. She had not made a comment about anything for the longest time, but now, when everyone was thinking about sending her into a possible trap, she suddenly spoke. It seemed odd. The idea that Miriam may be able to read their thoughts sent chills through one and then another of the Travelers. No, this was ridiculous. It couldn't be … it just couldn't. Even though she was not likable in any measure, surely she was not one with such specific powers. It was likely nothing more than a coincidence.

Jennifer knew differently. She knew that Miriam was a Reptilian Mindbender. But as she rubbed the scars on her cheek, Jennifer knew better than to try and say anything about it. She could feel Miriam's eyes burning into her skin and so, with no other option, Jennifer remained quiet. She did wonder, though, if a Mindbender could also be a Mindreader?

No, that's ridiculous. There's no such thing as a Mindreader, she decided and let the entire thing get lost somewhere in the back of her mind. It was safer, after all, being lost.

"Yes, Miriam," Bella said. She hated when she had to agree with the wicked girl, but this was one of those times. Bella had to let common sense take the reigns, and clearly, common sense said to keep going, even if it was Miriam who had pointed it out. "Let's leave it and move on."

"Then let's go," Pierce said and off they went. It seemed from the tone of his voice that his patience with the girls was wearing thin.

It was easier to see the path now, but also easier to see everything else; things that they didn't want to see. Since the sun had now been allowed to shine—although not as brightly as one might hope—and Trilleah was awakened, the humming of the land quieted down. It was barely noticeable now in the light.

But the shadows that were darting around were very noticeable. There were hundreds of them flitting this way and that, looking for somewhere to hide. The unveiling of the sun had caught the shadows off guard; with the sun so bright now, they moved quickly, searching for cover. Of course, shadows can't live in sunlight, so each headed for dark corners. The Travelers pretended not to notice the shadows, for fear that if they acknowledged such things, those "things" might acknowledge them right back.

The shadows did not wish to be noticed by the Travelers any more than the Travelers wanted to be noticed by the shadows. The Travelers moved ahead, focusing on the path before them and wondering where the path might lead them.

Judah had picked up one of the sticks from a while back, one that had pretended to be a pillar of fire. He was surprised to find it not even warm when his skin touched it. Even though he knew it was just a stick, he still felt it cautiously, half-expecting it to be hot enough to burn him and half surprised to find it wasn't.

As they walked, Judah dragged the gnarled stick behind him in the dirt. It was leaving quite a deep trail which, Sam, who was directly behind, was staring at. His eyes were on the trail being made in the dirt instead of on the back of Judah, where he should have been watching. He couldn't look away from what was peeking through the ground. Every now and again, Sam thought he'd see bits of bright orange just below the dirt … like sparks dancing and looking for a way out perhaps … yet … different.

If he really let his imagination go, he'd say it looked like the eyes of a thousand horrid dragons peering from an underground lair, watching them from somewhere below.

Good grief, Sam, you are a crazy one, he thought. But while Sam thought many such things, his gaze never left the trail.

He didn't feel it was anything worth saying to anyone else, but more of a "hmm, there it is again, how interesting, " kind of thing. Sam didn't realize that what the stick was actually doing was revealing something that was indeed keeping itself hidden just below the trail … something that should have gotten his attention … something that would undoubtedly become the greatest danger they'd ever come across in Trilleah … eventually. Perhaps his imagination wasn't as crazy as he thought and he should have mentioned it to the others.

It seemed as though the stick was exposing a concealed wound to reveal the innermost parts of Trilleah, and Trilleah did not wish to have such parts exposed. So, the dirt trail that was being sliced open by the dragging point of the stick—like a zipper undoing a sweater—quickly pulled itself back together to shut up whatever it was so painstakingly hiding. It could not do so fast enough, though, to keep from being seen by Sam's peering eyes. This is precisely why no one other than Sam saw it.

He certainly should have been alarmed, but he was much too busy not being alarmed. Sam blamed his imagination for being too busy; too overactive. He said nothing.

"Pierce, do you remember where the map drew the path?" Judah asked. "Look how low the sun is getting already … now that we can see it."

"I'm getting nervous," Jennifer added.

"So am I," Bella agreed.

"Me too," came the voices of Sam and Tahlia.

"No need," Pierce said calmly before answering Judah's question. "I remember the path and it's not much farther until we're going to turn into a vineyard of some sort. The map showed loads and loads of sharp rocks, so we will have to be careful where we walk, but the clay tablet must be in that vineyard; that's where the path ends."

The Travelers considered how wonderful it was that it seemed this journey was nearly over. They pondered such things a little too soon, however, for whatever those flying savages were that had zoomed up to the sun and removed the veil, had returned. They were hovering above the Travelers, high enough so that no eye could get a good look at them, but low enough so their presence could not go unnoticed.

It seemed the creatures knew exactly where to hover so they could be seen, but where they could easily get lost in the rays of the sun and not be visible if they chose to hide. They weren't flying, exactly, and seemed to have nothing to fly with. There were no wings or anything of the sort that the Travelers could see; just wisps or something that looked like storm clouds with a long tail. Then again, it was hard to see them. When the sun was veiled, these savages looked completely different than they did now. The brightness of the sun had somehow faded them.

The Travelers' eyes were confused; the air was hazy.

It was tricky really, trying to walk quickly in such long cloaks, their eyes mostly covered by thick hoods, with heavy boots on their feet. That was tiring enough, but trying to look into the sky directly above them without walking into the back of the ones in front was downright dangerous. More than once, one Traveler would smack into the back of another, causing both to stumble.

Jennifer worried that these things hovering above were quite possibly what had grabbed her before. Although she couldn't see any sharp claws or talons on these beings, her heart raced, and she tried to hide completely between Judah and Matt … just in case.

There was no need, though; no need for her to hide nor fear at all, for whatever these were, they didn't stick around. After hovering above the Travelers for a short time, they vanished; no sign of them anywhere. It seemed like whatever those very odd beings were, they were here to help the Travelers. Maybe they'd make an appearance again but for now, they were gone.

Jennifer recalled briefly seeing creatures similar to these sitting outside of their Hollow on a different journey but quickly put it out of her mind. She would wonder about that another day.

It felt like the Travelers had walked a long way in one direction before Pierce finally made a slight turn to the west. Before very long at all, they entered what seemed like an unusual area for this land. They'd never seen anything like this here in Trilleah. There were giant vines everywhere. It did look very much like a vineyard, at least in pictures anyway, as most of the Travelers had never seen an actual vineyard.

It was one of the only places they had been in Trilleah where the true colors were not hidden beneath a thousand shades of gray. They had entered through a stone archway, and this vineyard was completely separated from anywhere they'd been before—like a land within the land. Even the ground had some color to it with the vines running thick, nearly covering it. The path had been covered over completely now with the thick running vines. It was tricky to walk on them, but they were careful and their boots were helpful.

If anyone had let their imagination wander even slightly, this place could almost have been described as lovely. As far as their eyes could see were vines—enormous vines. There was this shade of green and that shade of purple. There was no fruit on the vines that they could see, but perhaps, with any luck, they might find some deeper inside the vineyard.

22

MOTION DETECTED

Judah let go of Jennifer's hand, but she continued to hold tightly onto Matt's. She felt reasonably safe so had no real need to hold onto Matt, but she enjoyed having him close to her; so she was in no hurry to let go. It didn't last long, though. Matt moved up to speak to Pierce and let go of her hand anyway.

Bella reminded the Travelers of something Pierce had said earlier; something that made them slightly excited and a whole bunch frustrated. "You said the map showed that the tablet is in these vines, Pierce?" she asked.

"I said I *thought* the tablet must be in the vineyard because the path ended here," he replied.

They had all stopped walking and started looking around. This didn't seem like any of the vineyards they'd seen, after all. In the ones they'd seen in books or on TV, the vines were in neat rows. They were orderly, with wide spaces to walk between. These were vines alright, but there was no order whatsoever to anything. Now that they were deep inside the vineyard, it looked more like an overgrown mess that had run amuck, filling up every possible space.

The deeper into this place they wandered, the darker it became because of the disorderly wild vines climbing every which way. They could see the sun shining, but few of its rays were able to wiggle through. The vines covered the floor like a thick carpet, tripping the Travelers and grabbing their feet. They snagged their cloaks and hung over the top of their heads, poking into their hair. It had quickly gone from a calm, colorful place, unlike anywhere else in Trilleah, to a prison of grabbing, snagging, poking invasion of out-of-control vines—like everywhere else in Trilleah. Judah turned to look at what they had wandered through, but all he saw were vines. The vines had moved in behind them, closing off the way back … and any way out.

The vineyard had a stuffy feeling now, something that none of the Travelers appreciated. They moved farther and farther inside until there was nowhere else to go. It was like they'd wandered straight into the heart of something they should have stayed out of.

"I see why the path stopped," Sam complained.

So here they were, standing in a disorderly group, waiting for the stragglers to catch up, and hoping the vines had no intention of enveloping them.

"Where have you led us, Pierce?" came an angry voice from the back.

"Oh, Miriam, perhaps you should begin leading us if you know so much better," he barked back to her.

Judah, who'd been quiet most of the journey, now spoke up. "Arguing won't do any good. We need to stay still until we can figure this mess out."

As they stood still for a few moments, the vines eased up. Quickly the Travelers had plenty of room again; the vines seemed to calm down and get back into some sort of order.

"Hmm," Pierce hummed.

"Odd," Bella added. A bit of the path had opened up, so Pierce began moving again.

"Here's the path." He sounded delighted.

But as he took some steps and everyone started following, the vines reared up and filled the space again.

"Stop," Pierce shouted. Everyone stopped and the vines backed off.

"Move," Pierce bellowed, waving his hand and motioning for the others to follow. Straightaway the vines stood up, hovering around the group, grabbing at them and closing them in again.

"Oh dear," Bella sighed. "What are we going to do?"

"Let's think," Judah said. "We need to calm down and think this through." It had become evident that the movements of the Travelers annoyed the vineyard; the more they moved, the more upset the vines became. The Travelers felt like flowers in a weed patch, doomed to get choked out.

Nobody was calming down even slightly. In fact, the longer they stood trying to calm down and think, the less calm they felt. When the vines backed off, the Travelers could see glimpses of the sun. It had long reached its peak above and had begun making its way back down. It had reached that time of day where, even though the sun was still hanging in the sky, the moon decided to peek it's head out as well. It was dim, but could be seen; a sure sign that the Travelers did not have any time to "stop and think."

Simeon, Jennifer cried. *What do we do?*

While she waited impatiently for an answer, something grabbed her ankles. Even through her boots, she could feel it. The small girl tried moving her feet but the more she moved, the tighter whatever it was that had a hold on her became.

SIMEON, she screamed silently. *HELP ME!*

Since they had passed through the stone gate that led to the vineyard, neither Judah nor Matt had continued holding onto Jennifer's hands. When they first stepped into it, with all its colorfulness, they felt reasonably safe and, mistakingly let their guard down.

Unfortunately, because everyone was so preoccupied with the shock of the vines hedging them in whenever they moved, neither of the boys had thought to grab ahold of Jennifer again. It might have been because every space around them had vines and really, how dangerous could a vine be? The open sky they had feared previously was now entirely covered over with vines … they never considered what may lie below the vines. Jennifer was left open to all sorts of quandaries and conundrums.

So, when whatever it was that had wrapped itself around Jennifer's feet yanked from below, she quickly slipped right through the thick covering of the vines and disappeared into an abyss below. It happened quickly; so quickly, in fact, that it took a few seconds for any of the other Travelers to notice she was gone.

"Kaija Mae," Judah turned around. "Is Jennifer back there with you?" he asked.

"No, of course not. She is up there … between you and Matt," Kaija Mae answered. Judah looked at Matt. Matt looked at Judah.

"She most certainly is not," Matt shouted back to Kaija Mae. He turned around. Everyone turned around.

"Where is J?" Bella demanded. "Judah, where is Jennifer?"

"I … I … don't know," he stammered. First, he looked up, but seeing the vines directly above, he knew she didn't get picked up or taken by the flying savages. He looked below and kicked his feet stubbornly at the vines.

One vine he kicked particularly hard, moved slightly. As it did, he caught sight of the most horrible of any possible sights. Judah caught a glimpse of a crevice just below the vines that was slowly closing itself up. He managed to grab a view of it just as it came together and disappeared. Not even a scratch in the ground remained, but Judah knew what he'd seen.

The last thing his eyes took in before the dirt had closed itself up, the very last thing, was his sister. Judah wished he hadn't seen what he did because the look on her face would terrorize him for all of eternity unless he was able to get her back … somehow.

Judah fell to his knees and began clawing at the ground where he had seen the crevice.

"What are you doing? Pierce hollered. Judah did not reply. He kept digging.

"Judah!" Bella shouted. She moved toward her nephew, expecting the vines to puff themselves up and hold her in place. They did not. In fact, the vines recoiled, giving her plenty of space to take the few steps back to her nephew.

"Judah," she put her hand on his shoulders. He kept clawing at the ground but said nothing. Bella knelt down and grabbed his dirty, bleeding hands, in her own. "Judah, what is it?"

"JUDAH … WHAT HAPPENED?" she screamed.

The moment that Judah's eyes met with his auntie's eyes, the weight of unbearable grief fell upon his shoulders and he fell to the ground, weeping.

"Jelly Bean!" he sobbed. "I'm sorry … I'm SO SORRY!" he screamed, and ripping away from Bella, continued clawing at the merciless ground.

Without anyone else knowing what Judah had seen, the others began weeping as well. They knew it must be horrible, whatever it was, for the usually tough and tenacious boy to react this way. It was completely against his character to do so and the hearts of everyone who was now moving quickly to where he knelt, began to shatter.

"Judah," Matt said firmly and grabbed his friend's bloody hands to get his attention. "What did you see? Tell me what you saw. Where is Jennifer? Tell me, Judah."

The broken boy pulled himself together enough to share with the others what he'd seen, and while he tried his best to describe the look Jennifer had as their eyes met, just before the ground covered her over, Judah broke down again.

"There are no words … no words …" he kept mumbling.

"JELLY BEAN!" he shrieked and threw himself to the ground, wailing uncontrollably.

23

SEA OF BLOOD

Immediately the Travelers dropped to the ground and began digging and clawing at the dirt. The vines had withdrawn so much now that they looked like they did when the Travelers had first entered through the stone gate. The ground was still covered with vines, but instead of the swollen thicket that hid the dirt moments ago, now was just an orderly mess of thin, twisted, knotted-up vines.

Any progress the Travelers would make digging into the ground was immediately erased by the ground itself. It was thoroughly covered with sharp and jagged rocks; like razor-wire. With each motion, the flesh on their hands would tear open; the ground was becoming damp with their blood.

"Just like the map showed," Pierce mumbled to himself as he dug and clawed at the unrelenting ground.

"Pardon?" Bella said. She heard his words but misread what they meant. "The map showed this?" Her voice was angry, but before she could say any more, Pierce recognized the misunderstanding and explained what he meant.

"The rocks, Bella. Remember the map showed a vineyard with sharp rocks?"

"Oh," she said, and her voice returned to sullen brokenness. She stopped clawing and slumped to the ground next to where Judah still laid sobbing, her body shaking with grief.

Pierce didn't know how to help Bella. He loved her greatly and it ripped his heart apart to see her broken. He carried on talking about the map because he feared that if he stopped talking, he'd be lost. At least, if he continued rambling on about the things he did know about, Pierce felt like he was helping, even though he knew he wasn't.

"I thought they were larger. On the map, the rocks grew to be a large size, but I wonder now if they were disproportioned on the map." He was quiet and pondered for a moment. "I know they were large on the map." The poor boy was clearly flustered and felt responsible for the situation in which they now found themselves.

What he didn't realize was that the size the rocks were on the map was the weight of their danger and not the weight of their size.

As Pierce was talking about the map, even though he was only speaking to himself, Miriam spoke up. "Pierce, you said the path that was drawn on the map ended here in the vineyard, didn't you?"

"Yes," Pierce snapped.

"Maybe this is why," Miriam spouted off.

It always seemed to be Miriam who pointed out things like this, especially when it came to the demise of Jennifer. It was odd; most odd. She always managed to stir up rage in the others when she did so. One of these times, that rage was going to bubble over and Miriam would get what was coming to her.

"Huh?" Sam stopped digging and looked up; first toward Miriam and then toward Pierce.

She tried to explain.

"Perhaps the path ended here not because the tablet was here but because we would only get *into* the vineyard—and not *out* of it." All the digging stopped as their minds pondered Miriam's words. While they were furious with her for saying such foul words out loud, they couldn't say so because the nonsense she was rattling on about made some sense. Maybe she was right. Maybe they would all be dragged down below by the vines. None had thought of that … not until now.

No, that couldn't be right. If that were the case, the vines would not have backed off and left them alone. When the immediate horror of such a thought subsided enough for them to find their minds, it seemed clear that the trap was set solely for Jennifer.

Some stood with their heads drooped. Others, like Aviel and Matt, continued to kneel in the dirt and dig frantically. They both knew their digging made no difference and that they were not even making a dent in the ground, but it didn't matter. They were digging because they didn't know what else to do. Surely they couldn't leave this spot. They would NOT leave this spot.

SPLAT

Something wet fell on Sam's face.

SPLAT

Another and again, another.

SPLAT

It hit Bella. She looked up as a second drop fell on her nose.

SPLAT

"It's raining," she grumbled and wiped her nose.

"It's not rain," Judah complained. A few more drops fell on the Travelers … one here, one there. A few more and then a few more and then a few more after that.

"It's blood!" Sam shrieked. "LOOK!!!"

He pointed to the moon, which had now found its place in the sky without any of them even noticing. It wasn't time for the moon to be revealed so clearly, yet since the sun was still clinging to one corner of the horizon. Nevertheless, it seemed the moon was making decisions of its own and had turned itself into a sea of blood.

Of course, the Travelers did not yet realize where all the blood had come from. They didn't know that there had been many Travelers before them who had been brought to Trilleah for the same reason they were here now. They would not have remained in the Dark Land now if they knew that most of the ones before them had been captured by King Shrailzhar and his army. They didn't know that the moon had scooped up the blood of those before them … those who'd had their souls stolen by the Trows as their blood escaped their bodies … right on this ground … in this very vineyard.

A few drops here … a few drops there. Some landed on the ground … most found their way to the noses or the cloaks of the Travelers. The moon was indeed throwing great drops of blood down onto the group. It was the most sickening sight one could ever imagine. In fact, it was not likely that any sane person would even have the imagination to dream up such a thing.

"What do we do?" Sam screeched.

Kaija Mae began singing her enchanted songs in an unknown language, but it did not carry any peace in its tune at this particular moment on this particular day.

"GET OUT!" Miriam shouted.

"Miriam, shut your mouth," Judah bellowed. He stood and headed to where the girl was still standing. She was the only one who never moved to where the others had been frantically digging. She was the only one who was disinterested in Jennifer's disappearance.

Matt caught Judah and held him back from taking any more steps toward Miriam. "Judah, leave her," he whispered. "We don't have time to deal with her. We've got to get back to the Hollow; there's no other way." Matt said the words that Judah had already known in his heart. His breath left him, and he slumped down. Matt had to struggle to hold him up.

"I can't leave her," he sobbed. "You go, but let me stay." There was no consoling the ruined young man. No matter how hard they tried, Judah refused to leave the spot where he lost sight of his sister.

"Judah, NO. You will do her no good here, and we cannot lose you too." Matt tried to convince him, but he would not be convinced. "Bella," he said, looking at the girl who was weeping beside her nephew. Bella did move toward Judah, however, and grabbed his hands in her own. It had been a while since she held her nephew's hand, and at that moment she realized that somewhere along this terrible, horrible, deplorable journey, the boy had become a man.

Through sobs of her own, Bella spoke wretchedly. "Judah, we must trust that J's Shailma will protect her." Even as she heard her own words, she knew they sounded crazy. She hated saying them. They tasted like vomit in her mouth. She hated that it was her voice that was having to speak sense to her nephew. She also knew this was their only hope.

"Simeon, help Jennifer," Bella wailed as countless more drops of blood splattered against her hands. It seemed as if the moon was crying as well, shedding tremendously thick, red tears. She looked up to the sky and with her fists balled up, shook them at the moon, and wailed loudly … painfully. Many drops of the moon's bloodied tears fell on her face, but she didn't care. Finally, Bella took a deep breath and held it for as long as her lungs would allow.

"Judah," she finally shouted, "WE MUST LEAVE NOW!"

The drops of blood being thrown down by the moon were becoming bigger and more steady. As Bella looked up again, taking in such an unbelievable sight, she was perplexed. The moon looked as though it was about to drown; as if it was throwing down great drops of blood to keep from drowning itself.

"WE HAVE TO GO NOW!" she shouted, fearing the moon would turn itself upside down and drown them instead.

Together, as one huddled, broken, dissolving group, they left the vineyard … they left Jennifer. The vines moved out of their way and it was clear that the vineyard was the trap set for Jennifer. The trap had won … Jennifer was gone.

As they stepped quickly toward the Hollow, which was not nearly as far away as expected, Judah had a thought. "Why is the land so concerned with Jennifer's presence?" he asked through broken words and shattered sobs.

"You're right, Judah. There were no traps set for us, only for her," Sam added.

"What is it about Jelly Bean that makes her such a threat to Shrailzhar?" Judah repeated his question many times on the quick trip back to the Hollow. No one could tell whether he was asking them and hoping for an answer, or whether he was just repeating a question to which he knew there was no answer. He continued to feel heartbroken and every few steps a painful wailing would escape his lungs. All sorts of imaginations played around his mind of what his poor sister might be facing … alone.

But this new thought—mere wonderings really, of the tremendous threat that Jennifer was to the king—was so intriguing that it played a distraction to the terror in his heart and the nightmares in his mind.

It was a good thing too, or Judah might never have left the vineyard.

24

RED DRAGONS

The Travelers were trying to be brave for Judah and Bella, but it was hard, since they were all deeply broken—and terrified—by what had just happened. The strong arms of Pierce and Matt were helping Bella to walk, since her legs had become weak and her heart weary, and Judah was surrounded by Sam, Tahlia, and Kaija Mae.

Judah was glad that Kaija Mae had come to visit him in Westlock and that they had spent some time together. There was something different about that girl; something unnamable. Something peaceful and soothing. Her singing, usually the distributor of peace, was entirely empty this time. The unrecognizable words that slipped from her tongue and danced around in the air were beautiful, but not helpful.

Today the song had a sound of mournful lament. Despite it all, Kaija Mae kept right on singing.

Then, of course, there was Miriam. She hadn't said much since the ground had opened up and swallowed Jennifer. She had remained at the back of the group … a little too far back some may have thought. But it was not far enough back for the liking of others. Kaija Mae hadn't seemed disappointed at all about the recent happenings, which only caused more questions to arise in the minds of those who had noticed.

To make matters even worse, if such a thing could be possible, the ghostly hum had returned to the land. It sounded like Trilleah was breathing—whimpering perhaps—but, of course, that was silliness.

A small white serpent slithered across the trail and didn't even notice the Travelers; then another, and finally one more. They paid no attention to the Travelers and the Travelers paid no attention to them. There was a repulsive smell in the air as well. The girls covered their noses; the smell hanging in the air was vile. Besides those few oddities, most of the journey back to Asphelia's Hollow was dull and without any mentionable incident.

This lack of anything out of the ordinary only made it all the more apparent that the land—or King Shrailzhar—was not at all concerned with these remaining Curse Breakers. Perhaps they were not the Curse Breakers after all. Maybe they were just Travelers in a foreign land and Jennifer had been the only true Curse Breaker. *Is that why the traps were set only for her?* Judah wondered. *Is that why he and Bella knew that she must come to the Land? It makes no difference now, I suppose.* Judah thought and lamented deeper than he ever had before.

Judah, came the soothing voice of Shemaiah. The Shailma had seemed absent for much of this journey and because of it, Judah hesitated to converse with him now. Shemaiah had not shown up when Jennifer most needed him, but while he thought this angry thought, Shemaiah reminded him of a forgotten truth.

Judah, I am not Jennifer's Shailma. I am yours. Her Shailma was with her then and continues to be with her now. Don't you know? Have you forgotten there is nowhere Jennifer can go that Simeon will not be with her? You must trust and believe that if Simeon allowed her to go where you could not travel, there was a reason beyond your understanding and he will go with her. I assure you, Jennifer is not alone.

Judah heard the words and pondered them, but he didn't want to believe such things. Believe that a Shailma would allow his Jelly Bean to be stolen away to such a wretched place? He would have to consider that for a long while before he decided whether or not to believe it. Furthermore, if he did choose to believe such a thing, it would question his faith in Shailmas. For now, though, he put the speech from Shemaiah—and his doubts regarding it—into the back closet of his mind, locked the door, and went straight back to lamenting.

That lamenting abruptly turned into rage toward the land, the king, and anything else he could think of that may be responsible for such a horror—even the Shailmas.

No matter, you wretched king, he thought. *I will never leave my sister in your land. Traps can always be pried open, and prey can always be set free.*

Even while the thoughts circled in his mind, he knew in his heart that this was far from the truth. Nevertheless, a determination continued to take on a life of its own and was growing by the second. He would get his Jelly Bean back, even if it meant he had to give his life to set her's free. He didn't know how, but he'd figure it out.

However, no one in their right mind would ever choose to go to the place Jennifer went as she had been swallowed up, for it was far more horrible than one might have the words to describe with any amount of accuracy. But of course, it's to be wondered if Judah was in his right mind at the moment. The look in his sister's eyes earlier was now sadly reflected in his own, and quite possibly set his mind on a fast spin that would take him off course.

There were red dragons where Jennifer had gone—Judah had seen them—and with every breath, suffocating, sulfur-filled snarls filled the air just below Trilleah's floor. The air was already rancid enough, mind you. It had a strong scent of death about it, although Jennifer realized she never knew what death smelled like until it surrounded her. Though she hadn't smelled it before, there was no mistaking it now.

The trembling girl tried to hide in her cloak and pulled the hood as far as it would go around her face. This in itself was unpleasant because it was terribly hot here—wherever here was. A dungeon? Had she fallen into a deep crevasse in the ground or was she pulled into it? Was she chosen by the vines or was she simply the one who had stepped into the space where the vines were grabbing? Did she just happen to set her foot into the trap or was it set for her?

So many questions tried to swirl in her mind but really, that's all they could do was swirl. It was far too horrible to make any sense of the endless parade of nonsense.

Jennifer went from pinching her eyes closed to straining them wide open to get a better view. It seemed like only a few steps away she could see a large group of other people. No, that couldn't be right. A shiver ran up her spine turning the blood in her veins to ice. How could it be so terribly hot in the air and she be shivering? She was chilled from the inside and cooking from the outside; such a terrible combination.

She strained her eyes harder to clear the outlines that she was now certain were people, when suddenly, she remembered Judah. Jennifer knew he'd seen her. Their eyes had locked right before the ground closed itself up from above, swallowing her alive. The look on his face was dreadful. She wished she could erase it because it pained her soul greatly. She could hear him screaming as the ground sealed itself closed between them. Would that be the last sound she would ever hear from her brother? She couldn't bear the thought.

Jennifer, stop thinking that way, came a familiar voice. *Guard your mind, Little One; guard your mind. Take every thought captive, lest they take you captive. Being a prisoner in your own mind is far worse than being a prisoner of King Shrailzhar.*

SIMEON, she screamed silently. *Are you with me even here?* She was relieved to hear her Shailma, but looking around this dungeon she had been dragged in, the relief was shallow, shaky, and short-lived.

Of course, Jenny. I am with you always, even to the ends of the earth, and this is indeed the ends of the earth, wouldn't you say? Simeon asked.

I would, she thought.

Her feet were sore, so Jennifer tried shifting her weight and moved them a little to get the blood moving. As she did, a severe pain shot through her legs. She looked down and saw the thorn-covered vines which had wrapped around her ankles and pulled her down into this pit were still there. The girl could not move more than a few inches in any direction.

"Simeon," she whispered, but before she could ask him about the vines, another voice filled the air.

"Jennifer Lillian Elliot," came an audible yet undeniably familiar voice. Jennifer strained her head looking around for the owner of the voice. She was still far too afraid to let her hood down, believing she was somehow hiding in it.

"Jennifer Lillian," came the voice again.

It was so dark in this dungeon—like underground prisons she'd seen on television when Bella thought she'd been in bed fast asleep. But the breaths from the dragons, as well as the many other fires throughout, offered a little light here and there. Jennifer strained her eyes until they adjusted enough to the dimness that she could make out a few things.

"Those *are* people," she whispered. "At least … they *were* people."

Packed into the place like sardines in a can, were what appeared to be shadowy, sickly remnants of what might have at once been real human beings. Although they still had the appearance of being alive, something about them said otherwise.

Simeon, is that what smells like death? she thought.

It is indeed, Little One; it is indeed.

"Jennifer," came the voice again. Was one of these eerie beings calling her name? Did she know them? Did they know her? The voice was familiar. Then it happened. Her eyes settled fully on the shell of one she used to know.

"Mamma," she howled. "MAMMA!"

Even though her feet had been shackled by the vines, it was only now that she felt trapped. Jennifer saw the face of her mother and wanted to run to her, but couldn't. All she could do was reach out her arms—which was not doing anything at all—but she reached them out anyway.

Her mother moved slightly toward her, but not enough. Was she also bound by the vines? Maybe she was bound by something else altogether, but what? Jennifer could not see well enough to tell, but it was clear, even in the semi-dark, that this was as close as they were going to get to one another. Molly was weeping but kept calling out her daughter's name nevertheless.

"Where am I, Simeon?" Jennifer whispered. She felt frantic and was so panicked that it was becoming difficult to breathe. The sulfur wasn't helping either; it insisted on filling her lungs and choking her.

It's OK, Jenny, came the soothing voice of her dear Shailma. *I know it does not LOOK OK … or SMELL OK … or FEEL OK, but trust me, you're not here for long and you are not alone.*

Now she was torn. Was being this close to Mamma, who she'd longed to see for years, worth Jennifer staying? Maybe she did not want to leave now that she'd found her mamma, but maybe the choice wasn't hers to make.

Jennifer was reminded in an instant of the dream Bella had told her and Judah about, the dream she'd had only last night when Kaija Mae visited. Bella had said she didn't know why she was telling the twins, for indeed it was an atrocious nightmare, but reason or no reason, Bella said that she knew in her heart she must tell them. Jennifer had tried to tune her auntie out, to shut up her ears and not listen but still, some of the nightmare was pushed into her heart.

Now, in this place, Bella's nightmare had returned to Jennifer's mind and had come to life. There was no doubt that this was indeed that place, the very place in Bella's dream where her mamma was being held. Suddenly, Jennifer recalled clearly every detail of the dream that Bella had told. She remembered her Mamma said she'd remain in this place for eternity unless all the clay tablets were found and the curse was broken.

A switch flipped in the young girl's mind, and suddenly, she knew exactly who all these shells of people were. They were not dead, but neither were they alive.

THESE were the bodies of those whose souls were cursed and trapped in Malleana Forest … THIS was where the groaning came from … THESE were the Waiting Ones!

Oh, Dear God. Why was she here and how would she get out? Jennifer suddenly knew that she could not be kept here because her soul could not be taken; not yet.

SIMEON! she cried deep in her heart. *I must get OUT! I cannot break the curse from here. I need the tablets, Simeon. Simeon, please, PLEASE get me out of here so we can break the curse for Mamma—and the others.*

Jennifer wanted to run, but with her feet tangled in the barbs of the vines, all she could do was fall to her knees, which is exactly what she did. She tumbled with a hard "thwack" and began weeping. That young girl sobbed so hard that her stomach ached and she started choking and heaving terribly, throwing up whatever morsels remained in her belly.

All at once, she knew Simeon had heard her, for at that moment a bit of hope tingled in her toes. It was just a drop, but that was enough. As she waited for him to help her, that hope slowly—so slowly—climbed up through her veins and into her heart. A powerful determination came to her, and Sam's words came screeching back into her mind.

"Every lie can be overcome by truth; both cannot live in the same space at the same time."

That's it, Jennifer thought. As soon as the words filled her mind, Simeon agreed. *This place is for those whose souls the Trows have stolen, but your soul remains within you, Jenny.*

King Shrailzhar has no right to hold you here and he must let you go. He wants you to believe lies. He wants to convince your mind that because you are here, you have no power over being here or not being here. He wants you to think that because he was able to trap you that you are indeed trapped. These are all lies, my dear Jenny. All lies. Lies are only powerful when they are believed. The truth gives you the power to break free.

All of this seemed to make sense in her mind, but making sense in her mind and believing it in her heart are not always the same thing. She had no idea how to change her circumstances.

Jenny believed Simeon, but she needed more than that. She

needed wisdom to know how to use the truth to defeat the lies and escape this hell she'd been dragged into.

This entire time she had kept her eyes planted on the shell of her mother. Jennifer could nearly see right through her mamma. She was so thin, almost nothing more than a wispy shadow … a ghost maybe.

She is not a ghost, Simeon said. *Without their souls, they have no substance*, the Shailma explained. *It's the soul that makes the body a person, not the body. The body is what you see here, just the shell— the home of the soul.*

"Yes, that's it," she murmured. Jennifer remembered some of the elderly ladies at the lodge back in Westlock where she and her mother used to volunteer—before the accident. Jennifer dug back into the corners of her mind and reviewed a memory. She remembered the day when an old lady came and touched Jennifer's young arm. Jennifer noticed her old, thin skin and didn't want to touch it because it was so brittle that she feared it might melt away like wax.

She remembered asking her mother about it later, and her mamma explained that when a person gets old, their skin gets old too. Old skin is nearly see-through—like tissue paper—just like babies who are born too early. There was just something about a person's skin that it started out thin and flimsy and ended up the same way … transparent.

As Jennifer agreed with herself that this was the perfect description of what she saw now with her mother and the others, she felt every hair on her arms and the back of her neck stand at attention. Her racing heart was screaming at her to move deeper into her cloak, but she was already as hidden as she could be.

Coming toward her on the back of an enormous, black, indescribably ugly creature was King Shrailzhar. His fiery eyes burned right through her.

Oh, Simeon, this is the end for me, I fear, she wailed silently inside. But outside, she stood firm. Even as she watched the king move closer, Jennifer was altogether befuddled by the differences between her insides shaking and her outsides holding fast.

Simeon, she breathed in, letting the sulfur burn her nose. *Save me*, she breathed out, knowing he would.

25

NECESSARY CHAMBERS

Pierce put his foot into the small hole under the rock covering Asphelia's Hollow and the entrance opened to the Travelers. One by one they stumbled into the welcoming air of their home here in Trilleah. No welcome was felt this time—only bleakness and misery because Jennifer had not returned with them. Unlike when Matt had been inhaled by King Shrailzhar, they knew Jennifer wouldn't be there, waiting in the Hollow.

This time, the air was filled with dread and despair. It seemed as though the Hollow was expecting all the Travelers to return and when there was one missing, it noticed. The air inside, usually fresh, had turned sour. There was no peace either—Judah wondered if peace would be found anywhere. He was certain he'd never feel such a thing again.

Once inside, there was nothing to do; no reason for them to be here. The sun was still clinging to the smallest corner of the horizon, but the moon had finally found a place to settle. So unlike Trilleah. Never before had they seen both the sun and the moon in the sky together. But today, the sun had been veiled and the moon had covered itself in blood and neither seemed to have anywhere else to be. The moon had risen early and the sun refused to set.

They had thought the moon was throwing great drops of blood upon the Travelers, but now that they had a chance to think about it a little, some wondered if the moon was so filled with blood that it was overflowing and spilling over. There was no way to know, but they could not stop pondering such things. Their minds could make no sense of it. However, they decided that speaking of such things was far better than speaking of Jennifer's fate, so they talked about anything else they could think of, and hoped the Shailmas were with her.

Maybe the moon knew that Jennifer was going to be taken. Could it be that the sun was veiled so it could hide? Or the moon was crying tears of blood? Were even the sun and moon trying to keep Jennifer from being caught by that despicable king? Surely they saw the traps. Could they have been trying to warn the Travelers? Oh, if only they'd listened … if only … if only.

The thoughts were overwhelming, and Judah could not bear them. He became engulfed in anguish, put his hands over his face, and wailed; horrible, painful wails like none had heard before. Bella moved to him and put her arm out but then decided to let him be, and pulled it back to her side.

After a few minutes, Judah's lamenting calmed slightly; not because the pain in his heart eased, but more likely because he had wept so hard that his emotions were exhausting themselves.

"Judah," Pierce whispered. "Bella," he called. "Come with me." He took the hands of both, and the three of them disappeared into a passageway.

"Pierce," Bella sobbed. "What are we going to do?" Another wail slipped from her lungs, even though she was trying hard to keep them locked up tightly for Judah's sake. "We can't leave Trilleah. Not like this!"

"I won't go," Judah stated harshly. "I won't go back without her."

"Hold on, give me a minute," Pierce said calmly. A welcome side of this young man was peeking out of his hard shell, a side that none had seen before … a side no one even considered might be there, hiding … a side named compassion.

"Here it is," Pierce said and turned to face the rock wall. It was darker than usual in the passageway. Oh yes, the lanterns were casting their lights alright, but they seemed dull and without the twinkle they usually offered. Nevertheless, Pierce found what he had ducked into this passageway to find.

"The Chamber of Rest," Judah sighed. "I can't go in," he said, but Pierce insisted.

"Judah, what happened was not your fault and even if you believe it was, that does not make it so. Besides, feeling guilty won't help Jennifer right now. The best thing you can do to help her is to help yourself."

"I can't," Judah protested. "Pierce, how can I stand in the Chamber of Rest knowing that Jennifer is … is …" his voice trailed off, unable to finish his thought. "I just can't," he sighed heavily and slumped down hard against the wall.

Pierce turned to face Bella and Judah. "Now, listen here, both of you," he said firmly. "Jennifer will get out; I know she will. She has the strongest Shailma of anybody and even though she is just a tiny thing, she has more determination and wisdom and courage than the rest of us put together." He waited for any sign that they were listening, and when he saw they were, he continued. "Even greater than those things is the deep trust that Jennifer has in her Shailma, and THAT is what will get her out in time to return home."

"But Pierce …" Bella tried to protest, and Pierce would have none of it. He interrupted before she could continue.

"Have I misspoken?" Pierce asked. "Have I said anything that either of you knows to be untrue?" he demanded. Both Judah and

Bella shook their heads but said nothing. "OK then," Pierce continued, and extended his hands to help Judah up.

"It's not doing Jennifer any good for us to be mourning and unable to think." Neither Bella nor Judah responded. "This journey is not over!" he shouted. "We must believe in Jennifer, and we MUST believe in the Shailmas. We must believe that she will be returning shortly. We must hold onto hope." He waited for a response but still, none came. "We have to be prepared for her return, and spending a few minutes in the Chamber of Rest will give you both a head start on that." Still, no reply came, although Pierce could see they were finally pondering what he was saying.

"Listen, Jennifer will need you both to be strong when she returns."

"I guess," Bella finally shrugged.

"Punishing yourself by refusing to be filled with the peace that is behind this door, is ridiculous." Pierce's patience had been used up, and it was heard in his voice. "Now get up," he demanded.

Pierce had made his point and while both Judah and Bella felt deeply remorseful about where Jennifer was and horribly guilty about going into the Chamber of Rest while she had no rest at all, they knew Pierce was right. Judah grabbed Pierce's hands and pulled himself up. He stepped forward, slowly lifting the seat of the bench that was hidden in the wall, and stepped back again. Hand in hand, the three of them watched as the door concealing the Chamber of Rest opened wide and welcomed them. Straightaway, a deep peace swept over them.

"Why did we not want to come in here?" Judah asked.

"Can't recall," Bella answered. While the knowledge of Jennifer's whereabouts was still fresh in their minds, the fear and sorrow were absent. The peace in the chamber swaddled their knowledge and caused it to be just that—knowledge. The feelings it had been carrying were drowned out by the presence of peace.

They breathed in deeply, letting purity fill their lungs. There were no words to describe the air, but as they breathed it in, it drove every sad thought, every mournful feeling, every painful memory out of their minds.

Now, peace is peace, and while some make the erroneous blunder of thinking peace is happiness or peace is joyful thoughts or peace might even be freedom from sadness, only one moment in the Chamber of Rest tells the truth; peace is something entirely different. It has a life all of its own. It begins—and ends—in itself. There are no words to describe it, and it makes no sense to those who have not been swaddled in its embrace.

"My mind tells me that it's sad, and indeed it is," Bella muttered. She was thoroughly intoxicated from breathing the air of such purity. "Yet something greater covers the sadness and makes it seem so … insignificant."

"Mmmm," was the only sound Judah uttered. Pierce just sat there, grateful that his Shailma had instructed him to bring these two into the chamber and quite proud of himself for listening. He was not always great at listening to his Shailma and determined at this very moment, now seeing the results of doing so, to listen more, to seek more, to obey more.

A clamor interrupted Pierce's thoughts, and he looked up to see that Sam, Matt, Aviel, and the others had joined them. Everyone was there; everyone except for Miriam.

"Where is she?" Pierce questioned.

Sam shrugged and Kaija Mae, busy singing her songs, stopped briefly to answer. "We don't know," she said. "We hoped she had come here; that's why we came. We were looking for her, not trusting that she had good reasons for disappearing." Kaija Mae began singing again and now, unlike the deep sadness that was in her song on the way back to the Hollow, Kaija Mae's singing was filled with harmony and calmness. The words—even though none of the Travelers could understand them—knit their way into the hearts of everyone in the chamber, kissing their souls.

That was enough of an answer for Pierce, and he went straight back to breathing in the air and feasting on the restfulness that came with it. It was an added measure of peace really, not having Miriam here. She probably was so against peace of any sort, that there was no way her feet would carry her here even if her mind wanted to come.

For as much time as they could afford, the Travelers sprawled themselves throughout the chamber. Judah had slid down one of the deep red walls and had his eyes closed. He no longer looked sullen or mournful, just restful and maybe even momentarily untroubled. No one looking at him could tell, of course, but the truth was that Shemaiah had come to his mind, and the two of them were having a time together.

Judah, how proud I am of you, Shemaiah whispered. Judah wanted to answer—really he did—but he was so rested that his mind could think of nothing to reply. Instead, he just received the words. It wasn't that his mind was so empty that he had nothing to say, rather, that it was so full of stillness no words were required. So he sat, breathing the honesty of the air, and listened. His body was so possessed with peace that he was glad the wall supported him.

Shemaiah could not miss such an opportunity to fill Judah's mind with wisdom and goodness, so he spoke many things to him.

You have come such a long way, my boy. From your first journey until now, you have grown in wisdom and understanding. Judah smiled, causing those who were watching him to smile as well. *However, your fight is not over, Judah. Do not give up, for there are still tablets to find, journeys to take, and enemies to battle.*

BUT my boy, come here—to this Chamber of Rest—as much as you can. Be selfish in this chamber. Sneak away at every opportunity and fill up here. Drink it in ... it will give you the strength you require.

Shemaiah went on and on and on. For the time that he had the complete attention of Judah, Shemaiah filled the boy up with all sorts of necessary information he would need to complete the journeys ahead.

While Judah listened intently, soaking in every morsel of peace from the chamber, he did not realize his Shailma was also giving him valuable information that was passing straight through his thoughts and landing somewhere in his soul.

Later, though, when those thoughts would be needed, Judah would retrieve them and remember this moment and gain strength from it, knowing that his Shailma had prepared him.

You see, Shailmas always do.

26

SHRAILZHAR'S LAIR

Pillars of fire sprang up all over the underground dungeon that gnawed at its victims—actual pillars of fire, not the measly sticks that had been pretending to be pillars of fire earlier. While everything that was held together within her skin was withering and trembling fiercely, she continued to keep her eyes locked with those of the wretched king. Just behind Shrailzhar, in the line of her view but just outside the circle of her sight, Jennifer's heart begged her eyes to glance, even for a second, toward her mamma. Oh, how she wanted to look at her and smile and say everything would be all right. But she dared not look away from the king; not yet.

As Shrailzhar moved closer and closer, Jennifer stared. Her eyes were locked on his and even though his were hollow and lifeless and made her tremble, she did not look away.

Though inside Jennifer was shaking and her stomach threatened to turn itself inside out, though her hands were quivering and her breath was gone, at least her knees could not let her down because she was already kneeling on them. She couldn't run because the vines had chained her feet.

What a coward, she thought of the king. *What a pathetic scoundrel. What kind of king needs to have a frail little child like herself all bound up? Could he not overpower her and destroy her on his own? Did he need the help of such silly things like thorns and vines to hold her? Wretched and pitiful he was, this king ... horribly pathetic.*

As she kept her big, green eyes glued to his hollow, dead ones, all these thoughts galloped through her mind. The more she thought, the angrier she became. If her mouth was not so dry from the hellish temperatures in this underground lair, she'd have spit in his face.

Jennifer reached up beneath her cloak and grabbed her locket. It was closed, of course, and from Matt's explanation when he had given it to her, that meant she and Mamma were together and without a doubt, here in this unknown hell, they were. As she wrapped her fingers around the warm silver locket, they didn't steady even a bit, but she felt a surge of determination bubble up within her.

Perhaps seeing her mamma, even briefly, was from where her strength was stirring, but it seemed to come from somewhere else altogether. The looks from Mamma were grieved and wretched, so it didn't make much sense that any strength would come from such a dreadful sight.

Nevertheless, Jennifer was not about to let this wicked beast of a king take away her mamma's only chance of leaving this diabolical dungeon. Whatever this young warrior had to do, she set her mind to do it with all her might, trusting Simeon to help her.

King Shrailzhar was nearly upon her now, and she felt small —like a field mouse being hunted by a mighty lion. She was helpless and he, altogether powerful.

Oh, Simeon, Jennifer searched her mind for her Shailma. *Oh, that you would take me away, this instant.* She felt something move in beside her—something so great that she couldn't help but turn her eyes toward it. It was not that she could see it with her physical eyes, but somehow, without explanation, the eyes of her heart were open; so open, they looked straight through her own eyes, and she could see clearly those things that were otherwise unseeable.

It was as though, like the sun of Trilleah, a veil had been stripped away and for the first time in her life, Jennifer could see … really see. She blinked and smiled, for there, standing valiant and dauntless and large beside her, was Simeon. The sheer size of her Shailma made King Shrailzhar look like the mouse now, and every fear that was inside her belly vanished.

The Shailma turned his face toward her, and as Jennifer looked now into *his* eyes, she knew that she was indeed Simeon's Princess, his pride, his delight, his one. She knew that surely he was with her just like he'd said, "To the ends of the earth."

She looked back to Shrailzhar and wondered if he could see Simeon. It seemed he could, because in about three more steps the king stopped. He flared his nostrils like an enraged bull ready to charge. The beast he was sitting on stomped his feet … again … and again. The king dug his razor-laden boots into the sides of the creature, but that creature would not budge. Shrailzhar screamed commands but still, the beast would not take a step.

It dawned on Jennifer that perhaps the king did not see Simeon at all. It was clear that the beast which carried him did, though, and that beast was not coming any closer, no matter how many times the daggers from Shrailzhar's boots pierced his sides.

Jennifer looked up to Simeon and then back to the king.

"Little One," Simeon instructed, "look around you."

She did. Jennifer turned her head this way as far as she could and then that way. Surrounding her on every side were Shamar Shailmas. Each was smaller than Simeon, but only slightly. Some were silver; others red. There were a couple of black ones and a few dark brown ones, but Simeon was the only white one.

There were twelve Shailmas in all. Suddenly, Jennifer felt a bit bigger herself. She felt empowered and knew that even if King

Shrailzhar did not see the watchman who surrounded her, she saw them, and that was enough to fill her with bravery.

"I will take you up out of Shrailzhar's lair, Jenny, but you must demand the release."

"Oh, fiddlesticks," she whined. "Can't you just take me?" she begged. "Please, Simeon. And Mamma … We MUST take Mamma!"

"No, Little One, I cannot. Even in this world, there are laws one must follow."

"LAWS?" Jennifer shrieked. She sounded horrified, but also like she might burst out laughing. "How ridiculous!" she huffed. That was indeed the most absurd thing to be heard. King Shrailzhar seemed to have missed out on reading those laws as well because he didn't appear to follow laws of any sort.

"Jenny," Simeon began, enlightening her mind and filling it with understanding. "You see, just like in the world you come from, in Westlock, there are legal rules of the land here in Trilleah. Everyone must follow them or pay the penalty."

"For example, gravity," he said. He seemed proud of his example and waited for her to acknowledge it.

"Yes, I understand that kind of law," she said.

"Well, no matter who you are or where you come from or how very powerful you might think you are, everything and everyone in Westlock must adhere to the law of gravity. There are no exceptions."

"There is gravity here too?" she argued, still confused.

"Sort of; it is only a partial law here. However, another law here in Trilleah is that I cannot do for you what you can do for yourself." Jennifer scrunched her face and looked at Simeon.

"Huh?" she said. Jennifer wished that Simeon would quickly spit out all the information she needed and speed up this lesson. Even though the beast on which the king sat still refused to budge, Jennifer kept one eye on him and terror bubbled beneath her flesh.

"Have you never wondered why the Shailmas don't collect the tablets and break the curse of the Waiting Ones?"

"Well no, I have not wondered that. Not until now." Jennifer stopped and pondered for a moment. "I have wondered why you don't pick me up and take me to where the tablets are. It seems we could have gathered all the tablets in one trip and broken the curse. Why do you drop me at the edge of Malleana Forest?"

"You see, Little One, it is because of the laws of the land of Trilleah. I am unable to do such things; you must do them. I can help you, but I cannot do them for you."

"I don't understand," Jennifer wailed.

All the while this conversation of not understanding was going on, King Shrailzhar remained close. His gaze remained fixed on Jennifer. He continued to demand the beast beneath him to attack. The beast still refused to budge.

Now that Jennifer felt safer inside the ring of Shailmas, she was able to take a brief moment and look around. She was careful not to look at her mamma, though, as it was a purely dreadful sight, and she wanted to avoid it as long as she could.

The empty shells of the Waiting Ones which Jennifer had seen earlier were huddling together, wailing and howling and moaning. They had moved into tight groups when the king entered. They looked as though they were trying to hide from the wicked Shrailzhar—like his very presence made their translucent flesh burn.

"Oh," Jennifer groaned as she suddenly realized this was the very smell that horrified her nostrils.

Despite such wretched smells and daunting sights, Jennifer felt unusually safe inside the ring of the twelve Shailmas. Clearly, Shrailzhar's beast was aware of them too and was putting up quite a struggle to stay back.

"Well, Jenny, that is the beauty of all of this, I suppose," Simeon said sweetly. His eyes danced as they saw her.

"The beauty?" she shouted. "Simeon, there is no beauty here, except for Mamma," Jennifer added, still unable to force herself to glance toward the woman.

"The beauty is this," Simeon said. "That you don't need to understand everything. You need only to trust that I understand. Your job, then, is to listen and obey what you hear me say. I have a part—one that you cannot possibly understand, and you have a part—one that I cannot do for you."

"You're right, Simeon. I don't understand any of that. But," Jennifer added, "I trust you, so I will do whatever you say is my part."

"Great and wise choice, Little One," Simeon said. "I would pick you up and return you to Westlock, but I cannot do that yet."

"Oh, Simeon, let's go now," she pleaded, gazing deep into the eyes of her Shailma. She'd never had an opportunity to do this before, and as she moved her eyes from the dark pits of death that reflected in the eyes of the king to the eyes of Simeon, her breath stopped briefly.

The moment her eyes caught his, her heart was quickened, and her blood was warmed. Simeon's eyes were the greenest of greens that Jennifer had ever seen. They contained entire store-houses of depth and peace; pools of emerald that went on and on and allowed her to float inside of them for a moment. While she kept her eyes on Simeon's, all fear vanished and only peace remained.

Her mind went back in a flash to the first time she had seen Simeon. She remembered that his eyes—although she only saw them briefly from the side—were blood red. Also, she recalled the eyelashes that were like a thousand swords. He knew her thoughts, of course, and before she could ask about it, Simeon slowly brought down his eyelids. As he did, the emerald green seas disappeared behind blood red covers.

Jennifer sucked in her breath. Simeon opened his eyes again and looked right at her. She felt like she could dissolve in those eyes and was instantly filled with such a deep peace that she was convinced nothing could harm her.

"We cannot leave yet, Little One. There is a tablet here, in this lair, and you must retrieve it before we can go." Jennifer was sure she'd heard him wrong.

"A tablet?" she sulked. "In hell? Really?"

"Oh Jennifer, this is not hell," Simeon whispered softly. It seemed he did not wish to talk about such things, or maybe he did not want the others to hear him. Either way, his voice had become quiet and had returned to the silent conversation only heard inside of her mind.

Jenny, this is only King Shrailzhar's kingdom. Hell is a thousand times more horrific than this pathetic pit in the ground. No imagination can bear to consider it. We need not take the time to speak of it.

Her mind was certainly going to be considering it now. She had been sure this was hell; it was only Shrailzhar's kingdom? Who would want this as their kingdom? Her mind refused to go any farther into pondering such things, and it snapped back to Simeon and the clay tablets.

"How am I supposed to find a tablet here?" she asked.

"You will know, Jenny," Simeon whispered. "You'll know." And with that, he and the other Shailmas faded. She knew they were still there, surrounding her. She knew because even though her eyes could no longer see them, the beast that carried Shrailzhar still refused to budge.

Hmm, she thought. *If my eyes can't see the Shailmas, but the beast's eyes can, then I shall keep watch of the beast and trust Simeon and the others to lead the way and keep me hedged in on all sides. Now, what did he mean by, "I'll know?"* she contemplated.

Jennifer looked one way and then another. Finally, she mustered the courage to look her mamma in the eyes and in a second, her heart shattered into a thousand bits and a million pieces.

"Mamma," she sobbed loudly. Too loudly it seemed, for immediately the king turned to see who it was, Jennifer was crying for.

"So that's your mamma, is it little girl? Well, if I can't get to you, I can get to her. There's always a way to get what I want," the king spewed, throwing his head back and laughing a dark, skin-peeling sort of laugh.

"Mamma … RUN!" Jennifer screamed. Her mamma did not run. She didn't move. Molly stood still and kept her eyes on her daughter.

"Oh, Little One, there is nowhere to run where the king will not find me," Mamma whispered in a faint, hopeless voice. For the first time, Jennifer realized that Simeon wasn't the only one to call her "Little One." Mamma had been calling her that same name all her life, but she'd never noticed—until now.

It confused Jennifer's mind how, even though it was horribly loud in this place with screaming and wailing of the Waiting Ones, and snarling from the dragons and hideous sounds coming from the beast carrying Shrailzhar, that the small voice of her mamma was able to weave through all the ruckus and find its way into Jennifer's ears.

"Mamma," was all she could cry out. Jennifer was still on her knees, now throbbing painfully from the jagged rocks beneath them. She fell forward, hitting her face on the ground with a thud. She didn't care. She could not rescue her mamma, and she could not find the tablet, and she would never break the curse. Jennifer begged death to come, but even death turned its ear away and refused to listen.

"Jenny," Simeon whispered. "Get up."

"It's too late, Simeon. It's finished. I can do nothing more." Jennifer was no longer wailing or crying or even whimpering. It was as though she had decided to believe that it was over and accept that the king had won. She accepted her fate.

"Jenny, it is not. You are believing lies and deceiving yourself." Simeon sounded slightly impatient with the girl and repeated himself. "Now, get up."

Jennifer got up. She had no need to dry her tears for she hadn't shed any. She stood up and looked for her mother, but Molly was no longer there. Jennifer looked at Shrailzhar, who hadn't come any closer to her but there, held by the king, was Mamma.

There were no words to describe what happened next—in that instant, Jennifer had a sudden knowing fill her. That was the only word that would describe it; a knowing. It was nothing that Simeon had whispered to her mind. It was not seeing her mother there, held prisoner in the hands of the king.

It was something else altogether … something she never knew before, but now, she suddenly did—in the pit of her belly, in that place where nerves give birth to butterflies. Down deep in a place unknown, she knew. Jennifer knew that she would get the tablet and return to Westlock and hug Judah and dance with Bella.

Jennifer didn't know how, or when, or where she'd find the tablet, but she knew she'd find it. For the first time since the vines had wrapped themselves around her ankles, Jennifer considered that they might not be as limiting as she'd thought. She squatted down and began tugging at them. They were holding firm and tugged back.

"Simeon," Jennifer whispered. "Tell me what to do. I promise I'll do it." As the words formed themselves in her mind and rolled off of her tongue, she realized it sounded an awful lot like something he'd said to her earlier, and she replayed the words in her mind. *I have a part and you have a part. You need not understand my part, and I cannot do your part.* Over and over she repeated the confusing words until finally, she did the only thing she could do.

"Simeon," Jennifer whispered again, just a bit louder this time. "If you do your part, I promise to do mine."

Well done, Jenny, she heard in her heart. *You have yourself a deal, Little One.*

27

ALTOGETHER UNEXPECTED

After a long while of soaking in as much peace as one person could sop up, Judah finally stood and sighed. He stretched and stumbled, feeling a tad tipsy. Peace is an indescribable thing with indescribable effects on one's self. One can experience it but not accurately explain it. It satisfies the most wounded soul and quenches the deepest thirst. There is nothing comparable, except maybe intoxication but then again, perhaps it's the same thing brought about by different sources.

You see, a full serving of peace from the Chamber of Rest has many of the same effects as sweet wine. After one has drunk their fill of either, problems seem small and easy to overcome—sadness stings less, and mourning is lighter to carry.

However, there is also a difference, of course, between the two. A tall glass of peace has no harmful side effects, outcomes, or bitter aftertaste. Peace remains long after, although perhaps a bit less bold. A tall glass of the other is a mere impostor. It brings satisfaction for only a short time, but once it fades, the problems are bigger, the sadness deeper, and the mourning more heartbreaking.

Judah had his fill, and his breaths were so deep and pure and satisfying that it seemed like he was hardly breathing at all. He went to Bella, who had also spent much time drinking in the sweet nectar of peace; she, too, was completely saturated.

"Ready?" he said.

"Ready," she replied. Bella stretched her arms toward Judah and taking hold of them, he pulled his auntie to her feet.

The others in the Chamber of Rest did the same, and stood up. Now usually, the group would mutter and complain one to another … but not here. There was nothing to complain about here. The brilliance of it amazed every eye, yet, once outside the chamber, there were no words that would satisfactorily describe it and so, they never bothered to try.

Inside, however, the emerald greens and sapphire reds shimmering in the walls were stunning; breathtaking. Even the floor was spectacular. A few feet away on just the other side of the hidden entrance, the floors were cold, cracked rock. They were mostly flat and smooth, but there was the odd rough spot or jagged edge where they had to walk carefully. The colors were dull … gloomy. Nothing sparkled or glimmered or begged to be noticed on the other side of the door.

But here, inside this chamber, the floor was something else completely. It was like an endless sea of glass; the very deepest blue a mind might ever be able to imagine, yet crystal clear. The floor seemed to have no bottom. It looked as though it went on forever. The floor alone was something that would capture the eye and make it hard to look away. It was captivating; so inviting that it called out to whoever was near to dive in and let it wash the soul. There was no diving to be done, however, since it was solid and held up their feet, as floors always do.

Every nook and cranny, each wall and space and atom and molecule were the same way here in this chamber. There were no shadows, no dark corners, no hidden places. One might think the lighting was well laid out or the lanterns were perfect at casting their lights. But there were no lanterns, no flickering lights, and no windows. Just light. Brilliant light. Pure light. A light so thick that it would go straight through one's skin and wrap around their hearts.

But now it was time to go.

The Travelers didn't particularly mind leaving because the peace they'd feasted on was so filling that nothing could disturb it inside the chamber. Even knowing that when they left the chamber, the very moment they would step through the door and back into the

Hollow's passageway, the peace would begin to fade. Yes, the only way to hold onto this was to remain inside the Chamber of Rest continually.

Unfortunately, that was not going to happen and the time had come for them to return to wherever it was their Shailmas had gathered them from. One by one they stepped out into the passageway; one by one they were disappointed at how quickly much of what they had feasted on faded away.

Thankfully, small tidbits remained—for the time being—and each Traveler held onto as much as they could for as long as they could. Nobody said anything for a time, enjoying the aftertaste of the sweetness from the feast.

Judah continued to hold his auntie's hand as they stepped out after everyone else. As the air from the passageway filled their lungs, it also swirled around them, chilly and damp. Bella breathed in deeply and let her lungs fill up. She held that breath in for as long as she could and then let it seep out slowly. Once the breath was gone, she opened her eyes and accepted the fact that they had to keep going.

The two had not even taken the time to shed their cloaks yet, so Bella took hers off and held her hand out for Judah's. He handed it to her.

"I'm going to hang these up," she said and moved toward the Eating Chamber.

"I'm going to the kitchen," said Sam. "I'm starving. Does anybody want anything?"

"I'll come with you," Aviel said, and the two boys headed to the kitchen. They were all aware that the Shailmas could scoop them up at any moment, so as they each headed to wherever it was they were headed to, that thought was floating somewhere in their minds. No one spoke it out loud—no one needed to.

The Travelers each went in a different direction to a different place in the Hollow. Some headed to the Eating Chamber, some to the kitchen, some to their own Sleeping Chambers. Soon there was only Kaija Mae and Judah left in the passageway.

"Are you doing alright?" Kaija Mae asked. "Honestly, Judah, I don't even know what to say. I was sure we'd get through without anyone being snapped up in one of the king's traps."

"I'm OK, although, I wish I could take the Chamber of Rest home with me." Judah went quiet. "It's going to be unbearable going home without her, Kaija Mae. I'm not sure I can do it."

"Wait and see, Judah, don't think the worst. The sun hasn't completely set yet."

"I'm trying, really I am. I keep thinking that she's going to walk through the door or show up in the passageway … or that she's just making food or snooping around where she shouldn't be."

"I know," was all Kaija Mae could say. There were no words that would make Judah feel better, and thankfully much of the peace from the Chamber of Rest was still running through his veins.

"Have you asked your Shailma about these things?" Kaija Mae finally asked.

"No. I can't seem to straighten my mind out enough even to think. I haven't thought to ask Shemaiah about it."

"Perhaps you should," she said. "He might have something to say about it all."

"Maybe," Judah sighed. He didn't want to talk to the Shailma, if the truth were to be told, since the last thing Shemaiah had said to him was something about trusting. It was unbearably difficult —some might say downright impossible—to trust the Shailmas in such deplorable circumstances.

Instead, he decided to ask Kaija Mae a few things he'd been wondering about. Ever since the last journey to Trilleah, when they had met Kaija Mae, Aviel, Tahlia and the others, question after question had been piling up. This seemed a good time to ask. Maybe it would distract his mind.

"Kaija Mae," he began, "what is with these songs that you sing?" Judah stepped back and again slumped to the floor, letting the cool rock wall catch his back. "I mean, don't get me wrong, they are beautiful and soothing—like a healing medicine—but they are in such a strange language. What do they mean?"

She joined him on the hard ground and just like back in the garden in Westlock, Kaija Mae began drawing in the dirt with her fingers.

"Well," she said thoughtfully. "I was wondering when someone might ask about that." One thing about this girl, she was never in any hurry to offer information. Silence lingered in the air for a few moments. Typically, Judah would have become impatient and repeated the question but at the moment, he didn't care. He didn't care whether she ever answered the question—or any of his questions. He only asked because, well yes, he was curious, but also because he wanted to change the subject that she was on.

"To be honest, I don't know," she finally admitted. Kaija Mae looked at him, hoping to see into his eyes, but Judah refused to look at her. He stared at the floor instead; his eyes partially glazed over.

"I love music," she said. "Before I was wrongly dragged off to Trilleah, I couldn't sing at all," she laughed. "My grandfather used to say that it was my singing that made the chickens lay eggs. But even being so young I thought it was just something I wanted to do. It made no matter that I didn't have a pretty voice like the other girls, I sang all the time … usually as loud as I could."

Judah was too exhausted to interrupt her silly chatter, so he just leaned against the wall and only half-listened.

"When I came here, it was as though I was given a new voice and an odd sort of gift with these songs. I don't know the language either, or if it even is a language," she chattered on. "At least not one from home, but perhaps it's the language of Trilleah … I don't know." That didn't sit well, and Judah finally found something to say.

"I doubt that," he seethed. "Trilleah is a land of hateful darkness, and your songs have a soothing life in them. They are like salve for an injury or …" Judah searched his mind for the right words.

"Like glue for a broken heart." He rubbed his eyes and turned his face to the ground.

"Judah, I'll miss you some, you know."

"Huh?" he asked. Again she'd managed to confuse him.

"When the Shailmas come and take you all home," Kaija Mae replied. "Did you forget that some of us remain here? We don't get to go home. Although, if I could return home I'd not wish to, since what used to be my home was reduced to a pile of ash and rubble." Now it was Kaija Mae's eyes that needed rubbing. She didn't look away from him, though, and for the first time since they'd stepped out from the Chamber of Rest, Judah looked at her. She was rather fond of this handsome young man.

"I did forget. I'm sorry," he said. Judah reached his hand out to touch Kaija Mae and reassure her. Of what, he did not know, for his own heart was crushed, and his mind confused; so confused. He had nothing to say to her that would be the truth, so he said nothing.

"It gets horribly lonely, but I know you'll be back," Kaija Mae sighed.

"I want to say that I will never return to this disgusting land. There's no point now that Jennifer's gone. But I can't help but wonder if the Trows stole her soul. That gives me an even greater reason to return. Honestly, Kaija Mae, I'm so confused by all of this that I don't know what to think," he said. "I don't want to think."

"You'll be back, Judah," she said with a bit of a smile. "You and the others will all return; I know you will." Kaija Mae looked back to the ground, not wanting the young man to see the sadness that was beginning to cover her face.

Judah was about to say something brilliant when Sam and Matt came running down the passageway. The lanterns became confused, with some Travelers sitting on the floor and others running down the passageway. They didn't know which way to cast their light, so bits and pieces of light were being thrown all over the place, bouncing off walls and failing to light up the path for Sam and Matt.

CRASH … Right into Judah and Kaija Mae they collided and sprawled across the floor. Instead of becoming angry or frustrated, they jumped up quickly, sounding panicked.

"Judah," Sam wheezed, trying to catch his breath. "Come quick."

"Come where?" Judah asked.

"To Jennifer's chamber." Sam was so out of breath that it was a curious thing. The passageway to the kitchen was not that long, so it seemed clear that the boys had run from somewhere else altogether.

"You've been to Jen's Sleeping Chamber?" Judah asked. For some reason, the thought of that annoyed him yet excited him at the same time. *Was she there?* he wondered. *Had she made it back to the Hollow, after all?*

Judah sprang up from his place on the ground and without waiting for Kaija Mae, ran with Sam and Matt down the passageway. The boys ran past the kitchen, around a corner, around another corner, and down a windy passageway until they reached Jennifer's Sleeping

Chamber. There was a noticeable bit of a ruckus going on inside; they could hear it even through the thick walls.

Judah placed his foot into the hole in the wall and sucked in his breath as the door opened, welcoming them in. He expected to see his sister, even though he was nervous to even hope such a thing.

As he stepped inside, his heart skipped a beat when his eyes saw who was standing in the middle of the room.

"What are YOU doing here?" Judah demanded.

28

INTO THE SHADOWS

Judah's hopes of finding Jennifer behind the door were shattered. The racket he'd heard was not his sister, nor was it anyone that brought even a shred of joy. Furthermore, when he laid eyes on the unwelcome guest, the last snippet of peace vanished.

As the passageway to Jennifer's chamber opened, it was Miriam who was standing on the other side. The look on her face made it clear that she had no intention of being found there and furthermore, she had something in her hand she tried to hide it as the boys entered the room. Matt, Sam, Aviel, and Judah had all of their attention so focused on Miriam and what she was holding that they failed to see that someone else was also in the chamber.

Pierce noticed that none of them saw him, so he backed into a dark corner. He was close enough to the shadows that it was only a couple of steps back, and he took them quickly. Once there, he was well hidden by the dark. These chambers weren't like the Chamber of Rest where light came from the room itself, where there were no shadows or dark corners. If it were, Pierce would never have been able to cover himself.

These chambers were more ordinary … well, ordinary for Trilleah. There were lanterns on hooks throughout the room, throwing light wherever they felt it was most needed. Now, with all the ruckus and the focus on Miriam, the lanterns cast all their light directly toward her—leaving Pierce safely in the dark.

"What is that?" Judah demanded. "What's in your hand?" Miriam just glared. She neither answered the question nor acknowledged the item.

Matt was about to move toward her when he was interrupted and he, like everyone else, was startled. Kaija Mae and Bella burst into the room squealing.

"I ran and got Bella," Kaija Mae announced, out of breath. When the girls saw who it was in the room, they stopped, disappointed.

"We thought it was Jennifer," Bella sighed.

"So did I," Judah pouted.

"What do you have, Miriam?" Bella asked. She spoke with a strange kindness, which angered all of the boys. The attitude was sorely out of place, after all.

"She had it in her hands when we found her in here, but she won't tell us what it is," Sam snapped.

"Or from where she got it," Aviel added.

"Hand it over, Miriam," Sam demanded and took a step toward the girl. He would have taken two steps, or even three if that's how many were required, but truthfully, he was afraid of her. Instead, he took only one step and thrust his hand out, hoping she'd just toss him the item. Of course, she did not, and thankfully Bella came to Sam's rescue.

"How did you know where J's chamber was?" Bella asked. Her tone had changed now that she knew Miriam had not come into the room with the others but had snuck in on her own. "And why did you come here?" Still, no answer came from Miriam's lips. However, her stare did move from the Travelers to the item clutched in her hands.

It was a little green jar.

It was beautiful, with gold around the bottom and a thick glass lid with a gold ball on the very top. Miriam held it tightly and ran her fingers along the gold on the bottom. The truth was, she'd found it earlier in the Eating Chamber. It looked as though it had rolled into a corner, and while she knew where it had come from and where it needed to be returned to, she had been in no hurry to bring it back.

"Hey! That's the jar that J brought me here to look at on her first trip to Trilleah!" Bella announced. She seemed puzzled as she recalled Jennifer running into the Eating Chamber hollering at her to come and look at the green jar that had given warnings.

When Bella had come to look, though, the jar had done nothing—nothing whatsoever. Bella remembered scolding Jennifer about wasting time and letting her imagination get the best of her—or something like that. She was puzzled now, and curious as to why Miriam would be holding that same jar inside of Jennifer's chamber. Bella stepped up to take the jar, but it was obvious Miriam wasn't going to hand it over without a fight.

Miriam looked at Bella, and then the others, and then back to the jar. In an instant and quicker than lightning, she pulled off the lid and held the jar away from herself. Straightaway, an enormous cloud of fire shot out and hovered between Miriam and the others. Matt grabbed Bella and pulled her back. Aviel stepped in front of the rest. For the first time that any of the Travelers could recall, Matt spoke with an angry—and even slightly fierce—tone.

"Miriam ..."

No answer came, and they couldn't see the girl through the fire, so he shouted louder.

"MIRIAM!"

Still, no answer was returned. The fire was contained within the cloud but had a loud roar coming from it; not deafeningly loud, just loud. Sam began shouting at Miriam but again, there was no response.

Matt put his arms up to shield himself from the cloud of fire that had grown into a wall between the Travelers and Miriam. He took another step forward. As he did, the fire stretched from the floor to the ceiling; the green jar fell to the ground. The cloud that held the fire was sucked back inside and the noise it had made while hanging in the air became quiet. When the cloud had cleared, they all looked for Miriam. She was gone.

"Where'd she go?" shouted Sam. He ran over and picked up the green jar but let it drop again. "Ouch," he shrieked. It was much too hot to hold onto. When the jar fell, it rolled toward the dark corner Pierce was hiding in. He was concerned that someone might move toward him to get the jar but was thankful when no one did.

"Just leave it," Matt said to Sam. "We'll get it later."

It was unsettling to them that Miriam had vanished, but they understood how the Shailmas retrieved their mortals and carried each back through the portal, so her disappearance was not inconceivable. In fact, they were all waiting to be taken back to their homes. All, that is, except Kaija Mae and the others who had been wrongly imprisoned in Trilleah; but Judah was the only one who knew of their secret.

What was far more concerning was that Miriam had let herself into Jennifer's chamber and had refused to answer the Travelers' questions or hand over the little green jar. That became the topic of discussion.

"What would she possibly want in here?" Judah asked. He sounded genuinely perplexed. He began looking around the room, searching for anything that might be out of place or missing. It would be impossible for him to know, since he'd never been in his sister's chamber before now, if something was.

"Why did she have that jar? Why would she not hand it over?" Sam voiced more of the questions they were all wondering about.

Bella's memory was jolted back to Jennifer's first trip to Trilleah. Her niece was upset and had dragged Bella into this chamber to show her the jar. Bella remembered being angry with Jennifer and now felt remorseful that she hadn't listened to her.

Bella told the others how Jennifer was so worked up and went on about that little green jar. She said the jar was warning her about dangers within Asphelia's Hollow; dangers that Bella knew nothing about. Could Miriam have been the danger to which the jar was referring?

It all made sense now, and Bella jumped up and down, squealing and shouting. "Miriam must be that danger. It makes sense. She must have known about that jar and wanted to take it before it gave her secrets away."

"That may be right. However, it might be worth considering that Miriam is not the danger. Maybe she knew about the power of the jar and wanted it for herself," Matt suggested. "Either way, it doesn't look good for Miriam."

"Well, her Shailma grabbing her at that exact moment is quite a coincidence, wouldn't you say?" Sam asked. He blew on his burned fingers and walked over to grab the jar. Again, Pierce held his breath and crossed his fingers, hoping not to be noticed. Again, he wasn't.

Sam didn't even glance toward the dark corner. He only picked up the jar, which was cooler now, and jammed the lid on tightly, handing it to Matt as he did. Matt set it back on Jennifer's table and turned to walk away. He did not get far before turning back. He picked up the jar and turned it over in his hands for a time. Matt finally grabbed the gold ball on the lid and said, "I'm curious about you. Let's see if you have anything else to say."

None of them were sure this was a good idea but couldn't spout their concerns before Matt yanked off the lid. In an instant, the cloud shot from the bottle and hovered above them. It was smaller than when Miriam was here, but they were OK with that.

A powerful voice echoed from the center of the cloud.

"I have spoken my warnings to the keeper of the chamber, and I will speak to no other." And then, the fiery cloud returned to the little green jar and was silent. Matt set the lid on and carefully put it back on the table. His hands were quivering, making the lid rattle against the jar.

He stepped back, turned around, and looked at the faces of the Travelers. Their eyes were wide open and fixed on the jar. None of them had anything to say … the jar seemed to have said it all. As Matt stood facing the group of Travelers, he realized everyone was there except for one.

"Where is Pierce?" he asked. "Has anyone seen him since we were in the Chamber of Rest?" Matt had an odd feeling in the pit of his stomach but said nothing to the others about it.

Nobody had seen him, although it didn't raise much concern because truly, they had all stood or sat with him in that chamber only a very short time ago. His Shailma certainly could have retrieved him by now. Nobody realized that he was right here among them, listening to every word they said.

Although Pierce heard Matt's question and very much wanted to step out from the corner, he knew that none of the Travelers would understand him emerging from the dark shadows. He held his breath and remained where he was, quiet and hidden.

"Miriam's Shailma clearly retrieved her," Matt pointed out, "and likely so did Pierce's." Most agreed, but Kaija Mae knew full well that Miriam's Shailma was unable to retrieve her because of decisions she'd made long ago, and that she most certainly had not left Trilleah. Kaija Mae also knew that the time to say so was not now, so once again she kept her silence … and Miriam's secrets.

Judah sat down on the bed and was quiet. He was overwhelmed with all of these happenings. Jennifer was gone and now this crazy little green jar had warned them that she'd been given information no one else knew. Maybe it was that information that got her trapped. Perhaps if Bella had listened, Jennifer would be here now. Oh, the dread of such thoughts. They weave a web of uncertainty that stirs up feelings which should never be disturbed. Nevertheless, they were disturbed now and in the center of Judah's mind.

Judah picked up Jennifer's pillow and wrapped his arms around it, breathing in deeply. There was no trace of his sister in it, for she had not laid her head on it enough times. Not every journey gave them an opportunity to rest in their own chambers.

Judah wished his sister was here now, resting or grumbling or complaining; anything really. He wished he had never allowed her to come to the horrible land and he wondered a disturbing thought. *If Jennifer was needed to break the curse of the Trows, was the Travelers' entire purpose of being here useless without her? Would she get out of the hell that had trapped her? Was she able to get out or was her soul now cursed to the Malleana Forest?* So many questions without answers rumbled and tumbled in the boy's mind.

The time had come for Judah to find a quiet spot and speak to Shemaiah. He needed some answers, and if not answers, wisdom, and if not wisdom, direction, and if not direction, comfort.

Surely Shemaiah will at least give me comfort, he reasoned.

"Can I have a few minutes alone?" Judah asked the others. They were more than happy to step out and grant him his request.

While they all wanted to help and make his pain a little less, none of them knew how. While they too, missed Jennifer very much and were each ferociously worried about the young girl, they realized their pain was but a small drop in the sea of dread that was pulling Judah under; drowning him.

Quickly they stepped out into the passageway and walked in silence to the Eating Chamber. No one spoke; not even one word was uttered.

Pierce remained hidden with his fingers crossed. All he could do was be still and hope Judah didn't stay long. It wouldn't be long now anyway, because the Shailmas would be coming to gather their mortals; the sun had nearly finished setting. The last slivers of its light were about to disappear beyond the horizon, closing the gates.

Pierce knew if he could stay quiet and hidden for just a few more seconds, the Travelers would all be whisked away through the portal and his own dark secrets would continue to be safe.

29

FAMILIAR VOICES

As Jennifer was trying to loosen the grip of the vines, she kept her eyes fastened on her mamma. For the first time since she'd been pulled into this dungeon, Jennifer dared to look into her mother's eyes. What she saw made her cringe, causing the vines holding her to tighten their grip, ripping into her flesh.

Mamma's eyes were empty. There was nothing contained in them; no dancing, no sparkle, no glitter, no life. They were gray and hollow. Truly, the eyes were the windows to the soul and now, for the first time, the truth sunk into Jennifer. Mamma's soul was gone.

The pressure to find the tablet in this pit weighed heavily, and Jennifer settled in herself that no matter what Simeon asked of her, she would obey. Mamma's soul was at stake—she saw that now—as well as the souls of countless others. If it was up to her to find that tablet, then that was exactly what she would do.

As Jennifer struggled fiercely with the vines, she begged Simeon for help. She was listening intently in her own soul for the voice of her Shailma, but instead, she heard countless other voices calling out to her. She became distracted, which is never a good way to be when listening for the quiet voice of a Shailma.

"Jennifer," came a faint sound from behind her. She tried turning around but could not.

"Who are you?" Jennifer demanded. She had considered being silent, but the king knew she was here, so it seemed pointless to try and hide. This knowledge gave her a fierce boldness. Or perhaps Simeon gave that to her. Either way, it made no sense to be timid and hide. "Who are you?" she demanded again. Before the first voice could answer, another voice called out from in front of her.

"Jennifer, help us."

Then another and another and another. From seven or eight different places near her, she could hear voices crying out for help. This would have made sense, but the fact that they knew her and called her by name befuddled her and made Jennifer deeply anguished. There is nothing more wretched than having empty voices calling your name while their vacant eyes stare at you.

"Who are you?" she screamed.

One by one the hollow strangers began to identify themselves. As they did, Jennifer wished she'd never asked. Knowing who they were made it much worse, yet at the same time, this knowledge grew into a determination to keep fighting and find the clay tablet … no matter what.

"I am Tom," came one deep, male voice. "I'm Matthew's father." She could see him in the shadows and he was tall, just like Matt. His eyes, too, were gray and hollow. It was the eyes that taunted Jennifer more than anything else.

Then another voice answered her question; this one sounded much like her own voice; young and feminine.

"Jennifer, help me," the voice cried. "I'm Justice; Samuel's sister."

"Oh, dear God!" Jennifer screamed out. Her fingers worked on the vines around her ankles as one by one, the voices calling out to her each identified themselves as the loved ones of Jennifer's friends. Her head was darting this way and that, looking at the sunken faces and hollow eyes of all those calling her name. Then she saw one she knew instantly. Her fingers stopped working at the vines, and she stood up.

"You're Peter," she said, for there was no doubt that he was. He looked exactly like Pierce … there was no other one he could be.

"I am," was all the boy replied.

When it was just her mamma who'd been calling to her and staring at her with those hollow eyes, when it was just her mamma who was so painfully frail and horrid looking, it was bad enough. It ripped Jennifer's heart out and stomped all over it smashing it to bits. But now, with all these other innocent ones added, it was a thousand times more unbearable.

Jennifer had grown to love all those other Travelers who'd had the souls of their loved ones stolen. They often shared stories of the past and those whom the Trows had stolen, so in some way, Jennifer felt like she knew these, even if only through stories.

Listening to Sam speak of his sweet little sister, and how the Trows had stolen her young soul, had left a permanent grief in Jennifer's heart. Watching Matt tell stories of his father and how wonderful of a man he was left a whole other layer of anguish.

Even Pierce, though he was a bit wretched himself, had touched her heart with his story of watching his twin brother get hit by the car and running to get their mother. The desperation and guilt that wracked his words as he told the story made Jennifer's heart bleed for him. Being a twin herself, she couldn't begin to imagine seeing such a thing happen to Judah.

"Judah," she suddenly said out loud.

"JUDAH!" her mother screamed out. "Where is my precious boy?" Molly wailed in anguish.

"Mamma, he's safe," Jennifer said softly. There was such an oddity about this place in which she found herself. Even though the air screamed its painful song and the wailings of all those who were without souls was deafening, the quietest whisper could be heard. It made no sense but then again, Jennifer had become used to senseless things here in Trilleah.

"Simeon, help me with these vines," she pleaded and bent down to begin working on them again. "Please," she begged. Her fingers were bleeding by now as she dug and picked at the vines until the skin had become cut and worn through. She had made no progress whatsoever and was becoming frantic.

"Peace, Little One," Simeon said. "Stop trying so hard; it isn't in your trying that you will achieve freedom but in my leading you to it."

"Then LEAD ME, SIMEON!!!" she shrieked.

"Jennifer, you must calm down and trust me. The vines get tighter as you panic. The more anxious you become, the tighter they will hold you." Jennifer had noticed that they were, in fact, getting tighter and tighter and were beginning to cut off the blood flow. Her feet were starting to feel prickly and numb. But how was Jennifer suppose to not panic or be anxious?

Simeon heard her wonderings and filled her heart with wisdom.

Jenny, do you trust me, Little One?

"Yes," she sobbed.

Then tell your heart, he said somewhere to her mind. *Control the thoughts running through your mind ... if you don't control them, they will control you. I will help you, but you must choose to agree with what I am telling you before I can help.*

"Oh, this is too hard," she howled. "I'm just a little girl!"

As she wailed, she felt the vines tighten. It seemed Jennifer had no choices here whatsoever, so she took a big breath and pushed it out slowly. She forced all the overwhelming thoughts pounding in her mind to halt, and as she let the breath out, she imagined all of those thoughts and fears were carried in that breath. She watched in her imagination as every fear, and anxious thought was carried out in that deep breath, leaving her calm and tidy. To her complete surprise, the vines relaxed their grip.

Next, she focused on her breathing for a time and used her imagination to her advantage. Each time one of those crumbs of panic or overwhelming thoughts tried to sneak back in, Jennifer would hold her breath. It seemed that the ruinous thoughts were riding into her mind on the air she was breathing. As she held her breath, she imagined creating a web which caught each anxious and fearful thought like flies.

This took some time, but soon Jennifer realized the vines had become so loose and relaxed that she wondered if they were loose enough to pull away from.

"Simeon?" she called out.

Jennifer needed to ask nothing more; he answered her straightaway.

Calmly ... calmly step out now.

Jennifer picked up one foot slowly, set it down in front of her and then the other foot followed. She was free from the vines.

"That was almost too easy," she mumbled. Jennifer stepped away quickly, fearing the vines may reach out and grab her again.

Watch your thoughts, Simeon reminded her. *Be very careful which ones you let in.*

"Now what?" she asked. She had not yet taken her eyes off of her mamma, who was still held firmly by the king. Jennifer's ears rang loudly with the voices of the other Waiting Ones still calling to her for help; her heart began to race.

Jenny, Simeon warned. *Control your mind.*

Another big breath in and then out and Jennifer calmed enough to hear Simeon's quiet voice. She looked at the beast carrying Shrailzhar and her mother and saw the king was still unable to force it to move. She knew it could still see Simeon and the other Shailmas surrounding her and a bit more trust washed over her. "I trust you," she whispered.

OK, then we can continue. Jenny, do you see over to your left? Jennifer could not see to the left, nor the right, or any other direction for that matter, because she didn't want to take her eyes away from her mamma. What if she took her eyes off to look to the left, and when she looked back again her mamma was gone? What then?

Jennifer, you cannot get the tablet if your eyes are distracted. You must look at where you are going, so you don't stumble, Simeon warned.

"Ugh, I hate this Simeon. I hate this—all of it," she whined.

Yes, Little One, I am quite aware that you do, but you have the strength to do it; you have my help, and I trust you to finish the course, Simeon said calmly. He never seemed to get frustrated with her constant grumbling and whining, even when she would get frustrated with herself.

"Fine," she muttered.

Jennifer turned her eyes to the left, where Simeon had directed.

"What am I supposed to be seeing?" She didn't notice that while Simeon spoke his words into her mind, she continued to ask her questions out loud.

Look into the distance—it is dark and difficult to see. But if you look far enough you'll be able to see what looks like an enormous mound of sticks and branches and vines and brush. Do you see it, Jenny?

She searched but saw nothing other than dragons and vines everywhere. The dragons were at least nine feet tall; some even taller than that. They were a deep red color and while most had just one head, there were a few that had more. They all had forked tongues, like serpents, and horns were coming out of the tops of their heads and from under their chins ... like a spike had been driven right through them.

From the highest place on their backs and all the way down to the tips of their long, powerful tails, were thorns, like on the stems of roses, only a hundred times bigger. They looked to be razor-sharp, and Jennifer was convinced that if one of those tails caught her, she would be sliced into bits. On the lower backs of the dragons, right above their back legs, was what looked like the wings of flies—expanded a million times. Those clear wings flapped rapidly on some and were folded in on others.

The dragons were not roaming free, at least most of them weren't. The vines had most of them chained and they couldn't go far. Jennifer was exceedingly glad about that. However, there was the odd one that was loose and stomped about, snarling and gnashing their teeth at the Waiting Ones.

The dragons were dreadful-looking creatures, and Jennifer had to make herself look away. "Simeon, I cannot do this," she cried desperately. "I cannot!"

Yes, Little One, you are the one for this task, he reassured her. *Now, keep looking for the mound of branches and sticks and vines.*

"I don't see it," she snapped. "Do I need to be looking with the eyes of my heart, maybe?" The question was a genuine one, and so was the answer.

Oh, dear girl, have you not realized even still, that everything you are seeing is seen with the eyes of your heart? That is why you are the one who must be here and the one who will retrieve the tablet.

Jennifer was shocked at what she was hearing. *None of the rest sees as clearly as you do, Little One. Much of what you see is only air and space to the others, but it is real, Jenny, so very real. In fact,* Simeon continued, *what you see with the eyes of your heart is more real, more powerful, more genuine, than what you and the others see with your mortal eyes.*

Jennifer had never considered such a thing and didn't know how to consider it now.

"Oh," was all she could say. She tried desperately to imagine not seeing what was clearly surrounding her. No matter how hard she tried, Jennifer could not erase what the eyes of her heart had already seen, which only made her begin to get anxious again at the thought of what the eyes of her heart may yet see.

30

INTO THE NEST

Move a few steps forward ... watch your steps carefully, was Simeon's instruction. Jennifer took a few steps forward and then stopped to look again. Still, she couldn't see what Simeon was talking about. A few more steps; still nothing. A few more steps and ... and there it was, just as he had said. It was so large that she couldn't believe she had missed it the first few times she looked.

You didn't see it because you didn't want to see it, she heard.

"Well, I see it now, so what do I do with it?"

Indeed, it was enormous ... gigantic ... ginormous (if even there were such a word). It went nearly to the very top of this dungeon which Jennifer still thought to be hell, even though Simeon assured her it was not. As she considered it, Simeon heard her thoughts and responded to them.

Oh, this place is not hell, not at all. What you see here, this thing your feet are standing in, the smell that your nose is smelling, is nothing more than a snake pit.

Jennifer gasped and looked for something to jump onto, as she imagined snakes slithering around her feet.

Not that kind of snake, Jenny, Simeon said. *Shrailzhar is king of the vipers, and this is his domain. It is truly* THEE *snake's pit.*

Jennifer looked around, back to where she had last seen the king trying to force his beast to move, but he was no longer there. She looked around frantically, desperate to find him but couldn't.

"SIMEON!" she cried out.

All is well, Jenny, he said. *All is well.* Sometimes it angered her how Simeon was so calm when in her mind, clearly, all was *not* well … not well at all. The king had gone, taking her mamma with him.

"I knew I shouldn't have taken my eyes off of him," she cried.

While your eyes were on King Shrailzhar, you could not see what you needed to see. You were distracted. You cannot move ahead if you are focused on what is behind.

Sometimes, even when Simeon made sense, it still angered her. She continued to search as far as her eyes could see in every direction. Her mamma had to be here somewhere. Where else could the king take her that was worse than this very place? Surely, Mamma was here … she had to be.

Little One, you need to use the sticks and vines in front of you to climb to the top of this nest.

The only word that Jennifer heard was "nest."

"Um, what?" she asked.

You must pay attention and look forward. Focus, Little One; the tablet is in the nest.

"Nest?" she shrieked. "Nest of what?" She did not take hold of any sticks or branches or vines. She did not even reach her hands out to do so. She was too busy being horrified!

Does it matter? Simeon asked. *Will you go or not go depending on who's the keeper of the nest?*

"Well, uh, maybe," she stammered. All sorts of horrors raced through her mind. Some came and left. Others came and stayed. Jennifer couldn't seem to control her thoughts any longer, and she crumpled to the ground. The moment she fell, Jennifer felt vines begin to slither around her ankles and take hold. Others crawled up her back and moved quickly toward her throat.

In one quick move, she jumped up, threw the vines off, and grabbed on to the highest branch she could reach. Jennifer moved her hands quickly, one above the other. Although her fingers were raw from trying to free herself from the vines that had dragged her down to this snake pit in the first place, Jennifer gritted her teeth and ignored the pain that ricocheted through them.

She fumbled with her feet, trying to find anything to brace them with, but because her boots were so big and heavy, she couldn't feel anything. Without thinking it through, Jennifer kicked her boots off and watched them disappear into the matted vines below.

Don't look down, Jenny, look up. Keep going, the Shailma repeated over and over and over again.

The higher she climbed, the harder it was for Jennifer to guard her mind. The thoughts that hammered against her, trying to break down the walls and crash through, would surely destroy her. She could not afford, now that she'd climbed so high, to become distracted. Jennifer was so high, in fact, that she'd undoubtedly be seriously hurt if she fell. She knew that if that happened, her mind's barriers would crumble, and she would be finished. If the fall didn't kill her, the vines … or the red dragons … or the king … would.

While she climbed higher and higher, one thought kept fighting to push through and try as she might, Jennifer couldn't keep it out.

Surely you can see your mamma from here, that voice of distraction whispered. It was not Simeon, nor was it her own thought. The battle was on; she knew it was the voice of King Shrailzhar.

She's looking for you. Look around … you are above it all … your view is open … take a look … just a quick peek.

The thoughts kept coming, like cannons trying to break down the enemy's wall. And they were working. Her focus was being destroyed bit by bit.

You're nearly there, she heard Simeon's voice break through the chatter that was bombarding her mind. *Just a bit higher, Little One. Keep your thoughts on your task and your ears tuned to my voice.*

"Simeon," Jennifer said out loud, hoping to drown out the tempting voices, "I'm nearly to the top, and I still don't know what kind of nest I'm climbing into." She was hoping he would tell her, but she knew he probably wouldn't. The thoughts that were trying to break into her mind put a double portion of pressure on her now; now that she was feeling so weak. She wished she hadn't asked the question out loud, because it was clear that Simeon was not about to give her the information she wanted. Furthermore, asking the question gave the tempting voices more ammunition with which to blast through her mind.

Simeon seemed quiet now. She begged him to help her more, to tell her whose nest this was and if she was going to find any creatures inside. Jennifer heard nothing more from him, but her ears did pick up a voice she recognized.

Her mamma was screaming from somewhere below.

"Jennifer, NOOO!"

Jennifer stopped instantly and her foot slipped.

"Oh, Simeon!" Jennifer cried. "I can't do this!"

The moment she said the words, every fear and distraction that had been fighting against the barricades of her mind broke through. Her other foot lost its grip and while one hand held fast, the other was slipping. The pain was too much and she considered letting go. She felt vines reach out and twist around her ankles, pulling on her.

"SIMEON!!" she screamed as loudly as she could. She heard nothing from her Shailma but felt something take hold of her. In a flash, she was picked up and tossed into the nest.

Jennifer curled herself into a tight ball, hiding her face and pulling her feet up into the cloak. She lay that way for a long moment, trying to catch her breath and pull herself back together. Jennifer rocked back and forth, back and forth, curled inside her hot cloak. The terrified girl pinched her eyes tightly closed and stuck her fingers in her ears. Oh, how her fingers ached. Everything ached. Jennifer found herself begging for a quick death.

Jennifer, now that you're here, I will tell you this is a dragon's nest and there are nine babies here. Jennifer pinched her eyes tighter, if such a thing was possible, and tried to force her bloody fingers deeper into her ears. Now that Simeon was giving her the information she'd begged him for earlier, she didn't want to hear it.

The babies are the same color as your cloak, but as soon as you move, the mother will notice you. When the time comes, and that time is not yet, you must go quickly. It is so important that you listen now like you've never listened before. Jenny? Are you listening, Jenny?

Simeon waited for her reply and refused to give the information she needed until she did so.

"I'm listening."

OK. The nest is seven feet across so with nine babies, it's quite full. You need to unbutton your cloak before you get up. Do it slowly, without moving anything but your hands. Jennifer did what he had instructed. *Now you need to slowly—very slowly—wiggle your arms out of the sleeves but remain hidden underneath.* Again she followed his instructions with exact precision.

She very much wanted to grumble and complain and scream and holler, but Jennifer knew that right now she could do none of that. If she let herself think about anything at all, it would distract her enough that the mother dragon would be alerted to her presence, and come after her.

OK, Little One. Now, when you're ready, you are going to stand up and throw your cloak backward so you can move faster. When you do, you need to run to the center of the nest—that is where the tablet is. The king was convinced the tablet would be safe there. He underestimates you, Little One. He doesn't understand that your courage is without limits.

That seemed to be the end of Simeon's instructions. However, Jennifer thought it was not a good place for the Shailma to stop, and begged for more.

"What then?" she asked.

Trust me, was all Simeon replied.

No matter how she pleaded for further instructions, all Simeon would whisper were those two little words. *Trust me ... trust me ... trust me.*

"Oh, good grief," Jennifer spouted through gritted teeth. She pondered her options and realized she had none. She had to trust her Shailma; he was her only hope. Now that Jennifer was here, inside the dragon's nest, there was nothing else for her to do. Even if she could somehow climb out and back down the side of the nest, there was no way out of this snake pit. No; she had no option but to do what Simeon had said and trust him.

In one burst of motion, with the voice of Shrailzhar tempting her to come back to her mother, and the voice of Mamma screaming for her to stop, Jennifer sprang up and threw her cloak back as far as she could. She sped toward the center of the nest but careful to dart around this baby and leap over that one. In the blink of an eye, she saw the tablet ... right where Simeon had said it would be. She also noticed the dragon's claw resting on the edge of it.

She screamed for her Shailma at the top of her lungs. "SIMEON!"

As Jennifer shrieked, the enormous dragon was startled and turned toward her, moving just enough to uncover the rest of the tablet. Rage flared in its eyes and sulfur spewed from its mouth as the mamma dragon set her sights on Jennifer.

In a furry, the small and uncovered Curse Breaker dove with all the might she had left, which was not much at all, and grabbed the tablet with both hands. She rolled and landed on her back, looking straight up into the open mouth of the dragon, who was now hovering above her and spewing breaths of fire. The yellow, forked-tongue, which was larger than Jennifer herself, coiled out, revealing an outrageously huge bolt of fire spitting out from the back of its throat.

Jennifer covered her face, knowing that would not help one bit since the size of the dragon's tongue was ten times bigger than her.

She closed her eyes, knowing this was the end; a small part of her was glad that it was.

31

UNWANTED DISCUSSIONS

Judah watched as everyone left Jennifer's chamber. As soon as the door closed itself up, he flopped backward onto the bed, still holding tight to Jennifer's pillow. Judah stared at the ceiling. No words came to him, no thoughts, no ponderings. He felt empty. Part of him had been taken and whatever part was left seemed to shrivel into nothingness. No importance whatsoever remained in him without his sister.

Perhaps this was how it was supposed to be—having no thoughts or wonderings—it made it simple for Shemaiah to fill his mind with all sorts of truths and directions. Just like an artist with an empty canvas, the Shailma could start anywhere and end anywhere.

Often the problem the Shailmas had with their mortals was the constant interruptions. Judah's emptiness would make sure that didn't happen. Shemaiah knew that Judah's soul was tuned in, and the Shailma was well aware of the thoughts and questions that had been rumbling around in the boy's mind.

Judah, I see your pain, and I feel the anguish in your soul. There is nothing comparable to what you have witnessed—the look on Jennifer's face when she fell prey to the trap of the king.

So far, Shemaiah was not helping; only reminding Judah of something of which he did not wish to be reminded.

Take heart, my son, she is not lost, nor is she alone. This caused Judah to listen closer. *Her Shailma is with her and even now, at this exact moment as you lay here on her bed, Simeon has her in his clutches. Judah, you must trust the Shailmas to know what they are doing. They see the end of a thing from its beginning, and they are well aware of traps—traps that are all around you, which you know nothing about. Just because Kaija Mae warned you about the ones she saw, doesn't mean those are the only ones around. The Shailmas see them all.*

Again, Shemaiah was not helping Judah, but making him more concerned about future trips to Trilleah, if ever any were to be made. Without Jennifer, he saw no reason to make any more but then again, if she was trapped in Malleana Forest, that would bring Judah back, even if he had to come alone.

You are not finished your journey, came Shemaiah's thought. The Shailma had noticed Judah's ponderings. *There are more tablets to be gathered—though not many—and you will return for the next Summer Solstice.*

Judah's attention was stirred. *But the next Solstice is Winter Solstice,* he pointed out. If Jennifer was not going to be released today, if in fact, she was ever going to be set free from the trap, Judah would certainly be returning the very next Solstice to do whatever he could. If his sister was caught in the Forest of Waiting Ones, nothing would keep him from returning.

Yes, Judah, I am aware. There was an uncomfortably long pause, and from the tone of Shemaiah's words, Judah felt like he was supposed to be prepared for some unwanted information. Before too many minutes at all, that information came.

We won't be returning for Winter Solstices anymore.

Judah gasped. *But Jennifer ...*

Before he could finish his thought, which truly, he did not know how to finish, Shemaiah interrupted. Shailmas don't often interrupt, but Judah was glad for it this time. Shemaiah should have left him to dwell in his emptiness. But since he didn't, Judah was forced to think and feel and remember. Oh, how he wished he could erase it all, but of course, such a thing is not possible—even in Trilleah.

Judah, the remaining journeys will take every second of daylight and the Winter Solstices do not provide enough time.

This was not helpful, and Judah was becoming annoyed. "Shemaiah," he huffed, "you've always told me the truth, and you have never failed to rescue me. But this time, I feel that there is no way out."

He stood up and walked toward the little green jar, wondering if maybe, it might have more reasonable information than Shemaiah was offering. Judah picked it up and let his fingers feel every inch of it. He grabbed the gold ball on top of the lid but didn't have the courage to pull it off. He did not set it back down, however, and as he began wandering around Jennifer's Sleeping Chamber, he held the jar firmly.

"Put it down, Judah," Pierce whispered under his breath. "Put the jar down. Put it down." All the time Judah had been having the conversation with Shemaiah, Pierce hadn't once taken his eyes off of the boy. He wasn't especially fond of Judah. However, Pierce was not especially fond of anyone except Bella. He would do anything for her and if that meant pretending to like both Judah and Jennifer, so be it.

It wasn't that he didn't NOT like the twins, it was more like he was annoyed by them. Perhaps the reason for such an annoyance was that he had lost his own twin brother and felt responsible for the accident that took him. After all, it was Pierce who had thrown the ball to Peter. Even though they were young, that knowledge never lessened Pierce's guilt. It was unbearable some days. He should have thrown the ball straight. If he had not thrown it into the street, Peter would never have run after it. He wouldn't have gotten hit by that stupid car, and the Trows would never have had a chance to steal his soul. Pierce would never have had to come to Trilleah and would not be hiding now in the dark corners of a hidden hollow.

But Pierce did throw the ball, and Peter did run into the street, and the Trows had stolen the soul of his twin brother.

Yes, that was probably the reason the twins annoyed him so much.

But now, as he watched Judah wander around the chamber with the green jar, he felt a pang of compassion for him. Nevertheless, Pierce continued to beg, although under his breath, for Judah to put the green jar back down. Surely nothing good would come from that lid being pulled off again.

Judah picked up this, that, and the other thing on one of the little tables. It seemed as though he was looking for something but didn't know what. He would pick up an item, turn it over in his hand, look at it again, and set it down. With item after item, he did the same thing. Sometimes he'd groan or sigh, and other times he did nothing at all.

The one item he held onto for a long time was a picture of Jennifer and Mamma. There were many pictures on a long shelf in the chamber, but this one caught Judah's attention. He looked at it and sat down on the floor, leaning against the nearest wall. He never took his eyes off of the photograph; not even for a moment. There was something unusual about the picture, and it was clear to Pierce that Judah was pondering deeply.

"How odd is that?" Judah said to the photograph. "Where did you get such strange hats?"

Pierce felt like he shouldn't be there, lurking in the dark corner and truly, he shouldn't have been. But there was nowhere for him to go without making his presence known to Judah, so he stayed put but stepped forward a smidgen to keep a closer watch on the boy.

He tried not to listen to the conversation Judah was having with the photograph, but it was far too strange to plug his ears, and he became interested, stepping an inch closer.

"Mamma, I don't remember this picture ever being taken, and I don't remember you and Jennifer having hats like these. Although," he said, "I've seen these hats somewhere before." It hadn't entered his memory that these were the same hats that were in a basket in the Eating Chamber. Jennifer had recognized them in another photograph of her mamma and daddy but had never mentioned them to Judah. Now he was confused and pondering all at the same time. Pierce wiggled and stood on his toes, trying to get a glance at the photograph in Judah's hands. He wanted to see what was so odd about the picture.

Judah set the photograph on his lap and took the lid of the green jar between his fingers. He fumbled around with it for a few minutes, rambling to himself about whether or not he should remove the lid. The voice in the fire had said that Jennifer already had the necessary warnings and that it would speak to no one other than her.

"However," Judah said to the jar, "I am her twin brother and we share many things and countless secrets, so perhaps you might give me the warnings since she is …" His voice trailed off for a moment but then came right back. "Since she isn't here."

Pierce began his mutterings again, begging the lid to stay on the jar. He would never know, however, if the lid was removed or not, because in that very moment, as Pierce was considering coming out from his hiding place in the shadows and taking the little green jar from Judah, the Shailmas came and retrieved their mortals.

As Judah was whisked away, he tightened his fingers around the little green jar. The photograph of Mamma and Jennifer tumbled to the ground. As they soared up through the ceiling and into the open air of Trilleah, Judah heard the glass from the picture smash. There was no point in looking back, however, because the last pale light from the sun was about to fade to utter blackness. Terror gripped Judah, so a little breaking glass wasn't going to matter much.

"SHEMAIAH, WE'RE NOT GOING TO MAKE IT!" Judah wailed.

"Oh, my dear, Judah," the Shailma spoke, "when will you believe?" And with that, Shemaiah broke through the last crack of light just as the gates of Summer Solstice slammed shut.

The echo of the slamming gates ricocheted through the atmosphere, causing Judah to wobble and grip his Shailma tighter to avoid falling.

Judah did not wish to return to Westlock … not without Jennifer. He didn't see any reason to return, except for what Shemaiah had told him about returning in the Summer Solstice. Oh, the agony of the unknown was great, overwhelming Judah, and pushing him to the brink of a place to which one should never be pushed.

WRECKED

Simeon swooped in and gathered Jennifer up in an instant, just as the fire came rolling from the dragon's throat, catching three of the baby dragons and disintegrating them in an instant. The edges of the girl's hair were singed, but she was safe … and so was the tablet.

"Well done, Little One," Simeon boasted loudly as they sailed up through the snake pit. Even though Jennifer couldn't see him, she heard pride in his words. It didn't matter to her, though, as she was completely wrecked. There was nothing good about any of this journey. Jennifer was anguished over her mother, tormented about the Waiting Ones that had called out to her, and had great sorrow knowing there were more tablets to find before the curse could be broken.

"MAMMA!" she screamed in horror.

Judah and Bella are already back to Westlock and they will be excited to see you, Simeon said. This was the one thought that did calm Jennifer's heart, albeit only a small bit. Oh, how she missed them. She'd be grateful to have her feet back on Westlock ground again. *We'll be there soon,* Simeon whispered to her broken heart.

"Simeon," she sighed, "I don't want to return … ever."

"I know. You'll feel differently in time though, Little One."

She doubted that very much but had nothing left inside with which to argue, or even think, so she didn't bother to do either.

For the rest of the journey to Westlock, the ragged girl with the singed hair and bloodied fingers and shattered soul sat quietly, gripping the tablet. No thoughts went through her mind, no wonderings about any of the Travelers, no hope for the future.

Within minutes, Simeon delivered her safely to the rocking chair in the living room of their little house on the corner of Fairview Lane and Mitchell Avenue. The undone and shattered little girl sprawled motionless in the chair, clinging to the tablet. Simeon gave the rocker a few pushes to start it singing its usual squeaky tune and to let Bella and Judah know she'd been returned. He watched her for a few moments, speaking some words she did not understand. Simeon touched her forehead briefly, and then he was gone from her sight.

Bella was in the kitchen, pouring a warm cup of milk for Judah and herself, for there was not going to be any sleeping going on this night. She stopped, thinking she'd heard the familiar squeak. *It must be Judah, poor boy, rocking in J's chair.*

"Judah?" she hollered, expecting him to answer her from the living room. She was startled when the boy came instead from the basement. He looked at his auntie, who was looking straight back at him; she was as white as a ghost.

"Do you hear that?" she cried, tears beginning to stream down her face. "Could it be? Could it really be?" Bella shrieked.

"JELLY BEAN!" Judah sobbed.

Bella dropped the warm milk into the sink, grabbed Judah's hand, and together they ran toward the squealing chair … and the one they thought would never return.

That one had returned, although not without being irrevocably broken. Jennifer's body had been irreparably wounded, her mind fractured, her spirit frayed. This little one, who was the key to breaking the curse of Malleana Forest and freeing the Waiting Ones, had been returned indeed; undone and wrecked.

It has been said, that all things can be repaired, and time heals all wounds, and so forth and whatnot. The truth, though, is not always found in such silly sayings.

Sometimes wounds must get deeper, pain must become unbearable, and doubt must nearly overtake the soul before the healing can begin and the courage can be found …

… UNTIL THE NEXT JOURNEY …